May 1 '24

James Arnett has been a senior partner in a major Canadian law firm in Toronto and Washington, DC, CEO of a major public company based in Montreal and Chair of an Ontario public utility. He has advised the Government of Canada and the Premier of Ontario. He was born and raised in Winnipeg and graduated from the University of Manitoba and Harvard Law School. He lives with his wife, Alix, in Toronto. This is his first work of fiction.

D1596749

James Arnett

BEAN FATE

BASED ON A TRUE CRIME

AUSTIN MACAULEY PUBLISHERS™

LONDON * CAMBRIDGE * NEW YORK * SHARJAH

Copyright © James Arnett 2022

All rights reserved. No part of this publication may be reproduced, distributed, or transmitted in any form or by any means, including photocopying, recording, or other electronic or mechanical methods, without the prior written permission of the publisher, except in the case of brief quotations embodied in critical reviews and certain other noncommercial uses permitted by copyright law. For permission requests, write to the publisher.

Any person who commits any unauthorized act in relation to this publication may be liable to criminal prosecution and civil claims for damages.

This is a work of fiction. Names, characters, businesses, places, events, locales, and incidents are either the products of the author's imagination or used in a fictitious manner. Any resemblance to actual persons, living or dead, or actual events is purely coincidental.

Ordering Information
Quantity sales: Special discounts are available on quantity purchases by corporations, associations, and others. For details, contact the publisher at the address below.

Publisher's Cataloging-in-Publication data
Arnett, James
Bean Fate

ISBN 9781647500450 (Paperback)
ISBN 9781647500467 (Hardback)
ISBN 9781647500146 (ePub e-book)

Library of Congress Control Number: 2021915047

www.austinmacauley.com/us

First Published 2022
Austin Macauley Publishers LLC
40 Wall Street, 33rd Floor, Suite 3302
New York, NY 10005
USA

mail-usa@austinmacauley.com
+1 (646) 5125767

Author's Note

This is a work of fiction. However, it is based on real historical events and people.

It was almost one hundred years ago; a very different time. The ethnic slurs, and many of the attitudes and values found in this story, while common at the time, are considered totally unacceptable today.

Except as otherwise identified, all of the characters are white to the best of my knowledge.

The following characters in this story are real historical people:

Harry Bronfman, 37; Samuel 'Sam' Bronfman, 31; Allan Bronfman, 26; Paul Matoff, 35; Jean Matoff. Johnny Torrio, 40; Al Capone, 23; Dutch Schultz, 21. James A. Cross, 46; R.E.A. Leech, 63; Charles Augustus Mahoney, 52. Lee Dillege, 36; Jimmy Lacoste, 25. William Hale 'Big Bill' Thompson, 53; Amos Alonzo Stagg, 60; Charles Fitzmorris, 38. Meyer Chechik, Zasu Natanson, and Harry Rabinovitch. Gordon White; Colin Rawcliffe, 26; Dr. John Nicol, Colonel Johnson, A. J. Andrews, 57.

Among other real people referred to are the following:

Cyril and Vernon Knowles, Jacques Bureau, Frank Hamer, Dr. T. Albert Moore, Violet McNaughton, Nellie McClung, Avery Erickson, Fred Fahler, and Swede Risberg.

+ + +

Chapter 1

Big Bill Thompson just loved a parade. Just loved it, especially one featuring himself. And the completion of the Michigan Avenue Bridge over the Chicago River in May 1922 seemed like a good excuse for another one featuring himself. After all, it was a major milestone in the development of the bustling raw city of three million people on the shores of Lake Michigan, a city of many large such projects. Home of the world's first skyscraper!

And so it was that on a steamy day a parade approached the bridge, the city flag of only two stars and stripes flying from flagpoles atop the tender houses at the four corners of the bridge. It was an engineering marvel that Big Bill had built. Well, he hadn't built it but he had the good fortune to be the Mayor of Chicago when it was completed. It was a bascule bridge or drawbridge with leaves that met in the middle and could be raised to allow tall ships to pass under it to travel up the river. It was also double-leaf, which meant its leaves were divided in two along the axis so that it could be operated as two parallel bridges independently. And finally, it was a double-decker with a roadway on both levels, the upper intended for faster traffic and the lower for slower.

It was across the upper level with leaves down flat that Big Bill, sweating in a three-piece suit complete with gold watch chain and leather chaps, rode his horse at the head of the parade waving his trademark Stetson to the crowds. The city police marching band with various drums and brass instruments, and various floats, cars, and trucks, followed for two hours. The thousands of spectators, many the worse for wear from occasional guzzles of bootleg whiskey, known as booze, cheered and waved stars and stripes flags as the parade passed along Michigan Avenue and over the marvel of a bridge while they were showered with booster pamphlets from biplanes flying low overhead.

Goddammit! This is my town, thought Big Bill. *Wouldn't trade it for New York and all its fancy people. Look at all those people out there, WASPs, bohunks, darkies and they all voted for me. Well, not all but enough. The WASPS still do, most of them, because I'm one of them. Although not those arrogant anglophile McCormicks and their fucking newspaper. But enough, along with the bohunks and darkies.* It was tricky to be sure he ruminated while waving from high above the crowd on his horse. *While a majority of the WASPS want prohibition, the others don't. But so far, I've walked the line, kept a majority. And the truth is the WASPs are no longer a majority and there's no way we can really enforce it. Too many people want to drink when they want to drink. And I'm okay with that. Don't mind it myself.*

After the parade ended, he went back to his hotel suite and received a variety of good-humored citizens to celebrate the great civic event. While booze was served along with other drinks, it was done discreetly out of a pantry by a black waiter in a crisp white chef jacket with the hotel logo.

Thompson wasn't called Big Bill for nothing. He was a big man of an athletic, if now portly, build who dominated a room with his booming voice and outgoing personality. Some would say an outrageous personality, a dangerous personality with a strange populist showmanship for a Methodist and Republican of respectable upbringing. He stood shaking hands at the head of a small receiving line of well-wishers.

One of the first was the Baptist pastor with the big following.

"So glad to see you, reverend," said Big Bill with his signature handshake, pumping the preacher's hand with his right hand, small for a big man, and clapping him on the shoulder with his left hand.

"Glad to be here," said the pastor in a voice with still a hint of a lower-class English accent. "And I just want to thank you for all you're doing in supporting our crusade against crime."

"Nothing could be more important for this city. Glad to help. Anytime you need anything, just get in touch."

The pastor moved on.

Among those waiting in the line was a smallish foxy-looking man in a dapper three-piece suit. Finally, he reached Big Bill.

"Why, hello Johnny," said Big Bill heartily, looking around slightly nervously as he pumped Johnny's hand with his right hand and clapped him on the shoulder with his left hand.

"Hello, mister mayor," said Johnny in a quiet raspy voice with a thick southern Italian accent. "Thanks for all your help."

"Glad to help. Any time you need anything, just get in touch."

After another vigorous handshake, Big Bill hadn't let go, Johnny turned and left the room. He'd only been there for a few minutes, just long enough to remind Big Bill.

Johnny left the room, took the elevator down, and walked through the lobby. There were a couple of Chicago policemen at the door. After all, the Mayor deserved security. As he walked past them, Johnny made eye contact with one and nodded in acknowledgment. The policeman nodded back.

A lot of people were drinking a lot of booze in Chicago that night. Among them was a flashy-looking guy and a flashy-looking blonde woman in a downtown Italian restaurant.

At about ten PM, a big Packard car drove under the Loop, the elevated urban railway, along a side street and up beside that restaurant and stopped. Two men got out, one from each of the backdoors. They both wore homburgs and raincoats. One was beefy with conspicuous facial scars and the other was slim with cold dark eyes. The doorman noted their raincoats because it wasn't raining and nervously opened the door. He'd seen this picture before.

They walked in and saw at a table across the room the flashy-looking guy with the flashy-looking blonde. As he looked up, the guy's face registered instant dismay. He'd recognized the duo for what they were but it was already too late. Even as he pulled out the .35 caliber pistol, the beefy guy opened his coat and fired across with a sawed-off shotgun. The targeted guy crashed back off his chair in a spray of blood dead as a doornail. The blonde was hit too but was still alive. The slim guy with the dark eyes walked up and put her out of her misery with a shot from a big Colt 45 revolver. Then the two assassins turned and walked out and climbed into the waiting car.

As it took off, the beefy guy said to the other, "That's the way we do it."

Half an hour later, they walked into a red brick row building on South Wabash Street, not the saloon on the left but the staircase on the right. They ascended the stairs and, as they turned on the second floor landing to enter a suite of offices, they passed a cop descending from the whorehouse on the third floor who nodded at them. The ugly-looking thug who stood on guard at the entrance to the suite of offices ushered them over to an office, opened the door, and stepped aside to let them in, closing the door behind them. Foxy-looking Johnny sat behind a desk. They walked up to the desk and stood, almost at attention it seemed.

"You got the job done?" asked Johnny.

"Yes, we did, Mister Torrio," said the beefy guy with the scar.

"Should remind the street that we don't accept bad booze."

"Uh huh," nodded the beefy guy. The guy with the dark eyes was expressionless.

"Good job, boys," said Torrio. "Now, I have another one for you."

They looked interested, wondering if another hit was about to be ordered.

"Up in Canada. I hear it's wide open out west. There's a guy named Harry Bronfman in Saskatchewan just across the border from North Dakota. I hear he has booze for sale. Big quantities. I want you to go up there and make arrangements."

Chapter 2

"Don't worry, Jack. We'll be back home one of these days. I'll get you back."
That was what Colonel Cross had said to him that day in France and, sure
enough, here they were. *I'd do anything for that man,* he thought.

He was standing at attention on a parade square with nineteen other young
men. It was a pleasant day with a clear blue sky a few weeks after Big Bill's
parade, warm but not steamy like Chicago. They were in Jack's hometown of
Regina, capital of the Province of Saskatchewan, a thousand miles northwest
of Chicago across the line. Regina was a small but growing city of some thirty-
five thousand, roughly one percent the size of Chicago. Behind them was a
large one-story drill hall with a sign: *'SASKATCHEWAN PROVINCIAL
POLICE.'* In front and facing them, a sergeant-major stood at ease. Fluttering
in the breeze was the Canadian Red Ensign flag featuring the British 'Union
Jack' plus the Canadian coat of arms complete with maple leaves and fleur-de-
lis.

Jack was an ordinary but nice-looking young man, still solid like the
hockey player he'd once been. He was proud of his new uniform of the
Saskatchewan Provincial Police: British khaki long wool tunic with military-
type close neck collar, khaki wool (serge) breeches with red stripes, brown
riding boots, felt campaign hat pinned up on the left side, Sam Browne belt,
and a .38 caliber Smith & Wesson revolver in a buttoned-up holster riding high
on his hip. *Good to be back in uniform,* he thought. *And this one's a lot fancier
than the last. Almost like an officer's uniform with the riding boots.*

Led by the sergeant-major, the men paraded into the drill hall and stood
again at attention in formation, two lines of ten each, facing a raised platform
with a podium behind which stood two men, Colonel, the Honorable James A.
Cross, DSO, KC, the attorney-general of Saskatchewan, and Charles Augustus
Mahoney, the Commissioner of the Saskatchewan Provincial Police.

Cross, in civilian clothes, was slim and natty with clipped dark hair and lampshade mustache and was wearing a shirt with the wingtip collar favored by most serious men. The DSO stood for the Distinguished Service Order, an honor he'd received from His Majesty, King George V, and the KC stood for the honor of being a King's Counsel, one of 'His Majesty's Counsel Learned in the Law.' Being called 'the Honorable' was a courtesy style of address for being a member of the provincial cabinet. But being called 'Colonel' was what Cross prized most.

Mahoney was in uniform. A stocky man with a full chevron mustache and a close-shaven bald head barely hinted at below his campaign hat, he was a simple policeman without any social pretensions.

Right away, Jack saw his parents and brother. They were among the forty or so civilians seated on folding chairs set up at the side for families and friends to witness the little ceremony. His mother waved. Of course, he couldn't wave back but he caught her eye out of the corner of his and could tell she was thrilled. He also noticed an older man in civilian clothes standing off to the side who looked somehow as if he wasn't in the family-or-friend category.

The sergeant-major called each man to the podium in turn. When it was Jack's turn, he stepped forward and up onto the podium, placed his hand on a proffered Bible, and repeated after the sergeant-major:

"I, John Wesley Ross, do solemnly swear that I will be loyal to His Majesty, the King, and that I will, to the best of my ability, discharge my duties as a member of the Saskatchewan Provincial Police faithfully, impartially, and according to the laws of the Province of Saskatchewan and the Dominion of Canada. So help me, God."

Jack knew his mother and that she'd also be proud to hear in public the name of her son, whom she'd named after the founder of Methodism.

When all twenty men had been sworn, Cross gave a short speech to the new constables:

"You're joining one of the best police forces in Canada and the entire British Empire. At the request of the Saskatchewan government, five years ago the Royal Northwest Mounted Police were withdrawn from Saskatchewan except for purely federal matters like Indian affairs. We established the provincial police so that policing in our province would be directed and controlled here at home and could more accurately reflect the needs of our communities. That has worked very well so that we have an excellent force of which you can be proud to be members."

What an honor! thought Jack, who could almost feel his chest swelling with pride.

"You will have a key responsibility," continued Cross, "in keeping your fellow citizens safe. Saskatchewan is essentially a very law-abiding community based on the principles of peace, order and good government found in the British North America Act."

It sounded good to Jack, although he'd never heard of the British North America Act.

"In doing so," continued Cross, "your task will be to support British values, enforce the Rule of Law, and ensure British justice."

That part Jack got. That was what his parents and his school, even his church, had talked about.

"In this, you will from time to time have challenges because we are still a young province and some new Canadians don't fully understand our British ways and you'll have to help them with that. And of course, some immigrants living here are not yet Canadians. Again, that'll be a challenge you'll have to meet. But with assistance from the Commissioner and everyone at headquarters, I'm sure you will."

Jack had known some bohunks at high school but they all seemed to get along and view the world the same as he did. But maybe not their parents?

"One final word of advice," said Cross. "You are young men but you will be seen as figures of authority in the communities you serve. And many of the people there will have come from places, Russia, Austria, places like that where the police play a different role, a harsher role. We are not like that. We are a parliamentary democracy and our people have their rights as British subjects. And they *know* that they have those rights." "So, always remember that in your dealings with the public. And remember too: this is what we fought for in the war a few years ago."

Jack had a lump in his throat. He agreed with everything Cross said and he said it so well. He felt so honored to become a policeman and work for Colonel Cross.

Mahoney then announced that a special lunch would be served in the mess hall but, unfortunately, the attorney-general had another engagement and would not be able to stay for lunch.

As soon as the parade broke up, Jack walked right over to his parents and brother. His mother hugged him and his father and brother each shook his hand. Jack and his father had had their moments over the last few years but were close nevertheless and his father was obviously proud and undoubtedly relieved too that Jack had finally found a good position.

Cross walked up and took Jack's hand to congratulate him. Jack introduced Cross to his family who were a little shy in the presence of the great man. The attorney-general! A colonel! A war hero! They'd never actually met anyone like that before, although they'd seen Cross in church. Jack noticed this and, while he was aware of the class difference between himself and Cross, was surprised and a little sad for them to see that they were aware of it too.

Mrs. Ross said, "We're so grateful, sir, for all you've done for our Jack." While slightly embarrassed by his mother's reference to 'our' Jack as though he were still a kid, Jack quickly added, "Yes, thank you, sir, for helping me get this commission."

"I did it as soon as I could. Glad to help one of my men."

They all chatted for a minute or two and then Jack's family made a quick exit saying they'd see Jack later.

Cross looked at Jack and asked with a knowing look, "Everything's okay with you?"

"Yes, sir."

"I believe you've been assigned to the Estevan detachment."

"Yes, sir," replied Jack, surprised but flattered that Cross knew.

"Down near the border," continued Cross, "near Bean Fate. That's where the Bronfmans have an export house."

Jack had heard the name Bronfman and vaguely associated it with booze, maybe even bootlegging, but never from anybody who really knew like the Colonel presumably did.

Jack waited, wondering where this was going.

"In fact, Harry Bronfman is a good friend. He's a good man. You won't have any problems."

Oh, thought Jack, *I guess the rumors were wrong. Bronfman's a good man.*

"And when you get down there, go to meet Walt Davie in Bean Fate. He's our JP and knows the ropes. Any questions, just check with him."

"Yes, sir."

"And if he asks for any help in the community, you know, that's okay too. He's one of us."

"Yes, sir," said Jack, not quite sure what Cross meant by 'help.' *Maybe an emergency or something? And flattering to be one of us,* he thought.

At that point, the older man Jack had noticed in the drill hall walked up. He was still well-built if a little paunchy with thinning graying hair.

"Jack," said Cross, "I want you to meet Mister Leech, the Chairman of the Liquor Commission."

Jack and Leech shook hands.

"I'm sorry I can't stay for lunch," added Cross. "Good luck, Jack. I know I can count on you."

Turning to Leech, Cross said, "I'll see you later at Bronfman's," and he walked away.

Must all be friends, thought Jack.

He lined up in the mess hall for the buffet, chatting to his fellow rookie constables and when he'd filled his platter, he sat down at one of the tables. Leech followed him over and sat down beside him. He started off with a few pleasantries and Jack thought to himself, *He sounds more like a salesman than my idea of a chairman.*

"I understand you're going down to Estevan," said Leech finally.

"Yes," said Jack, surprised again.

"That's an important posting. It's so near the border and there are liquor exports going out from Bean Fate."

"So I hear."

"Of course, there may be some leakage into the local community but I don't think it's much. You don't really need to give a hard time to ordinary people living their lives."

Other men were sitting down but Leech kept chatting to Jack. Out of the blue, he said, "Harry Bronfman's a good man."

That's the second time I've heard that, thought Jack.

"I got to know him many years ago in Brandon," said Leech.

"Manitoba?"

"Yes. In those days, Harry and his father and brothers were scratching along, you know, doing a bit of this and a bit of that. And now... now Harry's got the biggest house in Regina!"

"So, when did you come to Saskatchewan?"

"Oh, even before I went to Manitoba. Almost forty years ago. Of course, it wasn't Saskatchewan yet."

Jack looked at him expectantly.

"Came out from Ontario to help capture Louis Riel. I was a young man then."

"You fought at Batoche?" asked Jack, impressed.

"I did. We had to put down that goddamn traitor. Else there wouldn't have been all we have now. We could have lost the whole bloody west. The Yanks wanted it and were just waiting."

"I guess so," said Jack, nodding in agreement and adding, "I guess you know Colonel Cross pretty well?"

"Oh yes, I met him before the war. Outstanding man and a real hero. And we're both Methodist."

"So am I."

"Heard that too. You'll be the right man for us down south. Anyway, good luck down there."

With that, Leech, got up from the table, said goodbye, and left, leaving his food untouched.

That's something, thought Jack. *The liquor board chairman himself taking the time with me. And Cross did too. I wonder if it's really as easy as they're saying. I wonder if they doth protest too much,* he thought, remembering a bit of high school Shakespeare. Not that he remembered much. *And Leech's comment about Riel and Batoche. Didn't that tie into the whole Metis problem?* Jack didn't really understand it, except that it seemed complicated. He'd always heard that Riel was a traitor and in fact had been hanged in 1885 for that. It was sort of in the air that the Metis people were all unreliable. The Indians were too. Hadn't some of the Indian chiefs gone to jail in 1885? But then he'd got to know Lenny Garneau. And he'd met a couple of Indians, like "Jim the Indian" as they called one guy, in the army overseas and they sure as hell weren't traitors. Everybody knew that after the last war. But it was all so complicated and Jack didn't really know what to think about all those things.

Chapter 3

Jack thought of Cross as a big man. He'd only known him as a commander, then as a feted war hero, and now, for all practical purposes, as the government. For Jack, Cross had always been an important and successful older man. He had no idea how Cross had got to where he was and had never thought about it, which was unsurprising because young people rarely do. He would have been surprised to know that James Albert Cross had come from a family not dissimilar to his own.

Cross reflected on that fact as he went back to his office. Meeting Jack's loving but plain parents and, indeed, preparing his little speech to the new constables had got Jimmy Cross thinking back to his own loving but plain parents as he'd grown up in Caledonia Springs halfway between Montreal and Ottawa on the Ontario side of the Ottawa River. The village had existed in support of a prominent resort, a spa and sanatorium based upon the allegedly salubrious qualities of the local mineral springs. His father had worked as a clerk in the grand hotel of one hundred rooms and, around the dinner table, would tell tales of the rich and famous patrons, many of them grandees from Montreal, although only later, when Jimmy was an adult, had he regaled Jimmy with the more salacious tales, like the bank president whose pretty secretary had been registered in an adjoining room.

Jimmy Cross had dreamed of going somewhere from the get-go. A wiry kid, he'd been a good hockey player but it offered no career for an ambitious boy. He'd attended the local Methodist church where he'd been more interested in its exhortations to do good works in this life than to prepare for the next. As he'd approached graduation from high school in the spring of 1898, he'd had a discussion one evening with his father at the kitchen table.

"What are you thinking of doing after exams?" asked his father.

"You mean after I matriculate?"

"Right. I guess that's what it's called."

"Well, I'd like to become a lawyer."

"Not easy. You'd need some money."

"I know."

"I'm not sure we can afford it."

"I know, Dad. I don't expect you to support me."

"But I could get you a job at the hotel. You could save some money."

"Thanks, Dad, but I'm thinking about going out west."

His father looked shocked.

"Manitoba? I do hear there's a lot of opportunity they say there, especially Winnipeg."

"No. The Northwest Territories."

"Why there? Is there even anything there?"

"Oh, Dad, there's a lot there. More opportunity than Manitoba now. The territories are just opening up. And the government is bringing in thousands of immigrants from Europe."

"That man, Sifton, is a whirling dervish."

"Yeah, and they say that the guy Haultain, who's the premier out there, wants to create a province out of it."

"If you went, where would you go?"

"I don't know. Regina is the capital. I'd head there for a start. It really depends on what I'd do."

"Well, what could you do out there? To earn some money."

"I assume I could find a job."

"You wouldn't know anybody. At least I know the people at the hotel."

"Dad, that's just it. Out there, it's not all tied up like here or Ottawa or Montreal. You don't need to know people. It's new, it's open, they need people, and they want you. There's way more chance to make a go of it. At least, that's what I hear."

"I see. Sounds like you've made up your mind already?"

"I have. And I've saved up enough for the train trip."

The next day, he'd gone ahead and booked a seat on the Canadian Pacific Railway, which everyone called the "CPR", for the three-day trip to Regina, then a small town of only two thousand but the capital chosen for the territories by the all-powerful CPR on the banks of muddy Wascana Creek in the middle of a flat and treeless prairie. A few weeks later, right after graduating, he'd said goodbye to his parents, assuring them he'd write.

The trip itself had been an experience to be sure. During the day, he'd watched the passing scene, starting with the deep forests, rich farm lots, and clear waters of Eastern Ontario. It did get monotonous through the boreal forest after Lake Superior west of Port Arthur and across the flat prairie west of Winnipeg. The train had stopped at Brandon, the home of a bright kid named Harry Bronfman, but that had meant nothing to Jimmy.

At night, the porter slid the seats down so that they formed a berth which was quite decent. But the air was hot and fetid and at least one baby always seemed to be screaming. So he'd arrived in Regina, exhausted.

He'd had an introduction to the Metropolitan Methodist Church in the center of town. Chance acquaintances there had led to a season's work on a farm outside Regina. He'd heard there was a great demand for schoolteachers, with no teaching certificate needed, only high school matriculation. So he'd secured a teaching position at a one-room school in a village down the road from the farm. An older parishioner in Regina had arranged an interview with none other than Frederick Haultain. They'd hit it off and Jimmy had ended up studying law with him. He'd also joined the militia, really as a way to make some friends. In time, he'd been called to the bar and become a successful lawyer himself. He'd chaired Regina's school board, been active in the Methodist Church, and was a founder of its Regina College. He'd arrived.

To top it off, when war was declared in 1914, he'd joined the Canadian Expeditionary Force and received the rank of a major because of his militia experience. He'd gone overseas and had a 'good war,' receiving the DSO for gallantry at the famous battle of Vimy Ridge and later managing a soldiers' camp in England. On his return, he'd been promoted to the rank of colonel.

While overseas, he'd been elected to the Saskatchewan legislature as a Liberal and the soldiers' representative. This had been a big step forward for a still-young man because the Liberals had been in power in Saskatchewan since it had been carved out of the Northwest Territories seventeen years earlier.

The key man behind the drive for provincehood had been his mentor, Fred, now Sir Frederick for his statesmanship. But then, poor Fred had had a falling-out with the Liberals and, notwithstanding his years of exemplary service, had been pushed aside when the province was formed. Such is political life. This had been tricky for Jimmy but he'd managed to distance himself from Fred just enough. People took notice. In politics, a bit of ruthlessness is an acknowledged virtue. He'd been re-elected in last year's election and, in April, he'd finally been appointed as attorney-general.

So, he was on a roll and he'd thought to himself: *KC and DSO so far and you know what? If Fred can do it, maybe I can too. Sir James has a nice ring to it. There's now a chance for it if I play my cards right. A big 'if'. As attorney-general, I'll have to handle a hot kettle of people and issues.* Of course, the majority, like himself, were more or less Anglo, mostly immigrants from Ontario. Added to these were a lot of American immigrants who were mainly WASPs or of Protestant Scandinavian background. So far so good. They would assimilate quickly. But then there were some French-speaking Metis, put in their place at the time of Riel but still harboring resentments and living largely apart. There were Indians, too, but few of them and largely invisible.

But the big wild card was all these immigrants that his colleagues in Ottawa like Sifton had recruited from Eastern Europe before the war, mainly Slavs of one sort or another, who knew? Plus quite a few Jews. *None of them knows our culture,* he'd thought, *let alone understands our laws. Not that I don't support Sifton's project. I do... assuming the immigrants seize the opportunity to become like us. They can become good citizens but it's a big assimilation project and seems to be getting more difficult.* He'd noticed an increase in feeling against them on his return from overseas. It was as though the conflict abroad had created a conflict at home.

Taking away people's right to vote hadn't helped, although he'd supported that. *But everyone's getting more defensive,* he thought, *like the Ukrainians who demand to be taught in Ukrainian. We just have to say no to that or there goes the project and social harmony with it. And there are social tensions not just with us but among all these foreign groups themselves. At least, they all remember who recruited them and vote Liberal now that they can vote again. That's the good news. The bad news is that it's a hot kettle and the lid has to be kept on.*

As if that weren't enough, he had these bloody liquor laws to enforce. Not that he was against the prohibition of drink; he was for it in principle: didn't drink at all, never had, not even overseas. He was a pretty staunch member of his church and had been the beneficiary of the anti-drink vote, a vote which reflected the exhortations of Dr. T. Albert Moore, a leading Methodist he'd met before the war at a Methodist conference in Toronto:

20

"The government (dominion, provincial, or municipal) that accepts money for liquor licenses becomes a partner in the business justly declared to be an enemy of God and men. We protest against the unholy alliance. The only proper attitude of Christians towards the unholy traffic is one of relentless hostility, and all members of the Methodist Church who possess the elective franchise are urged to use their influence to assure the nomination of municipal and parliamentary candidates known to favor and support prohibition and to use their votes as a solemn trust to elect such candidates."

That was all very well. The problem was the usual problem in the politics of liberal democracies like Canada: not everyone agreed, and compromise was required to get anything done. The actual laws as enacted reflected the attempts of the politicians of both the main parties, the Liberals and Conservatives, and both provincially and federally, to deal with the wide disagreement about the desirability of Prohibition all the way from Quebec where nobody wanted it to Saskatchewan where the majority did.

As a politician, he understood that. But the fact was it had resulted in a crazy maze of laws. Perhaps the craziest had been the one allowing the sale of booze to purchasers across provincial boundaries but not within a province. That one was gone now. And in fact it had settled down so that now it seemed pretty clear in Saskatchewan:

The focus was on sales, not mere drinking.

As to beer, sales of weak beer up to two percent alcohol, what everyone called temperance or near beer, were legal. Anything stronger was illegal.

As to the hard stuff, sales were illegal except for export which, for all practical purposes, meant export to the states.

And those exports produced hefty fees and taxes for the provincial government and Ottawa too. Although he was teetotal himself, he was also a man of affairs and was acutely aware of the importance to his government of those fees and taxes. Still, exports were a hot issue because they brought all those American purchasers up here, rough rum runners hanging around the export depots like the one in Bienfait. And since drinking booze wasn't illegal, there was a big black market for bootleggers to local drinkers.

As attorney-general, he'd have to try to handle this crazy mess without getting burned. Basically, he'd thought, *If I'm to have any chance of success, let alone working towards a knighthood, I'll just have to keep the lid on. That was why it'd be helpful to have someone down in Bean Fate I could count on if it gets complicated besides Walt Davie who may be a little dodgy.*

In addition to running the attorney-general's department, he had to do what all politicians have to do: raise money. And like most politicians, he disliked it, because asking for money seemed demeaning and required him to deal with some people he didn't particularly like dealing with. But, as he said to himself, *You have to raise the money from those who are interested in giving, mainly those seeking favors.*

So, on the evening after the swearing-in ceremony, Cross was welcoming a group of some twenty men standing in a semicircle, with non-alcoholic drinks in hand, in a large dining room with dark wood-beamed ceiling and Delft-type tiles in the fireplace surround. Leech stood beside him.

"Gentlemen," said Cross, "I first want to thank Harry Bronfman for hosting our party in this wonderful house."

Harry smiled and nodded appreciatively. He was pretty proud of his new house.

"And I want to thank Harry, and Sam Bronfman too, for their generous support."

Harry and Sam smiled and nodded in recognition.

If Jack hadn't thought about how Cross had got to where he was, neither had Cross thought all that much about the Bronfmans either. He thought of them as a couple of smart but unpatriotic Jew-boys from Winnipeg who'd made a killing in the booze trade while he was fighting overseas. And that they'd somehow ingratiated themselves with his slightly questionable colleague standing beside him. He didn't know, for example, that in fact they'd reported for military service but been rejected because of their flat feet. Nor did he realize that if he'd come a long way (of which he was rather proud), they'd come much farther.

In fact, Harry was reflecting on that as he listened to Cross and surveyed the room with a handful of Regina's most prominent businessmen. Young Harry had met Leech twenty years ago in Brandon in western Manitoba, by then a boom town of four thousand. Leech had already been in the west for twenty years. The Bronfmans had been there for only ten, having emigrated from Russia. Naturally, they'd moved in different circles. Leech was in the businesses of grain brokerage and land speculation. Harry's father was a peddler. But it was a small city and Leech and the Bronfmans had bumped into each other.

The Bronfmans had eventually gone into the hotel business which had morphed into a liquor business because they'd discovered the bars was where the money was. They'd navigated the maze of prohibition laws and their ever-changing loopholes. They'd made particularly good use of the one allowing interprovincial booze shipments from which they'd developed a mail-order business.

The Bronfman family had moved to Winnipeg but Harry had gone on to Yorkton, Saskatchewan, where it was said he could have been elected mayor. Meanwhile, young Sam had increasingly assumed responsibility for developing and directing their business on a Canada-wide basis with a cadre of brothers and brothers-in-law stationed across the country. He also spent a lot of time in Montreal.

Everyone had expected that the closing of the interprovincial loophole and the mail-order business would end the Bronfmans' business. But amazingly, Harry had found yet another loophole. He'd established the Canada Pure Drug Company and moving into the sale of alcohol for 'medicinal purposes,' both in pharmacists' medicines by doctors' prescription and in high-octane over-the-counter medicines like Dandy Bracer and Rock-a-Bye cough cure. Drinkers had laughed all the way to the drugstore.

Furthermore, all the while exports to the states had been allowed. Suddenly, this business had exploded after the imposition of national Prohibition in the states three years ago. It was where the real action was now. As well as dealing in imported legitimate brands, the Bronfmans had started producing their own stock in Regina with fake brand names and much better margins. And Harry had recently set up Dominion Distributors to pool their export business with some partners who had got into the business. They operated out of the Craftsman Building near Regina's CPR depot and distributed out of export depots near the border.

It was this export business that Harry ran now and, if Sam thought he was becoming their main man by flitting about the country from his home in Winnipeg, Harry assumed that he still was. After all, his operation was where the big money was. And he'd become wealthy not only from those operations but from dabbling in other businesses like a garage and the Gray-Dort car dealership. And he'd recently moved the business to the capital, Regina, and his family into the house where the reception was now being held.

As Leech had said, it was Regina's biggest house at five thousand square feet. Designed in the English arts and crafts style, its features included a buttressed tower and leaded windows. It also had a coach house and a string of stables which was so convenient for big cars. And it was conveniently located right across Wascana Park from the new provincial legislative building and where Cross and Leech had their offices. Both were so close, just a short walk away.

Meanwhile, Leech's Liberal connections had led him in new directions away from Brandon, first, as Chief Inspector of Dominion Government Land Agencies and, more recently, as chairman of the liquor commission in Regina.

Harry listened as Cross continued to talk about the government under the new Premier, Mr. Dunning, and what they were doing for Saskatchewan. As he did, it was apparent to Harry, and he took some satisfaction in it, that he, Harry, was obviously well-known and well-liked by the men in the room while Sam was neither so well-known nor well-liked. Along with most of the family, Sam lived in the prairie metropolis of Winnipeg, six times bigger than Regina. Indeed, until his recent marriage, Sam had lived in its fancy Fort Garry Hotel with their up-and-coming kid brother, Allan, a lawyer no less. It was the more polished Allan, not Harry, who'd recently been "best man" at Sam's wedding.

Sam was similar to Harry in looks, both being slight and short. Both had a Yiddish accent and a fondness for dark blue suits. Both had expressive eyes which revealed an underlying sharp intelligence but also the differences in their temperaments: Sam's was explosive and he couldn't have been elected dogcatcher.

After Cross finished his remarks and the group started to break up, he stood and talked with Leech and the Bronfmans. Harry told Cross he was expecting to make a new deal with purchasers from Chicago with much larger sales. "It'll be great for everyone," he said. They all knew this meant larger tax revenues too. Leech beamed approvingly.

But Cross looked uneasy. "You'll have to be careful with them," he warned. "Chicago's a rough town."

"Oh, I know," said Harry. "We'll be careful and play it by the book. And we're not going down there. All our dealings will be here. Strictly legal. Don't worry."

Cross raised his eyebrows to indicate some skepticism but thought to himself, *Well, the Bronfmans are big boys and smart. And the money will be good no doubt.*

As he was leaving, Leech pulled Harry aside, saying, "Thanks for buying that quarter-section."

"Which one?"

"The one over near Yorkton."

"You know I paid you five times of what it's worth."

"I appreciate that," said Leech, his hand on Harry's shoulder in a gesture of familiarity.

After everyone else had left, Harry and Sam sat down in the living room.

"It's good that you were here for that," said Harry.

"You know these guys pretty well."

"Yeah, I do," said Harry somewhat proudly.

"What's with Cross? Seems like a self-righteous schmuck."

"Not really. He's a big war hero, you know. But he is a teetotaler."

"Oh, that's it. One of those. But he's okay with us?"

"Absolutely."

"He was probably right about the Chicago guys. Who the hell are they anyway?"

"I don't really know. I got a call from a guy in Chicago named Torrio who said he was sending guys up. That's all."

"Torrio! He controls the rackets and everything in Chicago!"

"He does?"

"Yes! Jeez, Harry, you'll have to be really careful. He's a whole lot tougher than anyone in Regina or Winnipeg. You'll have to be careful with your buddy Dick Leech too."

"Our buddy."

"Harry, face it. He's your fucking buddy and he's like a piece of gum on your shoe."

Harry looked pained.

"If it turns sour," continued Sam, "those fucking goyim, and that includes Dick, will turn on you before you know what's happening."

What to say? thought Harry. He was used to Sam's hectoring.

"When do the other guys arrive?" asked Sam.

"Any time now."

"Paul?"

"He's in the kitchen. I didn't invite him to the reception."

"Just as well."

As if on cue, in walked Paul Matoff, and Harry thought, *He was eavesdropping*. Although like his brothers-in-law a short man with Yiddish accent, Matoff was a flashy dresser in a greenish check three-piece suit and sported a diamond ring and pencil mustache. Sam regarded him distastefully and said, "Hello, Paul," but didn't get up.

"So I hear you and Saidye are moving to Montreal," said Harry.

"Yeah," said Sam.

"Tell me about Montreal. I mean as a place to live d'you think. I've never spent much time there other than the railway station and St. James Street."

St. James Street was a reference to the small warehouse in downtown Montreal of the Bonaventure Liquor Store, a company Sam had set up a few years ago. Montreal was where the Bronfmans had set up the center for their mail-order business because there had been no restrictions on alcohol sales in Quebec and it was also where the major importers of alcohol were located. That was where Sam had bought the booze and alcohol from, which was then shipped across Canada. He'd spent a lot of time there.

"It's something else. You can't believe it. This house of yours, it'd just be the servants' quarters there."

Harry felt a little deflated.

"You should see the houses. There's so much money there. Harry, these are big guys, and classy too. You know what I mean? They know everybody, not just in Canada but London and New York. They live like royalty. Even some of the Jews."

Harry just looked at him.

"I met this guy, a Jewish guy, *Sir* Mortimer Davis," said Sam, emphasizing the 'sir.'

"Sam, I've heard of him. We all have. But helluva name."

"His family's from England," replied Sam as if in explanation.

"Sam…" said Harry, giving him an ironic look.

"Whatever, Harry. The point is I've met him. He's got a house in Westmount where all the rich English guys live. It's like a palace."

"Where's all his money come from?"

"Tobacco. He controls the market. Plus that pure alcohol I shipped out here? It comes from him. He's something, I tell you. He even belongs to the Mount Royal Club."

"What's that?"

"Where all those English guys belong, president of the CPR, bank presidents, shipping owners, everybody like that."

"Amazing. Not like the Manitoba Club. He couldn't get into that!"

"Exactly, I tell you, Harry, Montreal is different. Over half a million people. All kinds of people. Not like this chicken-shit town or even Winnipeg. Their English guys are not like these little tight-ass Methodists like Cross! We should be there, not here!"

"Aren't they mainly French there?"

"They just work for the English guys. And for some Jewish guys too. Like Davis. But you know the French, even here and in St. Boniface, they like to drink. Their church has no problem with it, so there's no Prohibition. Think of it, Harry. Quebec's the only place in North America with no Prohibition! And it's so close to New York!"

All the while, Matoff just sat staring sullenly at Sam.

"Well, we're doing pretty well here," said Harry.

"But it can't last. Allan and I talked to Jack Bureau."

Now it's always Allan and Sam noted Harry to himself, not like the old days.

Sam continued, "And Jack says they can't hold the line much longer. The anti-booze lobby is pushing hard."

Harry knew who Bureau was, the Honorable Jacques Bureau, Minister of Customs in Ottawa, and more or less on the Bronfman payroll.

"Soon as a province asks to close down the exports," Sam continued, "Ottawa will do it. So we've got to make hay out here while the sun shines. And keep the lid on as best we can so Regina doesn't ask Ottawa. Make sure we have no connection to local bootleggers. Don't fuck up our export business."

"We're careful," said Matoff defensively.

Sam gave him a sharp look and turned back to Harry. "So just keep moving as much stock out as you can."

"For sure," said Harry, thinking, *easy for Sam, the self-styled distiller and marketing genius, to say: Move as much out as you can while ignoring the*

27

local market. Actual sales are a whole lot harder than mixing liquids and designing goddamn labels.

"After that," continued Sam, "you can stay and piddle around here with that fucking City Garage if you want but there's much better pickings down east and that's where I'm going to be soon enough. Sir Samuel Bronfman. Has a nice ring to it! You can come along or not."

Harry gave him a bemused look.

"So," said Sam, "what's this partners' meeting about that's so important that I had to come all this way?"

"They're bitching. You'll see. I thought we should try to resolve it with a meeting and you should be here."

Ten minutes later, there was a knock on the door and Harry admitted Meyer Chechik and Zasu Natanson. Harry Rabinovitch arrived soon after.

Back in Manitoba, Chechik ran a little business raising and selling chickens wholesale, maybe some brokerage too. But he'd got into the booze business in Saskatchewan. *Smalltime compared to us but,* Harry had thought, *enough that he could complicate the market.* So, Harry had roped him in. Natanson was a junk dealer in Regina. You could tell just by looking at him. The roughest of the bunch, Rabinovitch was some guy who was based in Regina but spent a lot of time across the line doing who knew what. *Well, buying up alcohol stocks which he mixed up in Regina somewhere. Better not to know exactly,* Harry had thought.

Everyone exchanged halfhearted hellos.

Chechik immediately began complaining about how little he was getting out of the partnership while Harry seemed to be doing very well. "Look at this house," he said.

Harry tried to convince him there was nothing nefarious going on.

"The problem is," Harry said, "some of your booze is of poor quality." But Harry spoke smoothly and in an accommodating manner.

"Oh, so yours is great and mine's no good!" shouted Chechik.

"Some of it was even blue and had to be thrown out," said Harry.

"Bullshit!" said Chechik, "You just made that up to cover up what you're doing. I have good stuff and I'm not getting credit and you're just stealing from me!"

Sam exploded, "You're full of shit, Meyer, and you stop this or I'll throw you out!"

"You'll what?"

"And not just the company but this building… right now!"

The others quickly came between Sam and Chechik, who stomped out, all the way threatening to sue. Natanson and Rabinovitch soon left, shaking their heads after that, saying Chechik was crazy and that Harry was doing a good job and to just keep going the way he was.

Afterwards, Sam said, "Look, I have to catch the train back in an hour but I wish to hell you'd never got us mixed up with these guys. They're loose cannons. They're liable to blow everything up and then Regina will ask Ottawa. Like I warned. I don't know why you do these stupid things, Harry!"

Harry looked abashed.

Putting on his fedora, Sam turned to Matoff, whom he'd ignored the entire time, and said, "Paul, why the hell do you dress like that? You give the family a bad name. No way we're taking you to Montreal."

With that, he walked out the door leaving Harry and Paul looking at each other.

"That's Sam," said Harry.

Chapter 4

Jack took the train south to Estevan, a small city near the American border on the bank of the Souris, a small river in a wide and deep tree-lined valley that, on occasion, became a big river. It didn't respect the border of the forty-ninth parallel and ran a meandering looping course south from just north of Weyburn, Saskatchewan, into North Dakota past Minot and back up into Manitoba where it emptied into the Assiniboine River near Brandon. Although at Minot it was only seventy-five miles from the Missouri River which flowed into the Mississippi and down to the Gulf of Mexico, the Souris ran below an escarpment known as the Missouri Coteau and was in a watershed emptying into Hudson Bay.

He watched out the window. He was traveling through the garden of Saskatchewan. Under the big sky, lush crops of wheat stretched endlessly, it seemed, with the occasional stooked field heralding the beginning of the harvest. There were few other breaks in the broad flat landscape, with only the occasional slough of stagnant water surrounded by bulrushes and patches of scrubby poplar trees and shrubs like saskatoons and wolf willows. Out of one such patch close to the tracks bounded a white-tailed deer. He caught glimpses of the blue line of the Missouri Coteau on the horizon to the southwest. Occasionally, he saw cattle grazing and once or twice, a cowboy cantering along on a horse.

But while attractive in its spare way, the scenery became monotonous. The sound of the train's wheels on the tracks was a rhythmic clacking and as it went on hour by hour, Jack's mind wandered back. He was standing in a crowd on a street in Regina and the crowd was cheering and waving their hats. A military parade was passing. It wasn't quite up to Big Bill's standards, a few hundred people who said "sorry" if they bumped into someone. But they were enthusiastic and waved little Union Jack flags. In a Model-T Ford Convertible,

Cross was waving his hat at the crowd and they were waving back. Jack was too. Cross saw Jack and pointed at him and smiled and Jack felt proud.

And then too, he remembered that day in the trench, not the one at Vimy, after Vimy. He and Lenny were sitting in the muck, smoking. They'd both smoked a bit at home but by now they were smoking up a storm, any cigarettes they could get their hands on. And there were a lot, donated to the troops as a government-supported patriotic effort back home. They were smoking and talking. When they got out of there and got home, what would they do? They talked hockey and the Regina Pats. They'd both hoped to graduate to the Pats. That was why Lenny had boarded with the Jack's family, to play hockey for a team in Regina on the way up, just as Jack was doing. And they'd become chums, close chums, and in a way, Jack felt closer to Lenny than his younger brother. But now, as they talked, they both realized that going back to playing hockey wasn't in the cards. Younger kids would have supplanted them, and maybe some bohunks too who weren't overseas. They'd heard about homesteading. The government would give a man a quarter section and some help too. Maybe they could get a quarter section each and combine them or at least help each other. Yeah, that sounded like a great idea. They'd survived Vimy together and when they got home, they'd help each other and build lives together and grow old together.

And then Jack had heard the whistle of incoming mortars and they were hit and men were screaming. Lenny was not sitting beside him. He was dead with his arm and half his head blown off. Lenny wasn't screaming and they wouldn't grow old together. Jack was crying as Cross had come trudging along the trench and stopped and told Jack to put his helmet back on but gruffly tried to comfort him and said, "Hang in there. We'll be back home one of these days. I'll get you back." That was what he'd said and Jack had held onto it.

He eventually arrived at the Soo Line Railway Station in Estevan and was met by a provincial constable who introduced himself as Herb. He walked Jack back to a car. It was a Model-T, Henry Ford's revolutionary contraption which betrayed its horseless carriage antecedents, with a short wheelbase and width for only two high seats accessed by stepping up on the running board. Simmons drove over to a two-story yellow brick building. Above the door was a sign: 'SASKATCHEWAN PROVINCIAL POLICE, ESTEVAN DETACHMENT.'

They sat down in a little office, behind which was a small, empty, holding cell. Herb accepted Jack's offer of a cigarette and they both smoked.

Jack started off by saying he was a rookie and excited about his first posting. Herb didn't respond to that information, so Jack continued that he'd got his job because he was a vet.

"Me too."

"My old commander actually swore me in," said Jack with just a hint of pride in his voice. "Colonel Cross."

"Yeah, Regina gave him a big parade, but not us."

"He deserved it," retorted Jack indignantly.

Herb gave Jack a sardonic look. Then he filled him in. "The big issue down here is the booze. There's lots of it, all flowing out of Bean Fate and you never know for sure where it's going. You'll spend more time over there than around here. The town cop handles most things here but Bean Fate doesn't have one, so you're their town cop too. You'll get to know Walt Davie because he's the JP and runs things for Regina."

"Colonel Cross told me I'd be working with him," said Jack.

"I'll bet."

What's with his attitude about Cross? wondered Jack.

"Another guy you'll get to know is Paul Matoff."

"Who's he?"

"Brother-in-law of Harry Bronfman. You've heard of Bronfman?"

"I hear he's a good guy."

"Oh really," said Herb sarcastically.

"Yeah," said Jack in some surprise.

"He's tight with the big boys in Regina, that's for sure."

"But what about Matoff?"

"He's an arrogant little shit. Bit of bad news too. Runs Bronfman's so-called export house over in Bean Fate. You'll meet him and, matter of fact, he lives just around the corner, white house with green shutters. You'll see it soon enough."

Herb sure has a different take on the Bronfmans, thought Jack. *He must have had a sour experience down here somehow.*

"The thing is," Herb continued, "half the people want you to go after the booze and the other half hate you for it. No-win situation. It's best to not look too closely and keep your nose clean."

"So where are you going?"

"Buffalo Narrows."

"That's a way up north, eh?"

"Yeah, nothing but a few trappers and drunken Indians. Well, the trappers are usually drunk too."

"But you won't have to handle the Indians?"

"No, at least not theoretically. That's for the Mounties. They're up there too."

"How does that work?"

"Dunno. I'll find out. Probably the usual bureaucratic bickering."

"How do you feel about it?"

"The shits."

"Do you know how come you're going there?"

"I have a pretty good idea."

"Like?"

"I crossed some people around here. Last year, in the election. First, they asked me to help. Walt did."

"To help?"

"Drive voters to the polls, Liberal voters."

Jack was surprised at that and asked, "How does that work?"

"Walt gave me a list. No secret. Afterwards, I just filed my expenses as special duty. No questions from Regina. But I didn't feel good about it and the Conservatives around here gave me hell. Didn't help in the community. And I told Walt I didn't like it. Regina too. But that wasn't my worst sin."

"What was?"

"They were having a rally for the Liberal candidate, on a farm just outside Bean Fate. Big rally in the evening. I happened to see a truck heading there and I could see it had a couple of barrels of beer in the back. So I pulled it over. I mean what could I do? It was so goddamn open."

Jack listened, fascinated.

"I didn't know it was heading to that rally. Until the driver told me. But now I was committed. Anyway, I was a little ticked off with all this crap of being accused of helping the Liberals."

"So?"

"The driver claimed it was near beer. I took a sample. Felt like ten percent when it hit me, eh."

"And?"

"I poured it all out on the road."

"You did?" Jack almost whistled.

"Both barrels."

"Then what?"

"That Liberal candidate is a raging asshole and he complained upstairs, I guess. I got royal hell from Walt. Even Mahoney called me and said I should have just taken the driver's word for it and avoided all the fuss. Said it was very undiplomatic of me. That's his word: undiplomatic. Maybe it's an Ontario word. Undiplomatic. Herb almost spat it out. He's such a suck-hole anyway."

"I don't know much about him."

"Ontario Provincial Police. I don't know why they had to go all the way down east to find someone. Well, I do know, I guess. Everybody knows he's a Liberal."

"Anyway, so what happened after that?"

"Nothing more until Cross became the AG a couple of months ago. Mahoney warned me things were changing and next thing you know, I'm being reassigned to fucking Buffalo Narrows. So it's all yours now."

Jack didn't know what to say. His instinct was to be skeptical. For one thing, he didn't like the implication about Cross. For another, he didn't like the implication that he was stealing Herb's job.

He was saved by the whinny of a horse. Herb took Jack out back where there was a stable.

"That's Dolly," said Herb. "There'll be some days and some places you'll need her. Treat her nice and she'll treat you nice. By the way," he added, motioning towards the Model-T, "I'm afraid we don't have a new tin lizzie. You still have to wind this one with the crank."

Then they walked across the street to see Jack's new accommodation: a room above a dry goods store.

Chapter 5

The next morning, Jack thought he'd look around. He cranked up the lizzie. Around the corner from his apartment on the main street, he saw a white house with green shutters. He continued on and then out of town and slowly on a gravel road towards Bean Fate, eight miles east. As he came near an intersection with another gravel road, a big car roared across in a cloud of dust. There were two guys in it and it had North Dakota plates.

At another intersection, he saw a sign: *'WESTERN COAL MINE'* with an arrow pointed on a road headed towards the border. *That's where they are,* he thought. He'd heard there were small coal mines in the area and that the miners could be a problem come payday.

He soon approached a village, signaled by a line of trees on the flat prairie and a wooden grain elevator standing sixty feet tall above the flat landscape. A roadside sign proclaimed: *'WELCOME TO BIENFAIT.'* *Oh, that's how it's spelled.*

He drove slowly into town and down a wide and dusty main street, with buggies and vehicles parked in the middle forming a sort of median. There were no sidewalks or street lights. There were various one and two-story buildings housing various little businesses. Crossing the street at the end was the CPR line. On one corner was the CPR station, a long dark brown wooden building with a bay window and, for part of it, a second floor. The building faced a long wooden platform that edged up to the tracks.

Across from it on the other side of the main street also adjacent to the railway tracks was a two-story red brick building with white verandah and a sign: *'KING EDWARD HOTEL.'* Down along the railway tracks about a hundred meters was the grain elevator on the side of which was painted in large letters: *'LAKE OF THE WOODS MILLING COMPANY.'*

Jack parked in front of the CPR station, walked across the platform, and entered the building, the screen door slamming slightly as he did so. That brought out a man who identified himself as the station agent. Jack introduced himself and said he was just looking around and that he understood this was where there was a depot for the pickup of alcohol by American buyers. The agent said he'd show him around, first noting that he and his wife had living accommodations on the second floor. Then he took him outside and along the platform to the other end where there was cargo space and a separate express shed, which, said the agent, was the booze depot.

He unlocked and opened the door to show Jack. It was stacked with cartons marked: *'Black Horse.'*

"They belong to Dominion Distributors until it's properly released by us," he said.

"When's the next release?" asked Jack.

"Likely tonight. It's Wednesday and there's usually a pickup. Usually late."

Jack thanked him and walked across to the hotel. Above the door was a sign: *'WHITE HELP–WHITE SERVICE.'* He entered and the man behind the counter in the lobby looked up and introduced himself as Gordon White, the owner. He welcomed Jack to the community of which, he said, his hotel was the center. He proudly showed Jack around.

"We have the best equipped hotel in Saskatchewan. First-class beds, Simmons beds, electrical refrigeration, restaurant. Here, our billiards room has four first-class billiard tables."

"And," said White with pride, "look at this." He opened a door at the back to reveal a bowling alley with three lanes.

"Very well equipped," said Jack as he thanked him for showing him around.

"You're welcome. Any time you want to play billiards, it's on me, constable."

Next, Jack parked in front of a building with the storefront sign: *'WALTER DAVIE-GENERAL STORE'* and entered. He saw a large sales room stocked with a variety of groceries and dry goods. There was a long counter along one side, behind which stood a middle-aged man with short gray hair and wire-rimmed spectacles. He was jacketless with a shirt with armbands (sleeve garters) and a tie. He walked around the counter, stuck out his hand, and said, "I'm Walt Davie."

"I'm Constable Ross. Jack Ross."

"I've heard about you, Jack. Your Colonel Cross's man. I look forward to getting to know you. I'll call you Jack and you can call me Walt. That's the way we do it down here. Come on into my office."

So I'm Cross's man, thought Jack. *Very nice to hear.*

Above a door at the back of the store, there was a sign: *'WALTER DAVIE: JUSTICE OF THE PEACE.'* Jack entered to see a cluttered little room. Walt sat down behind a desk. Jack sat facing him across the desk. On the wall, there was a picture of King George V.

After a few pleasantries, Walt said, "It's pretty quiet around here."

Jack asked about the liquor situation.

"It's all legit except for petty local stuff that no one minds. The Bronfmans have an export house at the station. Their brother-in-law Paul Matoff looks after it. They're good people and what they do is all legit and blessed by the government. You'll see cars up from North Dakota sometimes and they're all legit as far as we're concerned."

Nothing new there, thought Jack.

"By the way," added Walt, "from time to time I can use a little help for the party. I imagine Colonel Cross mentioned that."

"Not really," said Jack, thinking to himself, *In light of what Simmons said about driving people to the polls, is that what Cross was alluding to? Surely not. Anyway, better shut this down at the outset.*

"Oh, well, I'm sure I can count on you."

"Actually, I'm not interested in politics."

Walt gave him a quizzical look but said nothing to that.

That night, Jack drove back to the CPR train station in Bean Fate. It was dark. A couple of men were loading heavy cases onto a truck. Maybe the same guys he saw driving along that morning, he wondered.

Two other men who were standing watching turned to look at Jack, who approached them and introduced himself. One of them responded with a handshake and said in an accented voice, "I'm Harry Bronfman." Jack was delighted. First day on the job and he'd already met Cross's good friend! He seemed pleasant and mild-mannered and Jack instinctively liked him.

Indicating his companion with the pencil mustache, Harry said, "This is Paul Matoff, my brother-in-law." Matoff said hello in the same accent and, as he offered his hand, Jack noticed the diamond ring. He'd never seen anything like that on a man! After the shake, Jack unconsciously wiped his hand on his breeches.

Everyone looked tensed except Harry, who said, "You're obviously the new constable. I'd heard you were coming down here."

Had Cross put an announcement in the paper or what? Jack wondered.

"So what can we do for you?" asked Harry.

"I just want to get an idea of what's going on."

"We're making delivery of our whiskey, Black Horse whiskey. Our best stuff! These are some of our customers," he said as the two men who'd been loading the truck walked up. "They have a standing order every Wednesday night."

Matoff introduced a wiry-looking guy as Lee Dillege and explained that he was from Lignite across the line. He introduced the other guy as Jimmy Lacoste who, said Matoff, lived locally. Lacoste was a big blond young guy with a flattened nose that had presumably seen better days.

Harry, Matoff, and Dillege headed into the station office. Harry turned back to Jack and motioned to him to follow. Lacoste stayed outside. The station agent was inside. So was a young guy, introduced as Colin Rawcliffe, the telegraph operator.

Harry showed Jack the papers Matoff and Dillege were about to sign for the station agent: *"From Dominion Distributors to Lee Dillege, Minot, North Dakota, U.S.A. via C.P Express Bienfait."* He pointed to the value of $6,000, saying pointedly, "That's the number the government cares about; they collect tax on it."

"A lot of money," said Jack, impressed, a bigger dollar number than he'd ever seen before.

Suddenly, they heard a loud disturbance across the street. Jack hurried out of the station and ran across to the hotel to find a drunken brawl among a group of some fifteen young men. But central to it seemed to be a big, older man in cowboy garb. Jack tried to break it up and seemed to get support from the cowboy. Soon, the fighting stopped and Jack turned to the cowboy to thank him. Then he demanded of the group, "What's this all about?"

No one answered. Jack saw several bottles, many broken, of Black Horse lying around plus some glass canning jars. He demanded where these came from. A heavily-freckled guy with a black eye and bleeding nose said, "Stud," pointing to the cowboy.

Surprised, Jack looked at the cowboy, who said, "That's bullshit." Jack looked back at the other guy who waved his hand to indicate he didn't want to talk further and shuffled away.

Jack walked over to the cowboy.

"Thanks for your help. You're Stud?"

"That's me, Bill Studwell. But what that kid says, it's all bullshit. He made a mistake, that's all. Don't know where it all came from, but glad to help you out."

Jack looked at him. Stud was older, maybe forty-five, taller than Jack and spoke with a drawl. He was obviously a Yank. By people like Jack, all Americans were called Yanks. Stud had a certain presence, in fact, swagger. He was a swaggering Yank, like the guys who showed up late for the war and then claimed they'd won it. Not the kind of guy Jack liked.

"Why were they fighting?"

"Miners and ranch hands and harvesters… they always seem to like to fight when they come to town. Just kids mainly. Nothing serious."

When Jack returned to the station, Dillege and his group had left. So had Harry. Matoff and the agent were just about to turn off the lights and leave.

"What was that all about?" asked Matoff.

"A bunch of drunks fighting. Drunk on Black Horse whiskey! That's yours, isn't it?"

"That's one of our brands," said Matoff guardedly.

"Where would they get it?"

"Dunno, maybe it fell off the back of a truck heading south."

Jack eyed him dubiously. Then he said, "There were jars too with maybe vodka in them. That yours too?"

"Absolutely not! Might be the bohunk's."

"Who's that?"

"Borys. Borys Adamchuk."

Chapter 6

Into a ranch yard wheeled a Studebaker Big Six Touring car, a big car with a six-cylinder engine, more than two feet longer than Jack's tin lizzie and more than twice as heavy. Stud got out. He was an imposing man, six feet plus and well-built with just a hint of a paunch. After all, he was in his mid-forties and it was a few years since he'd worked as a cowboy, although he still dressed like one with checked shirt, red bandana around his neck, sweat-stained Stetson hat, faded blue jeans, and scuffed boots with pointed toes and two-inch Cuban heels. He put a canvas saddle bag over his shoulder.

A tall, lanky man dressed not unlike Stud walked out from behind a shed and called him over. He and Stud greeted each other coolly but amiably. The man accepted a cheap cigar from Stud and they each stood smoking with a foot on the split rail fence looking into the distance.

The man was the ranch owner, Dave Anderson.

After a while, Stud turned to Anderson.

"I assume we'll keep to our arrangements? I'll make sure there's no problem with rustlers?"

"Yeah," said Anderson with a thin, slightly crooked smile. It was a bit of a joke but serious too. After all, it was extortion.

"And I could use a couple of bottles too," added Anderson.

Stud reached into his saddle bag, brought out two bottles of Black Horse, and handed them to Anderson. He opened one, took a snort, and handed it back to Stud who took a snort himself and handed it back. Anderson reached into his back pocket, took out some cash, and handed it to Stud. "Wonder what it'd cost if I bought directly from Matoff," he said.

"Forget it. I have exclusive rights."

Stud walked back to the car and roared off.

Chapter 7

It was early morning and Kate Roberts, dressed nicely but modestly in a trim blue suit with longish skirt, stood beside a passenger train on the platform of the Union Station in Regina, a new and handsome building with neo-classical façade in the popular limestone from Tyndall in Manitoba. Her parents were there too. The train's whistle blew.

Her father, Dr. Roberts, and her mother were excited, proud and a little apprehensive, too, about saying goodbye to their elder daughter, the first child to fly the coop. As a handsome and well-dressed Montrealer and McGill graduate, he was a prominent family doctor whose patients tended to be of the wealthier class, a 'society doctor.' But he made a point of devoting a portion of his time to poorer patients too, not charging them much if at all. This he did out of the expectations of both his profession and his faith, for he and his wife were prominent members of the Metropolitan Methodist Church which played such a leading role in the life of the community. If he helped the sick, she helped her 'sisters,' having worked with Violet McNaughton in the Saskatchewan Equal Franchise League a few years ago. They were both 'good people' and consciously so, and their expectations were that Kate would be one too. So, her becoming a school teacher and helping in the large task of educating an exploding population, including many foreign children who needed upgrading to British standards, was a source of comfort and even pride to them. And yet, she was leaving home and going to the hinterlands of southern Saskatchewan at the age of eighteen.

"I wish you weren't going quite so far away," said the good doctor, giving his daughter a hug.

"Oh, I'll be fine, Dad. I really want to see something different."

"We'll see how you like it without running water!"

"She'll be fine," said Mrs. Roberts, patting Kate on the arm. "But," she added, "you'll be meeting new people, some of whom will be very different from us. Always remember who you are."

"Of course I will, Mom."

The whistle blew again. The trainman shouted, "All aboard!" There was a last round of hugs and kisses and Kate boarded the train. It pulled slowly out of the station and she settled down in her seat for a trip of several hours south.

She, too, was excited but a little apprehensive. What she'd been planning for a couple of years was really happening. After graduating from Grade Eleven at Regina Collegiate, she'd taken the one year's teacher training course at Regina Provincial Normal School. Having graduated with her certificate, she'd applied for several teaching jobs and she'd received an acceptance from the chairman of the Bienfait school board. She'd never heard of Bienfait, nor had her parents, but they'd looked it up on a map of Saskatchewan and found it right down near the border sixty miles southeast of Weyburn.

That was something they did know about, the city of Weyburn. Last year, her parents had been excited to be among a crowd of over two thousand people, a majority of the city's population, who'd attended the opening of the new Weyburn Mental Hospital. The crowd had been enthusiastic. The hospital was said to be the largest building in the British Commonwealth with over six hundred beds for mental defectives and it was sure to put their little city on the map and create a lot of well-paying jobs too. If the city folk were interested in the economic benefits, the Roberts were interested in the benefits for public health which, they fervently believed, included mental health. As progressives, they were so encouraged to see the Mental Diseases Act replace the old Dangerous Lunatics Act. Surely, they thought the treatment of lunacy as a criminal matter was wrong and the emphasis should be on the curative. The new hospital was expected to move in that direction with pioneering work such as experimentation with electric shock therapy.

That location was about all they knew about Bienfait except that she'd be boarding with the school board's chairman, a man named Anderson, and his family. He'd said in his letter that he and his wife and two daughters would welcome her. He sounded like a nice man somehow, although it was just a handwritten letter and the handwriting was pretty awful. Anyway, she'd be meeting them soon and her new students, too, some of whom might be almost her age. After all, she was only one year away from high school herself. *I hope they're nice kids,* she mused.

The passing scene was the same one Jack had seen a couple of weeks ago, although she didn't know that. But she saw more stooks than he'd seen as the harvest was now well underway. They were so attractive. Sheaves of wheat propped against each other in row patterns that seemed almost artful. And she saw haystacks raising their heads here and there, more silver than green or gold. It was another garnish to the scene. And ducks gathered in the sloughs, their instincts preparing them for the autumn flight south. Her mind wandered.

She knew her parents were reluctant, in a way, to see her go, mainly from a sense of protectiveness. And her mother had given her that little admonition: remember who you are, really, remember who we are too! Don't get mixed up with any undesirable boys! And remember, we don't drink! Of course she would remember that; all her life it seemed she'd heard her mother talk about the evils of drink and her work in the Women's Christian Temperance Union. Well, she knew now she was leaving the cocoon of their world and that was exactly what she wanted to do. *Mom and Dad are great parents*, she thought, *and very progressive too. All that work they do in the community. Especially Mom who's so active about prohibition and women's rights. And yet, they're actually pretty confining and judgmental too. Especially Mom.* And Kate thought back to all the arguments around the dining-room table, her mother so fervent about 'her' causes and Kate challenging her just because she was young and trying out her ideas.

She hadn't challenged the drinking ban but there was the time they'd argued about electric shock therapy which Kate had said sounded cruel. Her mother had explained it wasn't cruel because the intent was to help people with severe mental issues. You wouldn't accuse a dentist of being cruel because it hurt when he helped you by extracting a bad tooth. And there was a bigger issue with mental health, which was concerned with not only the individual's interests but those of the broader community, and not just the old concern for its safety but also the new expectations of its improvement.

At that point in the argument, Kate had criticized some ideas her mother was flirting with, like the need to sterilize mental defectives... in the name of public improvement. Ideas associated with something called the Eugenics Movement. Her mother had replied hotly that this too was in the public interest: to upgrade the human species by modern science and to weed out unhealthy and unclean specimens. Kate had said it sounded uncivilized and, indeed, un-Christian. Her mother had replied that many eminent and admirable people wouldn't agree with Kate.

"Like whom?" Kate had asked.

"Some good Christian men. Like Winston Churchill," she'd said in reference to the brilliant Liberal politician in England, an Anglican. "Like Alexander Graham Bell," she'd said in reference to the genius who'd invented the telephone. He'd recently served as honorary president of the International Congress of Eugenics at the American Museum of Natural History in New York, to which invitations had been sent by the US Department of State. In fact, Bell was an agnostic but Mrs. Roberts had assumed he was a Christian from his name.

And as a knockout blow, she'd added, "Like Nellie McClung," referring to the great Canadian suffragette, prominent Methodist and current member of the Alberta legislature whom she knew her daughter admired.

It was indeed a knockout blow and Kate had backed off. But really, her mother could get so tiresome with her self-righteousness and uncompromising views, her dear mother whom she loved so much, of course.

But now, Kate thought, *I'll be glad to be on my own now. To have some freedom.*

Anderson and several other men including the station agent and the freight-car handler were standing expectantly on the CPR station platform at Bean Fate. Anderson chatted easily and casually with everyone.

The agent asked Anderson why he was there.

"Waiting for the new school teacher from Regina."

"Man or woman?"

"Woman."

"The last one was no looker. Let's hope this one's better."

Anderson grinned. Then he stepped over to the tracks, bent over with his ear nearly on the track, and, hearing the rumble, announced that she'd be arriving soon.

With smoke bellowing from its engine smokestack, the Regina train soon came roaring into the station and amazingly quickly ground to a halt. The uniformed black train porter stepped down from the passenger coach to the platform. It was a deep step and he set down a step box so the sole debarking passenger would have shallower steps to make.

Kate arrived at the top of the steps, hesitated, and looked around.

What she saw was a long, low brown building and a few plain-looking men, with no women, on the platform. A dusty-looking platform and a dusty-looking lot, all of whom seemed to be staring at her.

What they saw was a very pretty young redhead in a trim blue suit.

She stepped down, at which point a gust of breeze lifted her longish skirt. She saw the knowing looks and chortles along the platform. Guy stuff! She recognized it from collegiate days. A man in cowboy clothes came forward, greeted her, and asked if she was Kate Roberts and she said yes.

"I'm Dave Anderson. Very glad to meet you. Come along."

With the help of the freight-car handler, he got her luggage (a 'trunk') into his beat-up tin lizzie even as he looked over at the agent who gave him a thumbs-up sign. She saw that too and was flattered. She'd always known she was pretty, everyone said so, and she was proud of it and liked the attention in spite of herself. Of course, it meant she had to be a bit more careful than some girls, and maybe that was behind her mother's parting admonition.

They drove along, kicking up dust on a gravel road, across the wide-open prairie. She'd occasionally driven outside Regina with her parents, but this time, she was more aware of the prairie and felt a sense of freedom and purity.

"I love this," she said with a sweeping arm motion.

"What?"

"The openness. It feels so pure compared to the city."

"We'll see how you feel in a couple of months," he said wryly.

'I wonder what he means,' she thought.

He drove up to the front door of a weather-beaten ranch house and Mrs. Anderson came out to greet them. She, too, looked weather-beaten in her faded apron with hair awry. She stared a moment at Kate blooming with youth, beauty, optimism... and nice clothes. But Mrs. Anderson was welcoming enough and took Kate upstairs to show Kate her room. It was very simple with a single bed on an iron bedstead. There was no cupboard but some shelves, a chamber pot for night waste, a plain wooden chair, and a clothes' hook high on the back of the door. Kate tried to hide her disappointment.

Chapter 8

In the knee-deep April mud, his feet were cold despite the heavy boots and puttees wrapped around his lower legs and despite the thick and fiery over-proof rum the officers had broken out, which meant it must be near zero hour.

And then he heard the heavy allied machineguns roar from behind and shells start screaming overhead. Soon he was following too behind Lenny up the ladder and the rum was hitting now and he felt strong and he could take on anything. Machineguns from across no-man's land had already started. As he stepped over the top, Jack was hit by the body of a comrade being blown back and he fell into the trench too. But he picked himself up and climbed back up the ladder into the predawn maelstrom. The noise of all the machine-guns was shattering, and he was running across the scarred terrain. The sky seemed on fire. Bullets whined and thudded through the ranks of Jack and his comrades, splattering mud and shrapnel and shredding many of them. He came across a newly severed human foot lying on top of the mud, cut off cleanly above the ankle. There was no boot or sock. Where were they? The skin was white and clean. How could that be in all this mud? Where was the rest of the body? Who was it? Not his dad? Why would he be here? He picked his way through craters and around bodies. A German stuck his head above the lip of a sniper hole and Jack shot it clean through. Another German was climbing out of a hole and Jack bayoneted him. Where was Lenny? Oh, there he was over there. They'd reached the blood-soaked trenches which the Germans had just left. Except the many who weren't ever going to leave. Bodies were lying around, some in poses with hands raised and a look of terror on their faces. Did one blink? No, he was dead but there, a lone German was definitely alive and had lost his gun and fallen and seemed trapped in the mud. He looked up at Jack who pointed his pistol between the beseeching eyes. He was a boy like himself. He fired and blood spurted from the hole between the eyes. Oh, the horror!

Jack awoke screaming, sweating and his heart pounding. He got out of bed, unlocked a little case and took out a reefer. He lit up and settled back into bed, slowly relaxing.

Later that morning, Jack drove up to a church whose sign said: *'BIENFAIT METHODIST CHURCH: THE REV. FRANK SPARLING, PASTOR.'* Jack was late and sat alone in the back pew. The pastor was just stepping up to the pulpit to give his sermon. He was young, clean-cut, good-looking, and fiery.

He began by referring to the disgraceful brawl in Bean Fate just the other day. It was shocking, he said, to see such a thing after years of so-called Prohibition. He railed against the satanic conspiracy among society's deceitful leaders who failed to impose complete Prohibition, who always created loopholes in the law and who failed to enforce the law anyway. He spoke angrily against the papist and foreign forces supporting that conspiracy.

He talked about the misery brought by booze: ruination of marriages, violence in families, men beating their wives, children being deprived of safe homes and even the necessaries of life, men behaving foolishly and ruining their livelihoods, and so on. The other day, in a disgraceful brawl, young men being debauched by the dealers in booze, where did they get it? He didn't know exactly. Maybe some of the congregation did! And certainly some of the leaders in Regina must know. An absolute disgrace!

Although it was a good performance, Jack had heard this line before from other pastors and his gaze wandered around the congregation. He saw Walt looking up at the pastor, intently and sanctimoniously. He'd seen that sort of thing before too. Then he noticed Kate just a pew ahead and across from where he sat. That perked him up a bit. She must have felt his gaze because she looked sideways and their eyes met briefly before she looked away hurriedly. Did she blush?

Always remember, the pastor was saying, booze is a sin. But some people asked, he said rhetorically, about Jesus turning water into wine. Well, the translation in the Bible may have called it that but, assuredly, it wasn't alcohol. It was a drink, but not an alcoholic drink. Sparling knew that. You know how? Precisely because alcohol is a poison and He wouldn't want people to drink poison! Full stop. And so on. Jack saw many parishioners nod their heads in agreement. Even Walt.

After the service ended, people milled about. After saying hello to Walt, who left quickly, Jack approached Sparling talking to the Andersons and Kate.

Sparling had calmed right down, seemingly a different man than a few minutes ago. He was delighted to welcome Jack to his church and introduced Jack to the Andersons and to Kate. Jack was attracted to Kate. Who wouldn't be? He also hit if off immediately with Anderson and a warm feeling pervaded the whole group.

"I'm so glad," said Sparling, "that we finally have a constable who's one of us for a change. It's about time. That Commissioner doesn't seem to care about all the drinking. Maybe because he's a dogan. They all like to drink. Even the priests, in fact, especially the priests."

Jack didn't respond to that. He wasn't going to be a part of badmouthing his superior officer.

"Besides the dogans," continued Sparling, "there's the problem of the foreigners who all like to drink and don't seem to understand our laws."

Jack looked at him expectantly.

"For example, that man Adamchuk."

"I've already heard of him," said Jack.

"Yes, he's a farmer who attends that new funny-looking church down the road who I hear is a bootlegger. I hope you'll put a stop to him."

Jack was a little surprised by Sparling's bluntness but replied, "I'll look into it."

He and Kate drifted to one side.

"Looks like you've got your marching orders," she said with a mischievous little smile.

He was a surprised by this too, since he didn't know her. "Looks like it," he replied.

"At least we know where he stands on Prohibition," she said.

He regarded her in both amusement and admiration. She was obviously a respectable girl, being at church and all, but she was also very pretty and just a little saucy, a redhead after all. He knew right then that he wanted to get to know her a whole lot better. He'd have to figure out a way to do that. It would not be easy in a small town where she boarded with the school trustee's family.

Jack was not one to disobey his marching orders. So the next day, he decided to find out about Sparling's concerns. He drove to a farmyard where there was a small house and barn with thatched roofs and walls made of rough logs from small prairie trees. Although Jack didn't know it, the scene could have been on the vast Ukrainian plains. A youngish man, deeply tanned with dirty blonde hair, neither good nor bad-looking, emerged from the barn and stood there apprehensively as the man in the uniform with the gun on his hip approached.

"Are you Borys Adamchuk?" Jack said genially enough, remembering Cross's lecture.

"Yes," Adamchuk answered, in a heavily accented voice and with the wariness of the peasant's eternal suspiciousness with which, however, Jack was unfamiliar.

And that wariness made Jack immediately suspicious. After all, 'honest people don't need to be wary of the police' was the way he looked at it. But he would try to be open-minded.

"That's a nice-looking barn. When'd it go up?"

"Oh, I don't remember exactly," said Adamchuk nervously.

Jack didn't like this defensiveness. *Bloody bohunk*. "Probably," he said sarcastically, "while some of us were fighting for King George. Our king. You've heard of him?"

Adamchuk just looked at him and said nothing. *Looks nervous.*

"Anyway, let me look around," said Jack.

He headed into the barn and at the back, in an adjoining shed, soon found a homemade pot still and many glass canning jars, some capped. He opened one and sniffed. It smelled like alcohol.

"What's this?"

Before Adamchuk could answer, Jack took a taste. It was almost tasteless.

"Must be vodka," he said.

"I make some for myself," said Adamchuk ever more nervous.

"All this?" Jack gestured at all the jars. "For yourself?"

"For me and my friends."

"You sell to them?"

"No, no. Just give. Friends."

"You must have a helluva lot of friends. I'm going to have to charge you for this."

Adamchuk looked stricken.

+ + +

49

Jack had laid the charge against Adamchuk before Walt and the hearing was scheduled for a couple of days later. So, on a hot morning, Jack entered into the Bienfait drugstore. Mrs. Anderson was at the counter picking up a bottle of Rock-a-Bye cough cure. "Put it on the tab," she said to the druggist. She turned to Jack with a hint of embarrassment and seemed maybe a little high. They said hello and she walked out.

Jack introduced himself to the druggist and asked if Mrs. Anderson was okay. The druggist gave him a blank look and replied, "Yes, but she has a chronic cough."

Jack ordered a Coke which the druggist dispensed from the soda fountain in front. Standing idly looking out the window as he savored the ice-cold drink, Jack noted a big Studebaker parked in front of Walt's store down the street. As he was finishing his Coke, he saw Stud leave the store and drive off in the Studebaker.

Jack walked along the road and entered the store. Walt was not out front, so he walked back to the little office to find Walt sitting behind his desk. Standing in front of it and turning to look nervously at Jack was Adamchuk.

Walt conducted the 'hearing' across his desk. Jack read out loud the charge he'd laid against Adamchuk: making liquor for the purpose of sale for domestic use and not for export. Adamchuk swore he just made vodka for his personal use as he did in the old country and didn't sell it to anyone. Jack pointed out there were a lot of jars, so Adamchuk's claim sounded ridiculous.

Adamchuk looked straight ahead at Walt, saying, "Why does he give hard time to a poor man like me? At home? Why doesn't he go give hard time to that rich kike Matoff at the station?"

"That's a point," said Walt, looking at Jack. "Did you have a search warrant?"

"You know I didn't," said Jack in surprise. "I would've had to get it from you!"

"I think I'll have to reject your evidence then."

With that, Walt acquitted Adamchuk who walked out with a triumphant look in Jack's direction.

Jack was a little perplexed and a little angry too.

"Walt, why did you proceed with the hearing at all if you were going to reject my evidence over lack of a search warrant? You knew I didn't have one."

"I hadn't twigged to it. Anyway, Jack, all the bohunks drink and probably sell a bit to their friends, but so what? No harm. Plus they vote for us too. As you'll come to find out if you help us out."

"As I told you, I'm not really interested in politics."

"You're not a secret Conservative, are you?"

"No," said Jack, turning to walk away. Then he stopped and looked back.

"By the way, how come Stud was here with Adamchuk?"

"Oh, Stud wasn't with him," said Walt coolly. "He just came in to buy something."

Chapter 9

The Soo Line Railway ran from Chicago to Moose Jaw, Saskatchewan via Minot and the border town of Portal. It also stopped in Estevan where Stud was waiting in his Studebaker as the Soo Line's crack train from Chicago rolled into the station. Two men stepped down off the 'Soo-Pacific' as Stud walked up to meet them. They were conspicuous as city-slickers in three-piece suits and homburg hats. They were young guys, one beefy with conspicuous facial scars and the other slim with cold, dark eyes. Stud drove them over to Whites.

Soon after, Harry, accompanied by Leech and Matoff, arrived at Whites carrying a brown paper package. They walked up to the second floor and knocked on a bedroom door. They were admitted by Stud, to whom Matoff casually nodded.

Stud introduced them to Al Capone, the beefy guy, and Dutch Schultz, the slim guy. Both had broad Bronx accents.

Harry saw a couple of guns and shoulder-holsters hanging on the bedstead, not something he'd seen before. He also noticed Capone's diamond finger ring. That was something he had seen before... on his brother-in-law.

"Welcome to Canada," said Harry genially. "I understand you represent Mister Torrio."

"Yeah, we represent Mister Torrio," said Capone as he eyed the package suspiciously. A package could conceal a gun.

Harry saw this and opened the package to display a bottle of Black Horse. "This is our finest whiskey," he said.

"Mister Torrio is interested in large quantities," said Capone.

"Yes, no problem. We can handle whatever you need."

Harry turned to Matoff who produced a shot glass and poured out a shot and handed it to Capone.

After a gulp, Capone said, "Tastes pretty good. And I hear there's no problem with the cops here."

"I'm head of the liquor commission," said Leech, "and sales for exports are all legal."

Capone looked contemptuously at Leech. He'd seen a few like him in Chicago.

There was a feeling of nervous bonhomie in the room, guys wanting to make a deal but not knowing each other. Capone and Harry were the two big dogs. All the while, Capone was letting Harry know how rough and tough he was, trying to intimidate. But Harry, trying to emphasize it was his turf, said, "So, we have the law with us. Let's work it out."

"Okay," Capone said, "we want only good stuff. Like this. No shit. Understand?"

"Of course."

"A guy back home sold us some bad stuff... He's not around anymore... Understand?"

"Yes," said Harry a little nervously.

They talked money and logistics and confirmed a deal. Then Capone gave Harry a diamond stickpin (tie pin) to seal the deal as Mr. Torrio's partner. There was lots of false bonhomie again.

That night, there was a poker game at Whites. The regulars, including Stud and Matoff, played. Capone and Dutch joined in, but not Harry, who'd left town. Matoff played big as if to impress Capone and Dutch. They won big and he lost big. As he was leaving, he took Stud aside and said,

"So now you're working for those guys?"

"Just driving this one time."

"You're still working for me too?"

"Yeah, of course."

"Okay, but I didn't know you'd be here and when we arrived, I was worried you might show Harry that we were involved. Remember, it's just between you and me."

+++

The next day, Jack drove over to the outskirts of Estevan and parked on the lip of the wide Souris valley. A lot of cars and buggies were already parked there and people were streaming down the valleyside to the floor a hundred feet below. It was a magnificent scene, looking down and then across to the prairie on the other side stretching away to the horizon. There were lots of people down below. It was Labor Day and Lee Dillege had brought his barnstorming semi-pro baseball team, the Cubans, for an exhibition double-header with the Regina Balmorals.

There was a field on the flats down there. A baseball diamond was marked out with white base lines. Along the first and third base lines were simple plank bleachers already half-full. The lines had been freshly chalked and the grass had been freshly cut. The infield was lush green, for the valley bottom was moist. It was lush in the outfield too, although almost soggy in one or two spots nearer to the river. Many people had come from miles around including Burke County across the line. Most people parked their cars and buggies at the top of the bank but there was a road down to the field and some had parked down there. It was to be an all-day event and they were all there to watch a game, picnic, and just see friends and gossip on a nice late summer day. He drove the lizzie down and parked.

Since the Soo Line didn't leave for Chicago until late afternoon, Stud took Capone and Dutch to the game. "You might be interested," he said, pointing to a player surrounded by people and signing autographs. "Swede Risberg is playing shortstop for the Cubans." Capone was clearly surprised and impressed. Swede was the Chicago White Sox shortstop who, along with seven teammates including Shoeless Joe Jackson, had been banned from the majors for life for fixing the World Series three years ago for Arnold Rothstein, head of the New York underworld.

They ambled over to where Swede was signing autographs for star-struck fans near his current employer, Lee Dillege. Stud said hello to Dillege and introduced him to Capone, Stud explaining that Dillege owned the ball team. Capone and Dillege chatted for a couple of minutes until Swede could break loose to talk to them too.

Jack noticed this and wondered who the beefy punk with the scarred face was. *Where did he come from? Did Dillege know him?*

Kate was picnicking on the grass with the Andersons and Anderson called Jack over. He sat down on one of the blankets they'd spread on the grass. He accepted Mrs. Anderson's offering of an egg salad sandwich and iced tea which she poured from a glass jar. He and Kate talked easily. Apart from being pretty, she was bubbly, which melted his reserve.

"So, constable," she said coquettishly, "did you carry out your marching orders?"

"As a matter of fact, I did."

"What happened?"

"It didn't go very well."

"Did you find bootleg liquor?"

"I found liquor which I thought was for bootlegging. But Mister Adamchuk said it was just for him and his friends."

"Did you believe him?"

"No, I didn't but the JP, Mister Davie, did."

"You don't mean the man who has the store?"

"That's him."

"Isn't the JP supposed to be a judge?"

"A JP can be a layman and that's what he is."

"So what happened?"

"The guy got off."

By now, Mrs. Anderson was listening in.

"That's ridiculous," she said. "Everyone knows Borys sells liquor."

"That may be," said Jack, "but Walt Davie didn't agree."

"Not all that surprising," she replied without further explanation. "Anyway, Jack, you'll have to come to dinner with us sometime."

"That would be nice, thank you."

Kate looked pleased.

Out of the corner of his eye, Jack noticed Matoff escorting Capone and Dutch around, looking pleased with himself with a diamond ring just like the tough guy from Chicago.

Matoff took Capone and Dutch over to meet Walt.

Jack excused himself from the Anderson party and walked over so that Matoff had to introduce them to him too. Capone looked at him sneeringly. He clearly didn't respect cops and Jack was taken aback. That was not how cops were looked at in Saskatchewan.

He walked away and stood at the end of the first base line bleachers watching the game. It was only the fourth inning of the first game and already the Cubans were ahead: 6-0. Two were out and no runners on. At which point

Swede Risberg hit a long ball to center field. It looked like a triple but the Balmoral center-fielder had trouble in the soggy turf and Swede outran the throw to home-plate to cheers from the Burke County contingent. 7-0. *Oh well,* thought Jack, *it's not supposed to be evenly matched. Semi-pro versus amateurs.*

A man came and stood beside him and caught his attention. He was maybe forty.

"Hello, constable," the man said, "I'm Tom Stinson, Sheriff of Burke County, across the line." He was in civvies.

"I'm Jack. Glad to meet you."

They shook hands.

"Looks like you're hanging out with a couple of bad-looking guys," said Tom as they both stood watching the game. "Where'd you find them?"

"Came up on the Soo Line apparently."

"I don't recognize them and they look like Chicago. They'll be bad news."

They ambled along and came across Stud's Studebaker parked on the field back from the ball diamond.

"Nice car," said Jack.

"Looks a lot like one that was stolen in my county, although I see it has Saskatchewan plates."

Then Jack noticed Stud was sitting in it, window down. He stuck his head out the window and, grinning at Tom insolently, said, "Funny, you don't look so big without your sidearm, sheriff."

Jack looked at Tom who looked more annoyed than angry. They started to walk away.

"That's Bill Studwell," said Tom.

"I've met him."

"He's from Texas. Bad guy. Wanted for extortion in North Dakota and probably elsewhere. But it's not extraditable, so he's safe up her. Any time you want to drop him off at the border."

Jack didn't take it as a serious suggestion.

"What about Dillege?"

"He's a farmer in Lignite."

"Where's that?"

"In my county. And he's a smalltime rustler-bootlegger. He's a hustler too. Owns the ball team and everybody likes him for that. He's not that bad a guy. Why do you ask?"

"I met him when he was buying a carload of booze in Bean Fate."

"How come?"

"I'd just arrived and saw him doing some sort of deal at the railway station, so went over to check it out. His papers were in order and it was all legal. An export deal."

"Huh. We should get together sometime and compare notes."

+ + +

One evening a few days later, Jack drove into Bean Fate and saw activity at the station, obviously the same business of Matoff helping guys load cases of booze. Except it wasn't Wednesday and looked different from the other deals he'd seen. There was one big car, with Illinois plates instead of North Dakota plates, and the guys didn't look like hicks from North Dakota. They looked like hoods, nasty-looking with homburgs and bulges under the arms of their suit jackets. He thought he recognized one.

Jack motioned to Matoff to come and speak to him.

"Who are these guys?"

"They're from Chicago and that's Dutch Schultz who you met at the ballgame. Same as our other deals, only bigger. And I don't know why you're bothering me. You're even worse than Herb what's-his-name…"

You arrogant asshole, thought Jack, *you'll get your comeuppance someday.*

+ + +

The Estevan Police Station had a dedicated phone line. They didn't use the regular multi-party line on which the entire community could listen in. Jack placed a call to Mahoney's office. Mahoney soon came on the line, sounding surprised.

"What's up?"

"I thought I should let you know there might be trouble brewing down here."

"Is that supposed to be a joke?"

"No sir."

"You know shipments to the states are legal. That's the big thing, isn't it?"

"I know that and I checked out the Bronfman operation, which seems okay. But the situation might be changing," and Jack reported on meeting Capone and Dutch at the ballgame and then Dutch and other hoods picking up booze last night. A different crowd!

Mahoney said he didn't doubt there were lots of unsavory Americans picking up booze but to just keep an eye on it. The Bronfmans were smart and would be careful.

"The thing is," said Jack, "I get the feeling they're sort of tight with these guys. Matoff was buddy-buddy with the hoods at the ballgame. At the same time, he's buddy-buddy with the JP. And the JP himself was friendly with the hoods. Just seems a little strange."

"The JP is a member of the community down there, so he knows Matoff and there's nothing wrong with that. He can't be faulted for meeting people at a ballgame like anyone else."

"Well, this JP dismissed a bootlegging charge I laid on a technicality. It seemed he wanted to let the guy off!"

Mahoney enquired a bit and when he heard about throwing out the case for evidence obtained without a search warrant, said, "Well, that's a decision the JP was entitled to make. What of it? So you learned a lesson. Don't bother me unless you have any real problems you can't handle. But of course, if you feel you do need help, let me know right away."

Jack felt the implied criticism and said defensively, "I wasn't worried that I couldn't handle it. I just wondered if it sounded unusual."

"No, it's policing, that's all."

Chapter 10

Sam came to town to discuss the Torrio deal. He and Harry met in Harry's living room.

The opportunity to blow out large quantities of booze was huge, said Harry, and the terms he'd negotiated were excellent. Sam nodded approvingly. But Harry noted the two punks Torrio had sent were nasty, tough-looking guys and dealing with them hadn't been very nice.

"Nasty, how?"

"They basically threatened murder if there was any bad booze."

"Shit, Harry! You better be careful then because those asshole partners are careless about quality. You said so yourself to Chechik. So you better make sure that for Torrio, you only send our stuff."

"Easier said than done."

"You better find a way. Keep tight controls," said Sam. "And how's our stuff going?"

"Okay. But a guy from the Commission is sniffing around."

"What about?"

"Compounding."

"Fuck!"

Harry understood and had even expected Sam's reaction. Compounding was illegal. It was where whiskey was mixed with other spirits like gin, or with pure alcohol plus colorings and flavorings. On the other hand, blending, where different classes of whiskey were mixed, was legal. It was a fine distinction but all-important legally. Good whiskey plus bad whiskey was okay. Good whiskey plus other spirits like gin, or pure alcohol and other ingredients, was not okay. The motivation for mixing in either case was to reduce the average cost and increase the margin. But mixing legitimate whiskey with other much cheaper booze or even pure alcohol, which was even cheaper, made the margins that much higher.

The Bronfmans had originally just sold booze produced by established distillers. But a couple of years ago, Sam had got the idea of producing their own booze to increase both the quantity of sales and their profit margins. He was always thinking about the profits. Plus, Harry suspected, he'd also wanted to show that he knew more about the liquor business than his well-known and well-liked older brother.

There were two big issues: the quality of this mixed booze and whether it was blended or compounded. He'd bought all the necessary equipment to ensure good quality including redwood casks and bottling supplies. But his first batch had ended in disaster with barrels of bluish booze. Nevertheless, the relentless Sam had persevered and become quite adept at mixing. But rumors persisted that the mixing wasn't blending, it was compounding.

This was what had given rise to their first major run-in with the law in the person of a federal customs agent named Cyril Knowles. He was an unhappy little man and a former Conservative Party heeler, as political party workers were known. He and Harry had first crossed swords two years ago at a Bronfman outlet in the hamlet of Gainsborough back in Manitoba. Knowles had impounded a rum runners' car on a technicality and they'd suggested he deal with Harry. After all, they were legal in Canada. Knowles had met with Harry and afterwards alleged Harry had offered him a bribe, which Harry denied. When Knowles had reported all this to his superiors at the Customs Department in Ottawa, no one seemed to want to hear him. Instead, they'd revoked his right to bounty payments for seizing illegally transported booze!

Understandably, Knowles was angered. This past January, he'd retaliated with a real show of force, bursting in upon the Dominion Distributors premises in the Craftsman Building with some other customs agents on alleged suspicion of finding illegal compounding. He'd chosen to regard the distilling equipment as equipment for making illegal compounds. Maybe it was and maybe it wasn't. And he'd found labels which he took to be fake labels no matter what Harry said. Harry had watched in consternation as they had gone about smashing Sam's redwood casks and breaking open cans. Booze and various other liquids had been spilled all over the place, running out into the drains and gutter as, to Harry's embarrassment, a jeering crowd had gathered outside.

Nor had that been the end of it. Ottawa had followed up by launching a prosecution against Dominion Distributors. The American government had even got involved, being only too glad to assist in stopping the flood of booze across the border. The U.S. consul in Regina, Colonel Johnson, had even arranged for an expert to come from Washington, D.C., to testify as to forged labeling.

But the Bronfmans had counterattacked. Knowles had been summoned to Ottawa to meet with his boss, the Minister of Customs, none other than Hon. Jacques Bureau. While he was waiting in the minister's ante-room, Sam and Allan had been meeting inside with Bureau. Knowles had met Sam and Allan coming out looking like cats who'd swallowed some canaries. When he'd entered Bureau's office, he'd been castigated for carrying out a personal vendetta against the Bronfmans. In fact, he'd basically been confined to barracks and had his career ruined. And the prosecution had been mysteriously abandoned!

"Are they still complaining about compounding after we got that thrown out?"

"There's a guy sniffing around," replied Harry.

"Tell him in no uncertain terms that we've already dealt with that."

"I did, but they know about things."

"Like what?"

"Like all that alcohol that arrived from Davis in Montreal."

"Can't you tell your big buddy Leech to back off? Isn't that why we're buying all that land from him?"

"Yeah, and I can handle it."

"Okay. Make sure you do. Back to Torrio. Just make sure he gets only our stuff. We can't afford any of Chechik's rotgut going there by mistake."

Chapter 11

The small wooden schoolhouse, weather-beaten white with a red pitched roof, stood rather forlornly in a one-acre lot on a gravel road a mile from the Anderson ranch and two miles outside Bienfait. Kate arrived for her first day.

She entered through a front door into a little hallway running across the front with an enclosure where she could hang her coat and with a little mirror where she could fix her hair. Beyond that was one large room with windows along one side. The light from the large but curtain-less windows revealed a room that was quite bare: three rows of eight desks, each facing the front and the doorway to the hall, a pot-bellied wood stove in the middle, a shelf with a water pail and a dipper, a teacher's desk at the front with a simple chair, a blackboard on the wall behind with a little rack along the bottom on which sat a few pieces of chalk, a few shelves with very few books, a map of the world with the British Empire identified in red on all five inhabited continents, a picture of King George V and Queen Mary, and a squeaky organ on which the teacher could play 'God Save the King' if she could, although it wasn't a job requirement.

She was disappointed and annoyed to find it all dirty, with chalk marks on the blackboard from last June. *Obviously, Mr. Anderson hasn't done his job*, she thought. *Come to think of it, the ranch is a pretty scruffy too. Nice man but a little slapdash.*

The children started to arrive to start their new year. Some of them were dressed in clothes not only threadbare but dirty. And there was the unusual and dreadful smell of garlic from some, to which she was unused.

But there was an initial air of excitement as the children surveyed their pretty young teacher, ranging from the bashful in little girls to something else in a couple of teenage boys. This soon changed. First, Kate ordered them to clean up the room, sweeping and dusting, and to wash the blackboard. Then she lectured them on hygiene based on instructions in a pamphlet issued by the

Saskatchewan Department of Education, which was mindful that there were lots of 'foreign' children whose parents might be unaware of Canadian cleanliness standards! Some of the children were embarrassed and some were angered too.

Later that afternoon, as the children were preparing to leave, Kate heard a car drive into the schoolyard. She went to the window and saw Stud get out of the Studebaker and amble toward the door. *What on Earth is that man doing here?* she thought.

She answered his knock on the door. Stud said "howdy". He'd seen her at the ballgame but they hadn't met and he just wanted to welcome her to town. Rather than inviting him inside, she stepped outside but left the door open. She didn't really know what to say and was embarrassed yet fascinated too. Here was a big older man, a cowboy, with an exotic drawl, good-looking in a rough sort of way, exuding a certain charm, and a hint of danger.

They made small talk for a couple of minutes until she became aware of the children crowding up behind her, trying to see what was going on. She said she really must get back to her class. Stud tipped his Stetson and started to amble back to his car while she turned to see the wonder and excitement on her charges' faces.

As Stud was getting into the Studebaker to leave, Jack drove up in his tin lizzie. This made the children even more excited.

Stud and Jack scowled at each other and Stud drove off. Jack walked over to the doorway and asked Kate why Stud had been there. She said Stud was just welcoming her to town. Jack replied with an edge in his voice that he doubted Stud usually did that. Wasn't she a little worried about it? Kate brushed him off airily and asked Jack why he'd come. He replied because he was driving by and thought maybe she'd like a ride home after her first day of school. "You're a dear," she said. "I'd love that."

As they drove along, he asked her how her first day had gone. She told him it was a little different from 'home,' with the plain and unkempt little school and children. In turn, he told her about feeling a little uneasy about the Bronfman booze operation which didn't seem to be shared by his boss.

The next morning, as Anderson was working in the ranch yard, he heard the clop-clop of a trotting horse. He turned around to see a horse-drawn buggy with two passengers and watched as it drove up close to him. The passengers were young women, one of whom was holding the reins. He recognized them as his voters, parents of school children.

"Ladies?" he enquired genially.

Ignoring the compliment, one of them said, "Dave, you're the chairman of the school board and we've come to complain about the new schoolteacher."

"Why, what's the problem?" he asked in surprise.

They seemed agitated and told him about the children coming home with Kate's lecture on hygiene and better clothes. They said they wanted an education for their children but not lectures on fancy city ways. And they reported on Jack, let alone the notorious Stud, arriving at the school. Imagine our teacher receiving men at the school!

By this time, Mrs. Anderson had come out of the house and walked over to the buggy too.

"Well, I'll speak to Kate but I'm sure it's just a misunderstanding," he said. "This is Kate's first job, you know."

"It was a mistake for Stud to show up," said Mrs. Anderson, "but you can't blame Kate for that. And Jack seems like a fine young man. I see him at church and I know he just went to the school to drive Kate home on her first day."

"I don't know," said the driver. "She'll want watching."

With that, she gave a clicking sound and the reins a small snap, said "gee" and the horse turned and they started off back down the lane.

"Thanks for coming over to help," said Anderson. "They were more ready to listen to you."

"Thanks, but mark my words: Kate's going to be trouble."

+ + +

A few nights later, Anderson was at home, sitting downstairs by himself, smoking a cigarette and reading a book. Mrs. Anderson and the girls had already gone up to bed, as had Kate. He heard what sounded like a gunshot. Then there were several more and then quiet.

Mrs. Anderson called down from the head of the stairs, "Dave, did you hear that?"

"Yeah. Sounded like gunshots. I'll go outside and see if I can see anything."

"Be careful!"

Stepping outside on the porch, he saw lights coming from a few hundred yards across his property.

He went back in and called up, "There are lights over towards the Portal Road. I'm going to check it out."

"Don't go!"

"Don't worry. I'll be careful."

He pulled on his cowboy boots and walked out in the cool autumn evening to the stable, quickly saddled up his favorite horse and set out towards the lights which were still glowing dimly in the dark. They looked puny under the arc of the Milky Way shining brightly in the black sky. In about ten minutes, he got close and reined in his horse. Sitting there, he could see two cars with lights blazing but they couldn't see him in the dark. A man with a shotgun was standing facing two men sitting with their hands behind their backs. Two other men were transferring cases from one car to the other. *A hijacking!* He knew they couldn't see him in the dark, but at that point, a small animal startled his horse, which whinnied. The man with the shotgun turned towards Anderson's location in the dark and fired twice. He felt pellets hit the saddle pad and for a split second wondered if he and his horse had been hurt but, no, they weren't, and they galloped home. As he anticipated, the hijackers didn't try to follow him in a car across rough country.

When he came into the house, all the females were there: Mrs. Anderson, the girls, and Kate, in their nightgowns and with worried looks on their faces.

"Don't worry, girls," he said. "There are some bad men over there but they won't be coming here. Some guys are hijacking a rum runner's car. But once they complete loading their car, they'll head south right away. They won't come over here."

"But we heard more shots when you went over there," said Mrs. Anderson.

"Yeah, they heard the horse and took a couple of pot shots in our direction but they didn't do any damage. Now everyone, go back to bed."

But he didn't take his own advice, not for a long while, not until he'd had a swig from the bottle he kept in the locked cupboard. *I'll wait till I'm sure.*

+ + +

A few days later, Sparling, in a suit of rough tweed and wearing no 'dog collar,' was standing at the counter of the Bank of Montreal's little branch in the nearby village of Ceylon. Hearing a big car screech to a stop, he turned around to see three rough-looking men walk in, holding handguns. A fourth was standing beside the car, holding a shotgun menacingly. People on the street stood agog. It was a holdup! In Ceylon, Saskatchewan of all places! No one in or out of the bank made any effort to stop the bandits who quickly convinced the young manager to open the safe and hand over its cash. Then the bandits ran out with bags of loot. All four jumped into the car and roared off.

Jack was immediately called over. Sparling was still there. Jack quizzed him, the bank manager, and the other witnesses. They were all both frightened and angered by the Yanks. The manager explained that he did not have a gun, nor did anyone else. So what could they have done to stop them?

"How do you know they were Yanks?" asked Jack.

A woman piped up, "Their car had North Dakota plates."

Sparling was particularly outraged. He said, "All this violence results from the booze laws which encourage gun-toting Yankee gangsters to come up into our law-abiding society. There's obviously corruption in high places."

Jack was taken aback and asked a little defensively, "Like who?"

Sparling took him aside and said, lowering his voice, "I don't know exactly, but maybe even one of our esteemed brethren, Mister Leech. They say he's very close to Harry Bronfman."

Jack looked at Sparling questioningly and thought, *could Leech be on the take? Wouldn't Cross know?*

+ + +

Jack, in civvies, drove Kate to a beautiful site on the south slope of the Souris Valley with sandstone outcroppings eroded into fantastical shapes. It was well-known to the locals as 'The Rocks' but its real name was Roche Percée and it had various historical associations. It had been a meeting place for Indian tribes complete with their paintings on the rocks. And then it had been the site of an encampment of the newly formed Royal Northwest Mounted Police on their initial march west in 1874 to establish law and order after the infamous Cypress Hills massacre of Indians by American whiskey traders.

They shared a picnic lunch under a blue sky with puffy white clouds. A perfect prairie fall day! The yellowing leaves of small poplars rustled gently in the breeze. It was a relief for both of them to talk of their recent local experiences. He told her about the Ceylon hold-up. She told him about the hijacking and they talked about the increasing threat of local violence. She asked if that was a worry for him and he said of course it was. She seemed sympathetic and he liked that.

And he was sympathetic to her problems at school and the complaining mothers.

"They complained about Stud showing up, which wasn't my fault," she said.

"Of course not, but you know he's dangerous."

"What do you mean?" she asked with, even he noticed, a certain brightness in her eyes.

"He's a fugitive from the states."

"Really? Why?"

"For extortion at least, although I'll bet even worse."

"He seems quite nice."

"Well, he's not!"

"They complained about you picking me up too."

"That's ridiculous!"

"I know. I know. Mrs. Anderson said that too."

Quickly changing the topic, she started to explore what they might have in common. They found Regina, Regina Collegiate (different years), and church. It was slightly awkward when she said her father was a doctor while his had a corner store. Bit of a class difference there. But they pressed on. She was a Girl Guide while he was Boy Scout. He told her proudly about playing hockey, although his hopes to play for the Regina Pats had been dashed because of the war and that was behind him now. Still, she was impressed; junior hockey players were stars in Regina.

"Did you ever fight?"

"Yes, of course," he said, looking at her almost incredulously. It was hockey!

"What about the war?"

"What about it?"

"Did ever see anyone killed?"

67

"Yeah. Lots," he said heavily. "But one was a guy from the country who boarded with us. Lenny Garneau. He was Metis, but a good guy. We were chums."

Jack looked a bit upset but Kate was curious and continued her interrogation.

"I never met any Metis. Did he speak French?"

"Yeah. Not around us. But in France, although he seemed to have some trouble making himself understood."

"Did you kill any Germans?"

Jack's face drained and he looked away and she could see he was struggling for control. He finally looked back with tears in his eyes and lips trembling.

"Yes."

She put her hand on his shoulder.

"Do you want to talk about it?" she asked softly.

"No."

She could feel him trembling and gave him a light kiss on the cheek and calmed him. They embraced. What started off as her comforting him soon became something else. There was real chemistry. Added to that was Jack's acute and vulnerable emotional state and her real compassion. But they'd both been brought up Methodist and Jack was just as 'proper' as Kate, although he'd had chances, some of which he'd taken, to experiment overseas in a no-risk environment. Well, not entirely no-risk. There had been disease risks for which, fortunately, the army had provided prophylactics. She hadn't had any such chances. So while they kissed and embraced each other with increasing ardor, they both knew when to stop. That was what good young Methodists did. Nevertheless, they both felt that suddenly they were starting a serious relationship, although they didn't say so.

Looking back on it that night, Kate felt very positive about Jack. He was a 'good person.' She could see that. Even though his family background wasn't quite what her parents would want for her, or even she for herself, he came from the same faith and, in that sense, same cultural background. And she felt he had potential. He wasn't just a dumb cop. He was sensitive and thoughtful enough with good instincts. In fact, he had potential, more than most of the boys at the collegiate. He'd been around and seen the big world. She could help him, even mold him. He'd be a worthy project. Yet, at the back of her mind, there were niggling questions: would he get boring? Should she jump at the first man who came along?

Looking back on it that night, Jack also felt very positive about Kate, although he had mixed feelings about having broken down in front of her. He always tried to control his emotions and present a face of manly stoicism to the outside world. That's what he'd been taught by his father. That was what guys like him aspired to. Yet, Kate had reacted warmly. It had broken the ice and now they were on different and more intimate terms. So that was a good thing. A very good thing! The other good thing about it was that she'd never got around to asking about his four murky years since he'd come home from the war. He'd have had to skate around that a bit.

As he'd more or less indicated to her, he'd been a happy, well-adjusted teenager when he'd left for overseas. Joining up had been the thing to do. There'd been parades and everyone had thought it was time to give the uppity Germans a bloody nose and show the world that the British Empire was still the big dog. Plus, for young guys it was seen as a chance for some adventure, and an adventure that wouldn't last more than six months. It hadn't quite worked out that way! He'd returned from that fiasco older and wiser, if somewhat ill. What to do?

He'd hoped that he could improve upon the lot of his hard-working father. Jack had been a good, not genius by any means but good, student in high school, although he hadn't concentrated much on his studies because a hockey career had beckoned. Now, supported as a veteran by his government gratuity money, he'd signed up to attend Regina College. But one day soon after entering the college, he'd had one of those flashback moments and had gone into the men's room to have a few drags on one of the reefers he bought from the Chinaman, not as good as the opium he'd tried overseas but easier to obtain.

Unfortunately, a teacher had entered and the end result was he'd been expelled. Distraught at this, he'd taken the liberty of contacting Cross at his law firm. Cross had sympathized with Jack, one of 'his' men, but had lectured him about the use of cannabis, saying that it was just as bad as booze and would soon be illegal too. Jack had been duly and honestly remorseful. Cross, who had a connection with the college, had then prevailed upon them to reinstate Jack on Jack's promise, to both the college and Cross himself, not to smoke dope again. And he hadn't. He'd kept his promise. But he'd lost his crutch and had been unable to concentrate on his studies. He'd failed out at the end of the first term.

The fact was he'd had a hard time settling down. While it was nice to be home and away from the nightmare in France, it had seemed somehow all different now. For starters, Lenny wasn't there. And he wasn't a kid anymore. He'd needed a job. He couldn't expect his parents to carry him. He and Lenny had talked overseas about going homesteading. He could still do that on his own. He could get land for a homestead like anyone else. But in addition, the Dominion Government had set up a Soldiers Settlement Board which would lend him money to buy government land plus stock and equipment. Pretty good in theory! The problem was that when he'd looked around the province, what was left in government ownership was marginal, either dry and infertile or wooded and needing clearing. It'd be a huge job.

Then he'd heard that some good and arable lands were being pried loose by the Dominion Government from Indian reserves to be made available for the vets. That sounded promising. But when he'd looked into that, he'd discovered that a lot less was available than he'd heard. The Indians felt they were getting screwed and didn't want to give up more land. They'd already given up pretty well the whole damn country was the way they looked at it. Now they were relegated to these few reserves. Sure, the feds said they were buying the lands, not expropriating them. Yeah, with offers they couldn't refuse. So, it was very controversial and had made him vaguely uneasy. Not that he'd worried about it too much. Like his family and friends, he wasn't heavily invested in the Indian issue. He'd kept looking.

But then there'd been the incident with Jim the Indian. One day, as he was having a coffee at a café in Regina, sitting a few tables away from the door and cash register counter, he'd heard a man say angrily, "Hey, don't bump me!"

"Sorry, sorry," someone replied.

Jack idly thought the voice had a familiar cadence.

As he started to turn around, he heard from the other voice, "Fucking Indian!"

"What did you call me?"

Jack saw Jim the Indian with his fist cocked and looking fiercely at the other man, a nondescript in workman's coveralls.

"Whoa!" shouted Jack as he jumped up and went between them.

"Jack!"

"Jim!"

"This man's a war hero," said Jack to the other guy. "Saved my life. Where the fuck were you?"

"Well, he bumped into me," mumbled the guy, backing off.

"By mistake," said Jim.

"Okay okay," said the guy who shuffled out the door.

"Thanks," said Jim.

"Not at all. How are you? Long time."

"Yeah, eh?" Jim spoke quietly, always had.

"Yeah, must be four years. On the boat back. Buy you a coffee?"

"Yeah, thanks."

Jack called the waitress over and ordered a coffee for Jim.

"So, Jim, what are you up to these days?"

"I work around on farms. You?"

"Well, actually, I'm thinking of going homesteading myself."

"Oh yeah?"

"Sort of complicated though."

Jim had looked down without a word.

"Have you ever looked into it?" continued Jack.

"Yeah."

"You can get a quarter section... anyone can... by applying to the government. Have to finance it yourself somehow. But as a vet, you can get another quarter section from the soldiers' board and they'll finance that and all the equipment and everything. But it's hard to find good land, it seems."

Jim was still looking down.

"That sound like it to you, Jim?" It seemed to be hard to engage him.

There was still no answer.

"Am I wrong?"

"I don't think you're wrong," said Jim quietly, "for you."

"For me?"

"I can't get that deal."

"How come?"

"Because I'm an Indian."

"But you're a vet!"

"But I'm an Indian."

Can this be true? wondered Jack. "Are you sure about that?"

71

"Oh yeah. I'm sure."

"Which part of it?"

"All of it."

"Even the homesteading?"

"Yeah."

"Jeez, that's not fair. You put out like the rest of us."

"But what can I do?"

"What about the reserve? Can you go back?"

"Yeah."

"You could farm there?"

"Yeah, but it's not the same deal, eh? It's not my own land like you could have. I kind of got used to being on my own overseas."

"But would the settlement board lend you for your own equipment and stuff?"

"Not the same deal either. They'd only do half of your deal, the deal they'd do for you if you asked."

"Jeez, Jim. That's incredible. So what are you going to do?"

"Just what I've been doing."

"Do you like that?"

"It's okay, eh, but I really wanted to try farming for myself. So I could build something up."

"I'm really sorry, Jim. I wish I could help but I don't know what I could do."

They were silent for a couple of minutes, nursing their coffee cups.

"By the way…" said Jim.

"Yeah?"

"I don't remember saving your life."

"No."

"Anyway, good to see you."

Jim drained his coffee. "And thanks for the coffee."

"You're welcome. Keep the faith."

They shook hands and Jim walked out.

Shit! thought Jack. *Imagine, the government had recruited Jim to put his life on the line for his country and was now discriminating against him as a vet.* Jack hadn't used the word 'discriminate' in his thoughts but that was the gist of it. It was just so unfair. *Imagine,* he thought, *if I went ahead and had a nice farm and everything and then met Jim again. How the hell could I look him in the eye?*

It was so disheartening that he'd finally dropped the idea of homesteading. Or maybe, he'd used that as an excuse for himself because, at the end of the day, in his heart, he knew he didn't really have the stomach for farming, out there on the land alone when he didn't know the first thing about it. He'd felt he really needed a job with some structure and where someone would teach him something – like he'd had in the army, with Cross.

That had not been easy to find and he'd spent three years doing odd jobs. His father had offered him work in his store but Jack couldn't settle down and irritated his father and they'd argued. So, Jack had left that and done other things like working as a clerk at the mail order depot of the Simpsons department store. But he'd wanted more than that.

Fortuitously, he'd chanced upon Cross this past April at a war veterans' event where he'd been honored as the new attorney-general. Well, Jack hadn't exactly chanced upon Cross; he'd attended in the hope of seeing him again after a couple of years. In fact, he'd been a little desperate to see him. And Cross had been helpful yet again, saying he'd find a job for him and that he had something in mind. Jack had never been so excited as when Cross had called his home to say there was an opening in the provincial police. The only thing Cross wanted to be assured about was that Jack was settled personally and not smoking dope. Jack had assured him on this.

Chapter 12

Jack drove the twenty-five miles south to Portal, a small railroad town which bestrode the border. For most local purposes, it operated as one town with people going back and forth, although the Canadian side was technically North Portal and there were Canadian and U.S. immigration/customs offices. Jack saw the stars and stripes flying and drove into the small U.S. office, not much more than a little booth beside a driveway off the main road. He identified himself and the Yankee officer said, "You must have replaced Simmons." Jack said that he was going for lunch with Sheriff Stinson. Suddenly conscious that he was wearing his holstered revolver, he asked if he should remove it. "If it's okay with the sheriff, it's okay with me," the officer replied and waved him on.

Jack met with Tom at a café on the main street on the American side. Tom was in a uniform not dissimilar from Jack's but his tunic had lapels instead of a close neck collar. He wore a shirt and tie, his campaign hat was not pinned up at the side, and the stripe in his breeches was blue, not red. And his revolver was in an open holster. They settled in for a talk over a simple lunch. Jack told Tom about Anderson being shot at by hijackers on his own property and about the bank robbery, and the general problem of American gangsters coming up to Saskatchewan. Tom was amazed that no one in Ceylon had a gun to try to stop the robbers.

"Our people don't generally have guns," said Jack a little sanctimoniously.

"Maybe if they did, they could've stopped it."

They started to get to know each other. It turned out they both were war veterans but Tom had served in a staff position and was impressed that Jack had seen combat and questioned him about it. Jack tried to avoid too much of that. But Tom persisted.

"How did you handle it all?"

"What I learned as a Boy Scout helped a lot."

Tom smiled, saying, "I'm a scoutmaster in Burke County. Do you remember your oath?"

Grinning, Jack put up his hand in the three-finger salute and chanted,

"On my honor, I promise that I will do my best, to do my duty to God and the King, to help other people at all times and to obey the Scout Law."

"Very good. Ours is the same... except for the king! Great stuff!"

"All that training about bravery and duty really helped."

Tom looked bemused.

"Let's see if we can help each other," he said.

"Like how?"

"We could start with Stud. What if you dropped him off here? I could take him off your hands."

Tom had made a similar suggestion at the ball game, thought Jack. So, he said, "Why would you want to do that?"

"Like I said, he's wanted for extortion in Minot, so anytime I can help the guys down there, it's a good thing."

"What kind of extortion?"

"He told ranchers he'd protect them from rustlers, for a fee, the implied threat being he'd burn down their stables, that kind of thing. I think he may have done the same thing to smalltime bootleggers, you know, guys who don't have their own muscle."

"I don't have any basis for arresting him or handing him over to you, even if I wanted to."

"Maybe there's another way."

"Like what?"

"Bail bondsman."

"What's that?"

"I think Stud was out on bail in Minot and skipped town so the bail bondsman can seize him and take him back to court. He could if he was here. So maybe if he found him in Bean Fate…"

Jack was shocked and said, "You mean a bounty hunter?"

Tom didn't get to reply because at that point, a big car roared past their window.

Tom jumped up and ran over to the café phone, called the Minot police, and alerted them that there was a rum runner's car heading towards Minot.

Then he said to Jack, "C'mon, these guys have come back from Canada. I'll show you how we deal with them down here."

They followed the rum runners in the Burke County Sheriff's Department car on the rough gravel road. The rum runners must have noticed they were being followed because they released heavy chains affixed to their rear axles which kicked up clouds of dust and slowed Tom down. But those clouds also identified their passage. As they go close to Minot, the car ahead obviously slowed down and headed into a ditch whereupon the dust subsided just in time for Jack to see that the rum runners' car was facing two big cars, one stopped on the road and one driving right into the ditch. Big cars, police cars with mounted Browning sub-machineguns.

Looks like we've got them surrounded, thought Jack, *and they'll have to surrender.* Sure enough, the front doors of the rum runner's car opened and two hoods started to get out, hands up. At that point, the machine guns started firing and the hoods were riddled with bullets, as was the car with blood and pieces of flesh splattered on its sides. It took less than a minute.

Jack sat with his mouth open in shock, and then said, "My God! Those guys were surrendering!"

"That's how we do it down here."

Tom got out of the car and walked over to where the Minot cops were standing and surveying the scene. Jack followed.

Tom greeted the Minot cops. They weren't dressed in quasi-military uniforms like Tom and Jack but in blue police suits with shirt and tie and blue peaked caps. They looked at Jack suspiciously. He was a witness to this little massacre, obviously a cop but not one of them. Tom realized the situation and quickly introduced Jack and explained he was from across the line and how he came to be there with Tom. Still, Jack made them nervous. One of them said defensively, "Ever since that son-of-a bitch Avery, we don't take chances with these bastards. It's them or us."

Jack looked at Tom, who said, "Avery Erickson. Last year, he killed Fred Fahler, one of these guys' fellow officers. Avery was a bad guy. One of these rum runners. The boys stopped him just like today but when he got out of the car, he started shooting and Fred was killed. Just down the road, a bit closer to Minot."

"Yeah, died in my arms," said one of the cops. "I still dream about it. Sometimes. He was my partner. I had to tell June. Now she's a widow with three kids. Goddamn shame."

They all stood morosely. One of the cops walked down into the ditch, opened the blood-splattered car trunk, and brought out a case. He opened it, took out a bottle of Black Horse, opened it, and took a swig. He came back up and the bottle was passed around. Tom took a swig and handed the bottle to Jack. He hesitated. *Be one of the boys? Become just a little complicit?* He shook his head and said, "No, thanks."

But the booze relaxed them and they started chatting – four Minot cops, Tom and Jack standing in a kind of circle on a gravel road in the open prairie, the wind blowing and occasional little dust devils whirling around on the road.

"Anyway, if you do arrest these hoods," said one, "one way or the other, they usually get off because the politicians and judges are crooked. Better to just take them off the streets."

"Yeah," said another, "we had a mayor who was recalled last year."

"Recalled?" asked Jack.

"Yeah, recall petition. He was being paid off by the guys who run the blind pigs and the gambling joints. People were fed up, so they threw him out. But the next guy's just as bad."

"They're all crooked," said another cop. They all shook their heads in agreement, and in self-justification too.

A raven swooped down and took a preliminary look at the corpses in the ditch. It'd be back soon enough. The men passed the bottle around again.

"Well," said one, "we kept the 'prohis' out of this one." He pronounced it *pro-ees*.

Jack looked at Tom questioningly.

"Prohis," said Tom, "Prohibition Agents. Feds. They have an office in Minot. Always sticking their noses in."

"Thanks for the call, Tom," said one. "Gave us a heads up so we could get out here without them."

"You federal or state?" one of the cops asked, looking at Jack suspiciously.

"Provincial."

"What happened to the Mounties?"

"They're up north," said Jack. *Otherwise it'd be too complicated to explain.*

"Jack knows where Bill Studwell is," said Tom.

The Minot cops perked up.

"Is he up in Canada?" asked one.

"Yeah," said Tom, "I'm trying to talk Jack into handing him over."

"That'd be a good thing," said another. They all nodded in agreement.

Jack, feeling very uneasy, said nothing.

"Or," said Tom to the group, "I suggested Parry could go and bring him back."

"Yeah, ol' Parry could do it. That's for sure," said a cop, "if Jack doesn't want to do it."

They looked at Jack. He said nothing, just wishing he wasn't there. He wanted no part of their conversation.

Afterwards, Tom and Jack drove back to Portal in silence, Jack turning over the shocking slaughter he'd just witnessed and Tom was obviously aware of that.

"You can understand why they did that," said Tom. "That Avery thing."

"Yeah, but it's against everything I've ever been taught about the law and policing. Innocent until proven guilty. Judgment by a court, not the police."

"Innocent until proven guilty? Proof? They saw the shooting, for Christ's sake!"

Jack just shook his head.

That night, Jack bumped into Jasper Leask, KC at a café in Estevan and they decided to dine together. While Jack seemed to spend most of his time in and around Bienfait, his days usually started and ended at the café where he sometimes saw Jasper, a lawyer with offices in Estevan from which he serviced the district. He was a middle-aged Englishman, a graduate of Wadham College at Oxford who'd started as a barrister at Gray's Inn in London. He let it be known that he'd been a classmate of 'F.E.', as insiders called F.E. Smith, now Lord Birkenhead, celebrated in the Empire as a lawyer and friend of Winston Churchill.

But Jasper's career had taken a considerably more modest path. He'd come out to the colonies, first Toronto, then Regina, and now Estevan – the end of the line. This path reflected the decline of his fortunes as his dependence on alcohol had increased. As a bachelor, he was overweight and seemingly always perspiring with a usually glistening head of thinning hair of indeterminate color. And he was unkempt, invariably wearing baggy gray flannel trousers with rumpled double-breasted blue blazer and stained Wadham tie be-speckled with cigarette ashes from his chain-smoking. But he was smart and, on a good day, he was a very good lawyer. His reputation was that he never drank when he was going to court so that his clients had confidence in him. Jack had once asked him where he got his booze and Jasper had told him about his dwindling but still substantial store from his orders from the Hudson's Bay Company over the mail, back in the day.

Jasper had already had a drink or two but was still lucid. Jack told him about the massacre, relieved to have someone on which to unload some of his stress, an officer of the court. Jack made the same points he'd made to Tom about the law and policing and how he was so distressed by what he'd witnessed.

In his fruity drawl, Jasper said, "Jack, never forget that, at the end of the day, Americans are very different than we British. They were founded in rebellion. They talk a good game about the Rule of Law but, in the end, they're always on the edge of mob rule and vigilante action. Washington himself realized too late what he'd done."

"Washington did?"

"Yes, dear boy, President Washington. The Whiskey Rebellion. All those wild American hill-billies. He had to send in the troops. Got up on his horse and led them himself!"

"I don't know anything about that."

"You should read some American history. You really should. A real eye-opener. Violent people."

Jack could only listen. His schooling had been pretty limited – Regina Collegiate, not Oxford.

As he drove into Bienfait the next day, in front of Whites he saw a parked car with North Dakota plates. As he got out of his car, a man ran out of the hotel and shouted that someone had seized Stud at gunpoint inside.

Jack entered Whites with his gun drawn. He saw an older rough-looking man with a pistol prodding Stud along with his hands cuffed behind his back.

"What the hell is going on here?" he demanded.

The man looked startled but then said he was Parry, the bail bondsman from Minot, and he'd come to take Stud to Minot where he was wanted for extortion. He added that the sheriff suggested it was okay.

"I don't care about your goddamn sheriff. We don't allow that here. Bounty hunting! Drop your gun. You're not allowed to carry it. This is not the American Wild West up here!"

Parry hesitated while Stud looked on in amazement.

"Drop your goddamn gun!"

Finally, Parry did with obvious reluctance and Jack arrested and handcuffed him. Then he freed Stud who thanked him.

"I'm not doing this for you," snarled Jack.

He phoned Tom from Whites and said he had something for him. Then he put the handcuffed Parry in the tin lizzie and drove down to Portal, waving at the immigration agent who didn't see Parry's handcuffs.

Tom was surprised. "I thought you were bringing Stud."

"We don't allow bounty hunting."

"This is not the time to play Boy Scout. You could have saved yourself a lot of trouble by letting Stud be brought back here."

Driving back up to Saskatchewan, Jack wondered, *What's with Tom and the effort to grab Stud?* He liked Tom, who was becoming in some ways a mentor, but his promoting bounty-hunting seemed at odds with his role as a policeman. The whole thing was unsettling.

Noticing the time, he drove over to the schoolhouse, arriving just as the last of the children walked out. Kate came to the door and waved him in. Out of sight of the children, they embraced easily as if that was where they now were with each other. She wiped the lipstick off his mouth with her finger.

"You know they'll all be talking again," she said with a little smile.

"Let them talk," he said as he embraced her again, hungry for more.

But she wasn't going to get into it in her classroom.

"Easy for you to say. I have to face those witches, even at church."

Then they talked, Jack sitting on the edge of her desk and she on her chair pushed back. He told her about the shootout in Minot and the bounty-hunter incident just now. She could tell he was perplexed and unhappy about it all. She knew he just needed someone to listen and that was what she did.

Then she took his hand and said, "In the end, all you can do is what seems right to you."

"Well, that's what I'm doing but it's difficult."

"I have great faith that you'll do the right thing and it'll all work out."

"I sure hope you're right. Can I drive you home?"

She stood up and gave him another quiet kiss.

"But people will talk," she said. "Just imagine that teacher receiving men at our school! Cluck, cluck, cluck."

He dropped her off at the Anderson ranch and headed towards Estevan feeling a lot less unsettled. *She's something special,* he thought.

That night, he sought out Jasper at the café. He told him about Parry and the fact that Tom seemed to be encouraging him to hand over Stud.

"That's illegal, isn't it? What is the law on that anyway?"

"It's illegal, alright," said Jasper. "It's all about extradition and what's allowed and what isn't. The Webster-Ashburton treaty."

"The what?"

"The Webster-Ashburton treaty, old boy – 1842 – between the old country and the states. It's still in effect."

"What does it say?"

"One country has to hand someone over to the courts of the other in certain specified cases."

"Like what?"

"Murder. Things like that. Seriously bad things. Of course, you have to go through the required court procedures and deal with the government too."

"What about extortion?"

"Not covered."

"Why would a sheriff think a bail bondsman could come up here and arrest Stud? There's no way that's allowed, is there?"

"Of course not. That's just kidnapping. As I said last night, the Americans pretend they believe in the Rule of Law but they really don't."

Chapter 13

One Saturday, Kate got a ride into town with Anderson to do a bit of shopping. It was arranged he'd pick her up in an hour. She stopped at the drugstore and Walt's and then walked along the road and into Wong's café. A little Chinese food would be an interesting change from the plain standard fare at the Andersons'.

She was pleasantly surprised by the interior of the café which was bigger and cleaner than she'd somehow expected. A counter ran along the right wall, in front of which were stools and behind which was shelving loaded down with all kinds of confections like chocolate bars and tobacco products, cigarettes, cigars, pipe and chewing tobacco. She'd heard that cannabis products were usually available in Chinese cafes too if you asked. Along the left wall, several booths were portioned off with seats for four. In the middle were several tables, each with chairs for four people. There was only one patron when she entered and he was seated on a stool at the counter. She elected to sit across in one of the booths.

Mr. Wong greeted her and handed her a menu. She chose the chicken fried rice and was halfway through a plate of it when in walked Stud.

"Mind if I join you?" he asked, sliding into the booth across the table from her without awaiting an answer.

"What if I did mind?"

"You do mind?" He looked at her in surprise, not used to push-back from a girl.

"Well, Mister Studwell, you didn't give me a chance to answer your question, but it's okay. You can stay."

She liked the exoticism of his deep drawl.

He asked how it was going at the school. She indicated okay. She wasn't about to confide in a stranger.

Changing the conversation, she asked about his background. He talked vaguely about ranching in Texas. She asked him why he was in Canada. It was vague again.

"So where do you live, Mister Studwell?"

"Everyone calls me Stud." The way he spoke it sounded like 'Stuuud'.

"Okay. Where do you live, Stud?"

"Oh, down near the border. Cabin in a coulee by the river. Pretty place."

"Near the Rocks?"

"Not too far. Have you been there?"

"The other day. It's beautiful down there."

"How'd you get way down there?"

"Jack took me. We had a picnic."

"Jack?"

"The constable."

"Oh, him," said Stud contemptuously.

"He's a very nice man," she said in some surprise and a little defensively too.

"If you like the Rocks, you'd love my place. Want to come along and see it?"

A big good-looking stud in a coulee, she thought for one moment.

"Thanks, but I couldn't today."

"Sure. Maybe another time, Miss Ross?"

"Maybe, thanks. And you can call me Kate."

"Okay, Kate. So how are you getting home now?"

"Mr. Anderson is picking me up in a few minutes."

"I can give you a lift in something better than that old rust-bucket of his."

"Thanks, but I should wait for him."

"Well, come out and have a look. It's a honey of a car. Here, I've got the tab."

After he'd laid some cash on the table, they started out and he, the southern boy, courteously touched her elbow as if to guide her through the door.

Nice touch, she thought nervously. *Not something Jack would do.*

"Here, get in and you can see what it's like," he said as he opened the car door.

So she did, just as Anderson parked alongside.

83

Stud started the Studebaker and called out to Anderson, "I'm just giving Kate a spin in the Studie. I'll drive her straight home."

Kate had a conflicting mix of thoughts and emotions at that moment. She knew he'd pulled a fast one. She was embarrassed in front of Anderson and yet, she was fascinated with Stud.

And he did drive her straight home. The game was just starting.

+ + +

That same day, there was a lot of excitement in Chicago, at least for Big Bill. He'd organized a weekend of police athletic competitions which, to no one's surprise, had been kicked off by a Saturday-morning parade featuring none other than himself on his horse. Also marching in the parade and getting a lot of cheers from the crowds was Amos Alonzo Stagg, All-American out of the Yale Divinity School and football coach at the University of Chicago. At various school grounds around Chicago that day, one hundred thousand spectators watched as participants engaged in tugs of war and hundred-yard dashes and similar field-day events, hammer throws and the like.

One of the spectators was Big Bill, attended by two of Chicago's finest, who stood watching one such event while talking to another spectator, an older but fit and fine-looking man with graying curly hair.

"Mister mayor, you've organized a great event here."

"Thank you, coach. And it's an honor to have you here."

"Not at all. Glad to do it. That's what we need in this country, more sports and just physical exercise generally. Sound mind in a sound body. That sort of thing."

"I couldn't agree more. Played football and coached it myself."

"I know. And very well too, I hear."

Big Bill looked thrilled at the compliment from someone like Stagg, the hero-athlete, winner of several Big Ten championships, as big as it got!

"But you can't rest on your laurels."

Big Bill looked at Stagg questioningly.

"At our age, we've got to work at it," and Stagg pointed at Big Bill's paunch.

"I know. I know," said Big Bill somewhat abashed.

84

"Never too old to start on a program. Come round someday if you want some advice from one of our trainers," said Stagg, clapping Big Bill on the shoulder.

As Big Bill watched him walking away, a handsome young man, in the company of two more of Chicago's finest with their treasured six point star badges, walked up and shook his hand. It was Charles Fitzmorris, the chief of the Chicago Police Force, who was dressed, as always, in civvies.

"Thanks for organizing this, mister mayor. It's great for morale."

"Sounds like you need it. The force I mean. That was a pretty damning statement you made."

"Which one?"

"The one where you said fifty percent of the force is involved in the booze business! That one!"

Fitzmorris moved a bit farther away out of earshot of his retinue. This was not something to discuss in their presence.

"Well, it's true."

"Even if it is, why'd you have to say it out loud?"

"To start getting the public's confidence back."

"You think that helps the public's confidence?"

"Yes. By showing I recognize the problem and setting the stage for what I've started doing."

"Suspending all those officers?"

"Yes, and what I'm working on, reassigning a lot more."

"Well, I'll support you. You know that. We can't have that kind of corruption in the police force."

"The problem is everybody wants to drink, so there's so much pressure on our men."

"Where's all this booze coming from anyway?"

"Right now, a lot comes from Canada."

"I thought they had Prohibition too?"

"They say they do but they don't. Bunch of hypocrites."

"I guess they're Brits. The worst!"

"But when you think of it, mister mayor, the real problem is the demand here in Chicago… I mean, it's huge! And the guy that brings it in. He's who we have to worry about."

"Of course," said Big Bill, thinking, *Is he pulling my chain?*

"Torrio."

"Right." *Yep, he's pulling my chain.*

"Listen, sorry, but I see someone over there I have to talk to."

With that, the chief walked away with his two cops.

Big Bill started to walk along trailed by his own cop retinue.

"Mister mayor."

Big Bill turned sideways to see who it was.

"Johnny, good to see you."

"I just wanted to say hello," said Torrio.

"Everything okay?"

"Yeah, it is."

They shook hands and Torrio walked away with a knowing nod to Big Bill's cops.

The chief saw that coming, thought Big Bill. *It's a game, the whole damn thing, and we all have a position to play. Not unlike Big Ten Football but with no referees.*

+ + +

The following Monday, Jack drove into the schoolyard. School was out and there were no children about. He knocked on the door and Kate opened it.

"Can I come in?"

"Oh, Jack. I was just about to leave." She thought to herself, *He looks like a thundercloud.* "But sure, is something the matter?"

"Yes."

He stormed past her and into the classroom and turned to face her.

"I hear you had lunch with Stud."

"Yes, so what?"

"I told you he's a bad guy."

"Yes, you did but he was very nice."

"Well, he's not."

What's going on? she thought.

"And I thought you and I had something going."

Kate saw his eyes were fiery and his lips were trembling.

"Jack," she said quietly, "I was lunching by myself and he just arrived and sat down. Nothing I could do about it."

86

He grabbed her by the shoulders, saying, "You could have told him to bugger off."

"Jack! I could not! And please don't talk like that!"

He looked so angry and he was holding her and it frightened her a little.

But then he dropped his hands and just visibly sagged.

"Sorry, sorry, he's just such a bad egg."

"Maybe he is, but please don't make a mountain out of a molehill."

"Can I drive you home?"

"Of course, and please just forget it."

They embraced gently and then left the schoolhouse.

But that night, Kate herself hadn't forgotten it. She didn't know about Jack. He was really a great guy with lots of potential but it was like there was something in there that she didn't know about and hadn't touched. *Surely not the dreaded shellshock. They're loony, aren't they?* she thought. He wasn't loony. No. He wasn't a candidate for Weyburn. But he was definitely edgy and surprisingly emotional. And was there a hint of potential violence? He might be a tougher project than she'd realized.

Chapter 14

Harry was hands-on and yet he wasn't. He was certainly the main man in the Craftsman Building, whether running booze production through Canada Pure Drug, or sales and distribution through Dominion Distributors. And he was smart and understood the business, especially operations. But, unlike Sam, he wasn't a micro-manager and had men working for him whom he trusted.

One of the men was Bob who looked after the details of distribution, filling orders, packing bottles of booze in cases and, in the case of exports, driving them to the CPR station and arranging shipping to Bienfait. Bob was a good guy and he and Harry liked each other.

One day, as Harry walked around, he came across Bob looking upset as he lambasted a boy whom Harry didn't recognize.

"What's this about?" asked Harry, adding, "I don't think I know you as he looked at the boy."

"That's my son," said Bob, naming him.

"Do you work here?" Harry asked the boy.

"Yes sir," the boy mumbled, looking abashed.

"What's the problem?" asked Harry, looking at Bob.

"I think we might have made a mistake on a shipment."

"What shipment?" Harry was suddenly alert.

"One of the ones to Bean Fate," said Bob nervously.

"Which customer?"

"The Chicago account."

"What was the mistake?"

"I don't think it came from our stocks."

"What? I told you…"

"I know."

"Whose stocks?"

"I think it was Chechik's."

"Godammit! You said you think. Do you know?"

"Pretty sure."

"You know! How the hell did that happen?"

"I was breaking him in and he got mixed up, I guess."

"How did he get involved? I don't remember hiring him."

"Remember, Mr. Bronfman, I said I'd like to give him a chance?"

"No, I don't." But Harry could see the boy looked terrified and added, "We all make mistakes, kid. I just hope this one isn't as bad as I'm afraid it might be."

Back in his office, Harry sat at his desk with his head in his hands, thinking, *who knows what was in that shipment. It might be okay and it might not. If not, I'm afraid I'll find out soon enough. And Sam will blame me. But that might not be the worst of my worries.*

+ + +

As Harry, Matoff, and Leech walked up to Whites, they saw Stud's car parked in front. Harry said, "All I know is Capone wanted a meeting." That was true as far as it went. While he'd told Matoff of his concern, he hadn't told Leech, nor Sam for that matter. But he'd asked Leech to come along for support as a reminder that he, Harry, was connected to high places. Maybe it was a little unfair to Leech but then Leech owed him.

Harry knocked and they entered a bedroom, same one as last time. Capone and Dutch were there, jackets off but this time shoulder-holsters on. They looked menacing. Stud was in the background.

Harry started to say 'hello' but Capone cut him off.

"Mister Torrio is very unhappy about a batch of bad booze."

"Really?" Harry feigned surprise.

Capone gave him the steely eye and said, "It was blue, for fuck's sake."

Matoff, trying his hand as the Bronfman heavy against the Chicago heavies, said, "I think there must be a mistake. Maybe it was stuff you bought from someone else. We don't do bad stuff."

Capone sprang at Matoff, grabbed him by the balls, and said, "Don't you fuck with us. It was your shit."

Harry and Leech stood back in alarm as Matoff wailed.

Letting go of Matoff's balls, Capone said, "This is a warning. No more bad stuff… or else."

"Maybe it was our stuff and maybe we made a mistake," said Harry. "It won't happen again. But remember you're in Saskatchewan, not Chicago."

"That's right," piped in Leech. "So don't threaten us. It's our town and our police."

Dick sounds angry, pissed-off and unafraid, thought Harry admiringly.

"You mean that fuckin' boy scout at the ball game?" said Capone nastily.

"He's got backup, I assure you," responded Leech.

Capone glowered at them. It was clear he wasn't used to being disrespected but recognized he was a long way from home.

Then he pointed at Matoff's diamond stick pin flashing in the light. "I thought I gave that to you, Harry."

"I just lent it to Paul."

There was silence in the room.

Stud hadn't spoken and was almost invisible, strange for a guy with a physical presence, the biggest guy in the room.

This could go either way, thought Harry.

Then he gambled. With a brave front, he said, "Okay, gentlemen. We'll make sure there are no mistakes again. And we'll be off now."

As they walked out of the hotel, Harry was shaking.

"You sure called their bluff, Harry," said Matoff.

"Yeah, but they won't be happy about that."

"You're right on that," said Leech. "Those kind of guys aren't used to being stared down. They take it personally. Maybe you should stop dealing with them while you still can."

"Not now. We're in too deep, and the money's too good."

Chapter 15

Bienfait's matrons kept an eye on Kate who seemed too immodest for their school teacher. Somehow, they'd heard of her picnic at The Rocks. Mrs. Anderson had tried to assuage their suspicions by saying that she herself had recommended it. She hadn't, but Kate, the foolish thing, needed protection. Kate's lunching with Stud and accepting a ride with him had not gone unnoticed, although the Andersons had done their best to dampen that speculation by saying Stud had tricked Kate. But it was difficult for Kate and Jack to be together. Even his driving her home from school seemed to draw criticism. Meanwhile, there'd been the incident at the school when he'd blown up over that lunch with Stud, although they'd smoothed that over. But it was all awkward and, so, they were both pleased when, true to her word, Mrs. Anderson had invited Jack to dinner.

Arriving in his best civvies, he was greeted warmly by Anderson and Mrs. Anderson, looking plain but scrubbed, as did their two young daughters, students of Kate's. Soon Kate came downstairs and made her entrance. And it was an entrance. She stood there, gorgeous, not in the trim blue suit of her arrival but a dress of deep green with rose bud trimming, green silk stockings, and green suede slippers. None of them had ever seen anything quite so ravishing. The daughters said how beautiful she looked. Anderson was more restrained but obviously impressed. Jack was speechless. So was Mrs. Anderson but she looked irritated.

Over dinner, the men talked and the women, at the outset, just listened. But the conversation turned to the provincial election last year and speculation on the influence of the women's vote. It was the second time women had been allowed to vote.

"Frankly," said Anderson, "I'm not sure it's a good thing."

Jack wasn't sure either... not sure he wanted to get into this discussion! So, instead of expressing an opinion, he asked Anderson a question.

"Why do you think that?"

"You know, I have the highest regard for womenfolk. But their place is in the home, where they do a great job. At least, anyone I know of," he said with a glance at Mrs. Anderson. "But they're not out in the world where we see the bigger things that are going on and the issues that need to be dealt with by the government."

No one else said anything. He was on his own but, politician that he was, liked the sound of his own voice. So he continued, "Also, we men tend to be realistic and hard-headed when it's needed. Women tend to be more emotional which, of course, is why we like them!"

At that, Kate could not contain herself. Anderson was just too much! And she knew all the arguments from the discussions around her family's dining room table.

"Mr. Anderson," she said, "I don't agree with you at all!"

They all looked at her in some surprise.

"And it's ridiculous," she said, "that we women weren't allowed to vote before. And I think the world will become a better place as the woman's voice is heard more."

"Why do you think that?" asked Anderson.

"Women won't follow the lines of the old corrupt parties like the Liberals and Conservatives. They won't be bound by the old ties of patronage where the politicians have to reward the vested interests who fund them. Instead, they'll form their own opinions based upon women's less adversarial and more generous approaches."

"What do you mean?" demanded Anderson.

"Women are always thinking of what's best for their children and the larger community, not narrowly of themselves. Not like all these men driven by worldly ambitions and their own egos, except present company of course! So there'll be less of these stupid fights, less conflict, and, hopefully, no more wars like the recent one which was caused by ambitious men for no reason but their own vanity."

The men were a little taken aback by her onslaught, a little annoyed too, but they didn't know how to argue with a pretty young thing. Mrs. Anderson finally gave Kate a 'look' as if to say she should just shut up, which she suddenly did, wondering if she'd gone too far.

After dinner, Anderson offered Jack a cigar. Kate asked if Anderson had a cigarette. He hesitated and looked at Mrs. Anderson, who frowned. It was Jack's turn to give Kate a 'look' and she said, unconvincingly, that she was just kidding.

Mrs. Anderson got up abruptly and headed into the kitchen, reached for the Rock-A-Bye cough syrup in a cupboard, and took a surreptitious swig.

Jack raised the problem of bootlegging and Sparling's rant about corruption in high places.

Anderson said, "I don't know about that. But the real problem is Prohibition itself. Lots of people will always want to drink and will find a way to get their booze." Mrs. Anderson regarded him coolly.

"Couldn't agree more," said Jack. "And the police are caught in the middle. I mean, there's the harvest dance Saturday night. I can't go because there'll be drinking and it'd put me in a difficult position. Anyway," added Jack, looking at Kate, "I'm going to my brother's wedding in Regina."

Kate looked surprised and then disappointed.

Turning back to Anderson, Jack said, "You know what's going on around here. What about Stud?"

"What do you mean?" replied Anderson guardedly.

"Well, I know why he's up here. He's avoiding an arrest warrant across the line. But what does he do? How does he survive? How does he drive that big car?"

"Good question, but I don't know the answer. I have nothing to do with him."

Did he see Mrs. Anderson give a funny look? wondered Jack as he responded, "The boys in that fight at Whites the other night said they got their whiskey from him and it was Bronfman whiskey, so I wonder if he's connected to them."

"I doubt it but I wouldn't want to know anyway."

"Do you even know where he lives exactly?"

"Way down south somewhere in some coulee, I think."

Did he see Mrs. Anderson give another funny look? wondered Jack momentarily. It was probably his imagination.

Kate could have confirmed it but said nothing. *No need to anger Jack!*

Jack looked at the clock on the nearby mantel and said, "Gosh, it's after ten. I should be going."

As he was leaving, Kate followed him outside. Mrs. Anderson watched as best she could through the curtain.

It was chilly in the autumn evening. Jack took Kate in his arms and they kissed for a while.

"Jack, do you really have to go to that wedding?"

"It's my brother!"

"Oh, I know, but it's the big dance too and it'll be a chance for us to have some fun together. For once in this town, it'd be legitimate."

"Kate, I'm his best man!"

"Why not take me then?"

"To the wedding?"

"Yes, why not?"

He felt awkward. He wasn't ready to introduce her to his parents. *They'd think she was too fancy. She'd think they were too plain.*

"I don't think it'd work. I have stuff to do and I couldn't look after you properly."

"You think I need looking after?"

"You know what I mean. Introducing you around and so on."

"Well, if I want to, I can always go and visit my parents!"

"Kate, please, don't make it a thing. I just want to deal with my family without having to worry about anything else."

"Okay, if that's the way you feel about me."

"Kate, please, c'mon, it's not that." He embraced her again and it seemed okay.

But it wasn't really, not in her mind.

+ + +

Jack didn't dare ask for marijuana from Mr. Wong in Bienfait. Word might get around. While its sale was not yet illegal like the sale of alcohol, its sale and use were definitely frowned upon in mainstream society, perhaps even more so than the use of alcohol which was, in fact, a staple for so much of European-based society. So, on Saturday, he was relieved to be able to return in his civvies to the café in Regina over the door of which was a sign: *'LEE'S CHINESE CAFE.'* Mr. Lee greeted him and Jack asked for 'the usual.' Lee reached below the counter and handed Jack a large package of reefers. Jack handed him cash, walked back to the entrance with a large brown paper bag, and, after looking carefully both ways, left on foot.

$$+ + +$$

The barn dance was held on a lovely fall evening. The Andersons drove up to the big Bienfait Community Hall in the old tin lizzie with Kate squished in the backseat with their daughters. The hall was a large barn-like structure painted a sort of silver with black trim. There were lots of cars and buggies parked out front and people streaming in.

As the Andersons and Kate walked into the hall, Mrs. Anderson looked embarrassed. Kate was in fuck-Jack mode: full flapper with a dress cut barely below the knee, dark red lipstick, a hint of rouge on her cheeks, and thick black eyeliner. No one had seen anything like it before except in magazines.

No booze was allowed in the hall but there was lots of open drinking by the men outside in the dark. It was accepted by those in attendance. How else would you get a party cranked up? And it was loud and high-spirited. The orchestra, which had been imported from Regina, played music for country dances like schottisches and square dances.

There were lots of young men, miners, farm and ranch hands, some of whom had been in the brawl. Kate was much in demand, to the obvious annoyance of some of the matrons and their plainly-dressed daughters, and she danced a lot. At one point, she asked the orchestra to play something from the Nighthawks. The orchestra knew what she meant. Like her and so many other young people in Regina, they had listened late at night to the Coon-Sanders Nighthawk Orchestra from radio station WDAF in Kansas City. So they played 'Red Hot Mamma.' She danced a fast-paced foxtrot with one of the young men. The matrons glared and clucked. Mrs. Anderson was doubly embarrassed, as she knew Kate was seen as almost her ward.

Stud entered the hall unexpectedly, dressed in his best cowboy outfit including snakeskin high-heeled boots. He took off his Stetson to reveal a full head of longish hair slightly streaked with silver. His was a striking presence and created a stir in the crowd and a thrill in Kate. He wandered casually over to her and asked her to dance. The orchestra retreated to country music. Stud obviously liked to dance and was surprisingly light-footed for a big man in cowboy boots.

They had several dances together, which was noticed by everyone. But he interspersed them with brief trips outside. By now it was hot and sweaty in the hall and he was getting a little drunk. He suggested to Kate that they go outside for some fresh air and she thought that was a good idea. He had a cigarette and offered her one, which she accepted. Then he offered her a swig from a small silver flask that he pulled from his boot. She hesitated and then decided, *Yes, I'll take my first ever drink of booze. Sorry, Mom.* She took a swig and spat it out. It was so bitter! He teased her and she decided on another one and this time swallowed it. The hit was almost instantaneous. And if it scared her a bit, she liked it too. She had another cigarette and another swig before they returned to the dance floor.

By this time, there was a general glowering from the assembled matrons including Mrs. Anderson. Anderson was a little worried. Kate looked a little out of control and he thought he'd have to have a word with her in the morning. The main thing now was to get her home tonight safely.

At midnight, the orchestra played 'God Save the King' to end the dance. People stood, some awkwardly, at attention. Then suddenly, there was confusion as people started to mill about and leave, but Kate was not to be seen. Anderson looked anxiously at his wife and said, "Let's split up to find her." In the dark outside, among the throng and parked vehicles, Mrs. Anderson suddenly came close to Kate, closing the door of the Studebaker.

"Kate," she called out. Kate looked at her and said that Stud was giving her a ride home. The Studebaker pulled away before Mrs. Anderson could reply.

She found her husband who asked anxiously, "Have you seen her?"

"I did just as she was driving off with Stud, the foolish little tart!"

"My God, that's bad. But don't you tell anyone!"

That same night, Jack was attending his brother's wedding celebration in a small hotel in Regina. He and his brother stood talking, arms linked and a little drunk, watching the dancing amid surreptitious drinking from mickeys.

They were close enough, Jack and his brother, two years his junior, but not as close as they'd once been. When Lenny had come to board with them, he and Jack had bonded. They were the same age and had the same aptitudes and ambitions centered around hockey. That had been amplified by their shared experience in class and then service overseas while Jack's brother was in high school. And then there'd been Jack's troubled return, his difficulties in settling down and his awkward introduction to the store where he'd clashed with their dad. And where he'd temporarily taken the spot in the store that the brother had been counting on. Still, they were brothers and no longer in competition.

Their parents watched from across the room, the brothers arm-in-arm. They looked as though they'd been drinking, although no drinking was on offer at the event and none was in evidence.

"Looks like they've had a couple of drinks," said their father.

"I know," their mother replied. "I don't know where they'd get it."

"I'm sure it's not that hard to get from what I hear."

"Oh well, they're careful and respectful of us and it's just one night. It's just so nice to see them together again, one boy getting married and the other holding a very good job finally. After all, he's been through."

At the other side of the room, Jack's brother asked him, "So how're you doing, Jack?"

"Fine."

"Not still smoking dope?"

"No."

"Any girls down there?"

"There's a girl, the schoolteacher. I like her and I think she likes me… In fact, she wanted to come to the wedding."

"Why didn't you bring her?"

"She wouldn't fit in. She's kind of fancy and she's outspoken and modern. You know, Mom and Dad wouldn't like her."

"Do you like her a lot?"

"To be honest, I'm crazy about her."

"Jack, don't do like you always do. Go back down there and propose before someone else does!"

"Maybe I should."

"Married life has its advantages."

They both laughed at the sexual allusion on a wedding night.

"But seriously, you're right."

They were interrupted by a friend of theirs, a teller at the main branch of the Union Bank. After some chitchat, he asked Jack if he had to deal with the liquor commission.

"Not really. I deal with the local JP, an asshole by the way, and my bosses up here in the police force. Although I did actually meet the liquor board chairman once."

"What's his name?"

"Mister Leech."

"Right, I thought so."

"You know him?"

"He has an account at the bank. A big account."

"Oh?"

"Big cash deposits."

"From where?"

"Who knows? It's cash! But it's pretty strange that a guy like that makes deposits like that, eh?"

"What are you saying?"

"It's just another example of how the big boys involved with booze always seem to have big money."

"Nothing I can do about it," said Jack, while thinking, *Maybe I can.*

Much later that same night Mrs. Anderson was sitting up waiting at the window in her nightgown, sipping Rock-a-Bye cough syrup. Anderson and their daughters had gone to bed.

She saw car lights come down the lane and stop before the yard, heard a door close, and saw the lights turn and head away. Then she saw a figure walking towards the house in the dark. Kate came in quietly. Poor Kate! She looked bedraggled, her hair was astray, her clothes were disheveled and she was silently crying.

Mrs. Anderson tried to comfort her but she pushed Mrs. Anderson aside and headed right upstairs to her room, stumbling once or twice on the stairs.

Mrs. Anderson went upstairs soon after, entered her bedroom and slipped into the bed. She nudged Anderson who woke up quickly as he'd been sleeping lightly, awaiting her.

"She's back?"

"I'm afraid so."

"What do you mean by that?"

"I think he's raped her."

Two days later, on Monday, Jack drove up to Kate's school just as the children were streaming out. He waited in his car. Some of the children got into a horse-drawn school van. Others just walked away, in some cases for quite a long walk home. And one boy untethered his horse from the hitching rail, mounted, and rode off. When all the children had left, Jack walked over to the school house and entered. Kate was sitting at her desk and looked up. Her face lit up. *Yet, did he see a cloud?*

He walked over, she stood up, and they embraced.

"I thought you might like a ride," he said, trying to sound light but he felt tense.

"Oh, Jack, that'd be so nice."

She seems a little tense, too, he thought.

"How was the dance?"

"It was okay."

"Not great?"

"Okay."

"Lot of people?"

"Yes, it was packed."

"How was the orchestra?"

"They were terrific. Came from Regina."

"I suppose you danced a lot?" He said this teasingly. Yet, he couldn't resist an edge.

"Yes. I did."

"Everyone would want to dance with you. I'm sure you were the prettiest girl there."

"Oh, Jack, but thank you for the compliment. And how was the wedding?" *Time to change the subject,* she thought.

"It was terrific too. Great to see everyone."

"Your brother must have been happy."

"Oh yes, very. My mom and dad too. They like the girl."

"Well, that's important. Girls and mothers-in-law."

"What?"

"It's often a difficult relationship. The oldest story in the book."

"I suppose."

99

"Boys have to think about that when they choose."

Why did she hit that button just now?

"Oh, I don't know. If two people love each other, what does it really matter what their parents think?"

"Believe me, Jack, it matters."

Damn! She was on the same subject he'd worried about with his brother.

"Listen. You know what?" he said.

"What?"

"It got me thinking."

She looked at him. He was such a lovely guy but so emotional. He was trembling almost.

"Oh?" She said it casually.

"You know I like you a lot."

"I know that, Jack."

"Well, I was wondering if we could get engaged." There he'd said it.

"Oh, Jack!"

Kate looked at him and burst out crying and he took her in his arms.

"Would you agree to that?" He felt sure she would.

But she just held on to him for a minute, thinking, *What would he do if he found out about Stud?* Then she backed away.

"I'd have to think about it."

"You're not sure?"

"It's just such a surprise, Jack."

He looked crestfallen.

"Oh, Jack, I do like you very much."

She kissed him and they embraced again and he felt so close to her and was encouraged.

"I know," he said, "I put it to you kind of sudden. Of course you can think about it. But not for too long," he said almost jocularly, his confidence restored. "Can I assume you're kind of favorable to the idea?"

"I am, Jack. But I just need to think." She was already thinking, too, *What would my mother think? Sons-in-law could be an issue too.*

"Okay, I'll hold on to that for now."

"But let's not tell anyone what we're thinking about. Not till I know for sure."

"Of course not. So, can I give you a ride home, Miss Roberts?"

"You surely can, constable."

Kate lay in bed that night, thinking it all over. She had a marriage proposal or, at least, an engagement proposal! A big deal! But did she love Jack? She'd certainly been growing to admire him, although he clearly carried a bit of baggage, but something that he was assuredly growing out of and she could help him with that. Yes, he was a lovely man really. The experience with Stud had put Jack's sterling qualities in sharp relief. What had she seen in Stud? Why, she asked herself, had she been so stupid as to flirt with him? Well, she knew why – precisely the hint of danger after the comfort of the bourgeoisie cocoon at home. But it had been foolish and she was lucky to have gotten out of it relatively unscathed. And it was close. She'd been initially thrilled, if scared, when he'd first fondled her but he'd moved so quickly and the next thing she'd known was that he was on top of her! But she'd fought him off successfully and, in fact, she'd been a little surprised at how quickly he had backed off when she made it clear. It was if he'd been genuinely surprised, mumbling that the senoritas back home liked a bit of horseplay.

Anyway, that was over now and, she hoped, behind her. Of course, the problem was that people had seen her dancing with him, she knew, a little recklessly, too, after the booze. And Mrs. Anderson had seen her leave with him and arrive home and who knew what she thought or was telling her friends? That could be a bit of a problem. If only Jack, lovely Jack, had gone to the barn dance, none of that would have happened and it'd be so much easier.

When all is said and done, she thought, *I think I'll accept his proposal. But I'll have to clear it with Mom and Dad. In fact, Jack will have to ask Dad. I'm only eighteen and that's the way it's done or, at least, the way they'd expect it to be done.*

She decided that tomorrow she'd write them and hint about Jack and tell them she was coming home for Thanksgiving weekend. She'd settle it then.

Chapter 16

Late some nights, Jack drove down to North Portal just to keep an eye on the occasional night runs by rum runners. And sometimes, he drove over to Bean Fate where there was often action around the train station, with the rum runners picking up booze from the Bronfman depot. Again, it was just to keep an eye on it all.

Wednesday, October 4 was one such night. It was dark and there were no streetlights. Lights were on at the station but all was quiet. He didn't see the big car parked with its lights off behind some bushes in the field with the makeshift ball diamond just across the railway tracks from the station. The lights were also on at Whites and several cars were parked in front. But all seemed quiet there, too, so he drove down to North Portal. Sometimes, there were problems there at the Grandview Hotel just like at Whites. But all looked quiet there, too. He turned around and headed back north.

Meanwhile, inside the poolroom at Whites, several men were drinking and playing poker, including Matoff, Lacoste, and the station agent. Matoff was in full peacock mode, ring and tiepin glittering. He was holding forth and the others put up with him because, as usual, he was losing, and poker is a zero-sum game. If he was losing, some of them were winning.

Half-filled glasses of booze sat on the table. One guy said, "Paul, what's with this horse-piss we're drinking?"

Another guy said, "Is this rot-gut what the Yanks are paying you the big bucks for?" Matoff ignored them with an indulgent air.

Someone came in and said, "Paul, you're wanted at the station. Lee has arrived."

Matoff and the agent hurried over to the station to find Dillege with a Cadillac car and a couple of men with a truck. They loaded fifty-six cases of Black Horse from the express shed onto the truck. Then Dillege, Matoff, and the agent entered the office. The natty-looking Colin Rawcliffe was there.

They stood around a desk beneath a ceiling lamp as Dillege counted out $6000 in $500 packets. Matoff watched closely, his diamond stickpin glittering in the light from the lamp. After that was completed, the agent headed upstairs.

Matoff turned to pay Rawcliffe for the express charges.

CRASH! The sound of the glass of the bay window being shattered. They all jumped and saw for a split-second the ominous barrel hole of a twelve-gauge shotgun stuck through the window... but before they could react further, *BANG!* It let out a fiery blast.

Matoff was blown back and collapsed. There was a hole in his chest the size of a dinner plate and blood and gore all around him. Rawcliffe and Dillege were momentarily stunned and then looked at each other. "Paul's dead!" said Rawcliffe in a choked voice.

In panic, he turned and ran up the stairs.

Dillege turned and ran out, leaving the cash on the desk. Looking to his right, Dillege saw the rear red lights of the truck leaving the driveway. His boys weren't waiting for him! Looking to his left, he saw a figure in the dark at the far end of the station platform.

Lacoste arrived running across the street from Whites, Dillege shouted, "Get in the car," and they both jumped into the Cadillac and drove off with a screech of wheels, Dillege at the wheel.

Moments later, a figure, indistinct in the dim light, entered the office and scooped up the cash into a satchel. It then took the diamond stickpin off Matoff's tie, hesitated, and then jabbed it in Matoff's right eye and pocketed it. Then the figure rushed out into the night like an apparition.

Minutes later, Jack was driving along in the dark on the gravel road back towards Bienfait, his being the only lights in a dark night. But then he noticed headlights in the distance approaching rapidly. *Must be a fast car,* he thought. *Unusual for late at night in the country. Maybe bad guys. I should check.*

He stopped and stood in front of his lizzie, signaling the rapidly approaching car to stop with left hand, revolver in right hand. But it kept coming and all Jack could see were its headlights bright in the surrounding dark. When it looked like it was going to plough right into him, he jumped aside at the same moment as the big car swerved to the other side into the shallow ditch. Jack managed a couple of shots at the car with his revolver as it passed the lizzie and heard a couple of pinging sounds. He'd hit it for sure, but the car didn't stop, regained the road, and sped off. *Was it a Studie? Or did he just imagine that?*

Jack knew his Lizzie was no match for the big car, so he continued on to Bienfait. Entering the town, he saw people standing around the station. They waved him over and pointed to the office.

Jack entered and saw the agent, Rawcliffe and a couple of other men looking at a pool of blood and Matoff's lifeless body with its big messy hole in the chest. On close inspection, Jack noticed an odd detail: one of Matoff's eyes, but only one, had a bit of blood oozing from it.

After calling long distance to police headquarters in Regina to report the murder, and to the coroner in Estevan, he interviewed the station agent and Rawcliffe. The agent recounted what he saw all the way from the poolroom to the station and heading upstairs after the cash had changed hands. Rawcliffe recounted the shooting, saying he never saw the shooter and that Dillege was standing beside him when the blast came from outside. At that point, said Rawcliffe, he ran upstairs and saw nothing more. He heard a car and a truck leave, presumably Dillege. Then he heard someone enter down below and then leave with a door slam and another car take off. He thought it was from the other side of the tracks somewhere. When he came back downstairs, the cash was gone. Six thousand dollars!

Jack noted that Matoff's diamond stickpin was missing, although his diamond ring was still on his finger. It seemed odd that a thief would take one but not the other.

"What about Paul's tiepin?" Jack asked Rawcliffe. "Did you see that anywhere?"

"I noticed that he had it on. It sparkled. But I don't see it now."

The agent's wife corroborated the accounts of her husband and Rawcliffe about coming upstairs, her husband before a gunshot and Rawcliffe after.

Jack talked to a couple of other bystanders who had come over from the poolroom. "Who was there?" asked Jack. The usual guys, they said, including Matoff, the agent, and Lacoste. They said Lacoste stayed behind when Matoff and the agent went over to the station and that he was just leaving when they heard the shotgun blast. They said that he ran over towards the station then and they saw him jump into the Cadillac with Dillege and drive off right after the truck.

"What about Stud?" asked Jack. "Was he there playing poker?"

"No," they said.

I'll have to have a look at his Studie, he thought. *I know I hit the getaway car.*

He saw Gordon White standing to one side and approached him. White said he'd been asleep in his bed in the hotel when he heard the gunshot and couldn't offer any information.

Jack told everyone to go home and back to bed, and the crowd broke up. He told the same thing to Rawcliffe. Then he sat down in the office with the agent to guard the body until the coroner arrived from Estevan. Into this grisly setting, the agent's wife brought down the stairs a pot of coffee for them. "Thanks," said Jack gratefully, wishing she'd brought a drink which, of course, she wouldn't, at least not for him. The coroner soon arrived with the undertaker and they took the body away in the undertaker's truck.

Jack followed them back to Estevan and drove up to the white house with green shutters. A light was on in the window. He steeled himself; he'd never had to do this before. But he remembered his training. Then he knocked on the door. There was no answer. So, he knocked more loudly and insistently. A youngish woman came to the door in her nightgown, obviously having been awakened. She looked shocked to see him.

"Mrs. Matoff?"

"Yes, why, what's the matter?"

"May I come in?"

She hesitated. She was in her nightgown. But it was a policeman and he was very polite.

"Yes, of course."

"Can I sit down?" He'd been taught that if he sat down, she probably would too. And she did.

"Mrs. Matoff, I'm afraid I have some bad news."

"Oh?" She said it with a tremor in her voice.

"There's no way to make this easy. There's been a shooting in Bean Fate."

"A shooting?"

"Your husband was shot. I'm afraid he's dead."

"Oh my!" she gasped. "What happened?"

"I don't know, Mrs. Matoff. But I'll find out."

She sat there looking crushed.

"Is there anything I can do to help?" he asked.

"No, thank you. I'll call my brother. He'll help."

Jack took his leave. It was well after midnight.

Jack awoke late the next morning and walked back to the Matoff house thinking he'd start by interviewing Jean Matoff herself and get that over with. In front of the house, he saw a big car. He knocked on the door which was opened by Harry, who looked like hell.

Jack introduced himself and Harry remembered him. Jack said he was sorry about Matoff's murder but he wanted to talk to the widow. Harry said she wasn't in very good shape and he was there to drive her up to Regina to stay with his family. In fact, he was arranging to take her away for good. Jack said all the more reason for him to talk to her now and that it shouldn't take long. In fact, he'd be happy to do it in Harry's presence.

Harry left and brought Jean Matoff downstairs and they entered the parlor. She looked distraught and a baby started to cry upstairs. Jack looked past her as a little girl came down after her. Jean turned around and told the girl to go back and look after the baby. But the little girl just stared at Jack.

"Why's the policeman here? Where's Daddy?"

"Daddy's busy in Bean Fate. He'll be home soon. Go back upstairs and look after the baby."

The girl backed up to the foot of the stairs, turned, and ran up.

"I haven't told her yet," said Jean forlornly.

Jack made the interview short. All Jean knew was that Paul had gone over to Bean Fate last evening and then Jack had awakened her with the bad news.

"Did Paul have any enemies, anyone that might do this?" asked Jack.

"Not that I know of," she answered.

Jack suggested that he and Harry continue alone, and Jean left the room.

"Did Paul have any enemies that you know of?"

"No. My brother-in-law runs a good, honest operation for us."

"Any ideas at all?"

"No."

"What about partners? Do you have any?"

"Just my brothers... Well, we have a couple in Distributors."

"What's that?"

"Our distributing company."

"Any problems with any of them?"

"No," said Harry while thinking of Chechik... *But he wouldn't do something like this. No need to open up that can of worms either.*

"The thing," said Jack respectfully, "is this, Mister Bronfman. I know you run a legitimate business."

"I sure do."

"But you deal with some rough customers. Like those guys from Chicago."

"Which guys?" *No need to volunteer anything*, thought Harry.

"Well, the ones I met at the ballgame."

"I wasn't there."

"But Paul was, and he was dealing with them. Their names were, as I remember, Capone and Dutch something. Later one day, I saw the Dutch guy loading up a car over at your depot. Do you know about them?"

"They're legitimate customers. We have a deal with them."

"Did you ever meet them?"

"Once. They came up here once. Paul and I met with them to negotiate the deal."

"That was it?"

"Yeah." Harry hadn't mentioned that second unhappy meeting or Leech's awkward involvement.

"What about local people? I've heard Paul was a big gambler; were there any problems there?"

"None that I'm aware of."

"Any ideas at all then?"

"Look, constable, people know about nighttime deliveries at our place over there and that cash changes hands. Lee Dillege comes every Wednesday. It was probably a robbery by some bush-league guys that went bad."

"Okay, and thanks, Mister Bronfman. But if you hear of anything, please let me know."

"I will," said Harry, showing him to the door.

Harry not only looked like hell, he felt like hell. He'd been called by Jean right after she'd been awakened by Jack and he'd driven several hours through the night to be by his sister's side. The Bronfmans were a very close family and he felt her pain deeply. And the question of how a young widow with two small children would survive was on his mind, although at least the family would look after her financially. He knew that. Also, Sam's admonition rang in his ears: *Don't do anything to fuck up the export business.* The murder would be big news and might trigger a call from Regina to Ottawa to shut it down. Shutting it down would be bad enough. But incurring Sam's wrath would be even worse in the long term.

Yes, he thought, *it's a disaster for the family and I'll wear it.*

Jack drove over to Bean Fate and the first thing he saw was Lacoste standing in front of Whites, so he conducted an impromptu interview with him. Lacoste's story echoed those Jack had heard from the bystanders last night that Lacoste was still at Whites at the time the gunshot was heard. Lacoste added that he left with Dillege in the Cadillac and that they caught up with Dillege's truck. But they were both hijacked before they got to the border. "So, Dillege was out of both the cash and the booze," said Lacoste. Jack looked at Lacoste skeptically.

"Really? Where exactly were you hijacked?" Lacoste was vague about where. He said, "Somewhere around the border."

It sounded a bit fishy to Jack but there had been that hijacking at Anderson's. Anyway, it was clear from witness accounts that neither Lacoste nor Dillege could be the murderer!

He walked back into the manager's office where White welcomed him.

"Coffee?"

"I'd love one."

White rang a little bell on his desk, a maid arrived at the door, and he asked her to bring in two coffees.

"That was something last night," White said expectantly.

"Yeah. I just wanted to go over what you saw."

"As I said, last night, I was asleep in bed."

"What about before you went to bed?"

"Paul was here, like he usually was, playing poker with some guys who'd showed up."

"Like who?"

White mentioned a couple of names Jack knew, a farmer, a ranch hand, and a miner.

"Lacoste?"

"Yeah, he was here too, like he always is."

"Stud?"

"Didn't see him last night."

"Is he usually here?"

"Quite often."

"Anything else?"

"No, I went up to bed around ten. Next thing I knew, something woke me up. I guess the gunshot. So, I got up and went over. That's about it."

"Any idea why Paul would be killed?"

"No. Other than the obvious thing that he was dealing with bad guys over there and a lot of cash was changing hands. I mean, we'd already had that holdup over in Ceylon. Beyond that, I don't want to speculate."

"Please try."

"Well, I heard he had big gambling debts."

"Do you know to whom?"

"I never heard anyone in particular. I think there were some miners but nothing lately."

"If you hear anything else, let me know."

"Of course."

"And remember, running a gaming house isn't covered by your license."

White looked surprised, as if to say, why now? Was Jack leaning on him?

"I don't do that. I don't take a cut. Plus, I live here. And I don't even charge for the room."

"What about the booze?"

"Jack, I don't sell booze, just near beer. And the food when they ask… if the kitchen's still open."

"That's all they drink? Near beer?"

"As far as I know. I don't search them."

Jack just looked at White for a moment.

"Okay, but let me know if you hear anything."

With that threat, thought Jack, *if he does know anything more, maybe he'll come back to me.*

White did know more. Only he didn't know that he did.

Jack got into the lizzie and started off when he saw Stud pumping gas at the garage. *There's that son of a bitch,* he thought. Then he noticed that Stud was pumping not into the Studebaker but into a big Packard Twin Six Touring Car. Jack drove up in front of the Packard, nose-to-nose, blocking the Packard. He got out and walked around to Stud.

"Different car," he said.

Stud just looked at him.

"Where'd you get it?"

"None of your business."

"Where's the Studie?"

"I said none of your business."

"I've got a couple of questions for you."

Jack waited until Stud finished filling up his tank, went into the garage, paid his bill, and walked back.

"What questions?"

"Where were you last night?"

"Why?" growled Stud.

"In case you haven't heard, Paul Matoff was murdered last night."

"What the hell! I'm not involved in that."

"Just asking. You weren't at the poolroom. Like you usually are."

"You can't come around asking people who have no involvement. Are you asking that pastor or Mrs. Anderson where they were last night? Now back out so I can leave."

"I'm a police officer and I'm asking you a question."

Stud turned, got into the Packard, backed up with the sound of gravel grinding, turned around, and drove off in a swirl of dust.

Seething, Jack walked into the garage. The owner/mechanic in greasy coveralls was just heading back to a car sitting on wooden blocks.

"When was the last time you saw Stud? I mean before just now?" asked Jack.

"Yesterday afternoon, he was here. Filled up that big Studie."

"You sure?"

"Yeah."

"Have you ever seen that Packard before?"

"Nope. Nice car though."

Jack got back in his car and drove along the main street where he saw a group of men standing and talking in front of the butcher shop. A beefy red-faced man with a bloody apron was obviously holding forth, his hand resting on a big knife handle in a scabbard hanging from his waist. Jack recognized him from the church.

Jack stopped and got out of his car.

"What's up?" he asked the butcher.

"We're getting sick and tired of all the goings on around here. The bank robberies and now Paul Matoff's murder. You obviously can't protect us. You're not doing the job. So we're going to do it ourselves."

Still seething, Jack walked right up to the butcher and demanded, "Meaning what?"

"We're going to set up our own group to look after our safety. And we'll guard the station. And we'll be armed."

Jack put his hand ostentatiously on his holster and said, "That'd be a big mistake."

There was silence with Jack and the butcher face-to-face. The other men looked uncomfortable. They'd never seen Jack like this. Turning to them, Jack said, "I'll get Matoff's killers but I can use any help you guys can give me."

"Like what?" asked one of them.

"Does anyone know where Stud was last night?"

They looked at him as if to ask 'why' and then all indicated 'no.'

"Do you know what happened to his Studie or where he got that Packard?"

They all indicated 'no.' And no one volunteered anything about Stud.

"Well, let me know if you hear anything," said Jack in disappointment. "Now get back to your jobs or whatever you were doing."

The men dispersed in a mixture of grumbling and surprise. He was tougher than they thought. And that was a good thing.

Jack drove back to Estevan and over to the Soo Line Station. He asked the manager if he'd seen Stud or any strangers there yesterday or this morning. The manager replied, "I haven't seen Stud for quite a while. Not since he was driving those hoods from Chicago a few weeks ago, in fact. You know, the ones who were at the ball game."

"You haven't seen them since?"

"No sir."

"Let me know if you do, or if you see anything else that might help my investigation."

Chapter 17

Jack attended church a few days later. As usual, it seemed, he arrived a bit late. He saw the Andersons and Kate a few pews ahead. There was space beside them but he thought it'd be less distracting if he just sat in the empty back pew. *Less distracting not only for the congregation and Sparling but also for Kate, who asked to keep things private, but only for now,* he thought optimistically.

Sparling gave another bravura performance about the failure to enforce Prohibition and the result in their community: the murder of poor Paul Matoff. He wondered darkly why the 'powers that be' in Regina didn't put a stop to it. Parishioners nodded their agreement, including the beefy butcher who looked over at Jack with an accusatory stare. Jack felt uncomfortable. He worked for those powers.

Afterwards, parishioners milled about, chatting about the sermon or just life in general. Jack saw the Andersons talking to a group of people but didn't see Kate. Then he noticed her talking over in a corner to Sparling, who seemed to be comforting her, after which she walked slowly up the Andersons. Jack saw people walk away almost ostentatiously. He saw Mrs. Anderson take Kate by the arm supportively and they started to walk towards him at the back of the church, with Anderson right behind. What was going on? Jack walked up quickly.

"Hello, everyone," he said, shaking hands all round, being careful not to betray his expectations with Kate.

They all responded with a sort of forced good humor, even Kate.

"Kate, I'd like to give you a ride home but—"

She looked at him.

"I just have to get back to Estevan for a veterans' luncheon where I'm the speaker."

"And we have to hurry away too," said Mrs. Anderson. "Reverend Sparling's coming to lunch and I have to get it ready, with Kate's help," she said, looking at Kate encouragingly.

The Andersons and Kate said their goodbyes. Kate looked so delicious that he could hardly restrain himself from kissing her. But of course he didn't. They did exchange knowing looks, which were not unnoticed by the Andersons.

Jack walked over to Sparling.

"Good morning, Reverend."

"Good morning, Jack. Nice to see you."

"I saw you talking to Kate."

"Yes. Lovely girl."

"Yes, she is."

"But I think it's tough for her here. Some of our good parishioners are pretty judgmental."

"I guess so," said Jack, thinking, *Some of those bitches are probably criticizing her again for my dropping by the school all the time. Well that'll change when we're engaged and that'll show them.*

"None of my business maybe," continued Sparling, "but I think you're one of her few friends here and she could use any support you could give her."

"Well, I'll certainly give her lots of support," and Jack looked at Sparling knowingly in spite of himself.

Sparling picked it up and said, "That's great to hear," and patted Jack on the shoulder.

+ + +

Sam arrived in Regina at the Union Station where he was met by Harry.

"This is a terrible thing," said Sam.

"It sure is."

"How's Jean?"

"Pretty shaky."

"You look bad yourself."

At Harry's house, Sam and Harry, Harry's wife, and Jean Matoff all sat around the kitchen table as families do in times of distress. Sam was obviously genuinely upset for his sister's sake in spite of his dislike of her departed husband. He suggested she should move back to Winnipeg where she had more family, including a couple of sisters. And he and Saidye were planning to take a trip to California over Christmas and wanted her to go with them. "That would be lovely," she said gratefully. Sam was a wonderful brother.

After a while, he and Harry retired to the living room and talked privately.

"Tell me everything," said Sam. "What happened?"

Harry went through it as best he could. That included what he'd heard about a shotgun blast through the window from an unseen assassin.

"Who do you think it was?"

"I don't know. The cop asked me if we had any problems with partners and I said no and I don't think Myer Chechik would do something like that."

"Of course not! He's a two-bit chicken farmer and a coward at that. Any other ideas?"

"Sam, it could be anyone of a million people. Rum runners, ordinary robbers, anti-Semites."

"Try harder."

"What?"

"Goddammit, Harry. It's got to be those hoods you've been dealing with. The Mob."

"Maybe."

"Shit, Harry. It's got to be them. I told you they'd be trouble."

"Yeah, but I didn't see you turn down any of their money."

Sam ignored the jibe and said, "Have you had any threats before?"

"Yeah," sighed Harry.

"About what?"

"A bad batch."

"Then you must have given them some of that rotgut from fuckin' Chechik."

"I tried to ensure that didn't happen but a new kid—"

"New kid?"

"Bob's son. He brought him in. I didn't know about it…"

"You dumb son of a bitch, Harry. That's it. Stupid kid gave them the wrong stuff."

Harry looked glum.

"You better get your fancy friends onside damn quick. They'll be wanting to shut you down."

"I'll be talking to them, that's for sure."

"I'd better head back to the station. Got to catch the evening train back."

"You just got here!"

"I've got to get back to Winnipeg. Things to do."

What's more important to us right now than this? thought Harry. *Seems like Sam just wants to get away from Saskatchewan.*

+ + +

Jack was having supper by himself at the café when he saw Anderson walk in.

Wonder why he's here, he thought. *I've never seen him here for supper.*

Anderson walked over and slid into the booth across from Jack.

The waiter followed him over and handed him a menu.

"I'll just have a coffee," he said.

"What brings you over here this time of day?" said Jack.

"Actually, I wanted to talk to you." Anderson looked uncomfortable. "About Kate."

"What about her?"

"Look, Jack, I don't even know if I should be here."

"Dave, what the hell is it?"

"I know you like Kate a lot. The wife says she sees it and she sees it in Kate too. And she said I should talk to you."

Oh, is Mrs. Anderson playing matchmaker? wondered Jack, actually pleased at the idea.

"I do like her a lot. In fact, it's kind of serious."

"That's just the thing. That it's kind of serious between you."

"Why?"

"It's about the dance on Saturday night."

"What about it?"

"Stud showed up."

"He did?" Jack was astounded.

"Yeah. Drinking and dancing too."

"Really?" *Hard to visualize Stud dancing,* thought Jack. That wasn't his image of Stud.

"He danced with Kate."

"Oh?"

115

"She danced with him a lot. And drank too."

Jack didn't like to hear that. But he wasn't about to be seen to criticize her. So he said nothing.

"That's not all, Jack."

"Okay, tell me all."

"She left with him."

"She didn't go home with you?"

"No, she left with him."

"I see."

"She came home very late."

Where is Anderson going? Again, Jack didn't respond.

"The wife's pretty sure that he raped her."

That was like a dagger to Jack's heart but he tried to hold on, saying, "Did Kate tell her that?"

"No, but she saw Kate come in. I'd gone to bed. She saw her condition, clothes all mixed up, hair all over the place. Crying. And she saw her the next morning. And women know these things, Jack."

Poor Jack! Anderson saw he was white as a sheet and obviously having a hard time controlling himself.

"That son of a bitch!"

"I know."

"Does everyone know?"

"We've told no one."

"That's good."

"But people suspect."

"Why? They didn't see her after, did they?"

"They saw her before, Jack, paying all that attention to Stud, dancing with him, obviously drinking. She looked a little drunk. And then leaving with him. Even if they don't know he raped her, they think she behaved badly. Very badly. It's not going to be easy for me to protect her as a teacher."

Jack looked at Anderson.

"Thanks for telling me this, I guess."

"We thought you should know, before you made any plans. In case you were thinking."

"Yeah. I needed to know."

"Well, I'd best be going."

They shook hands and Anderson left.

Jack walked back to his room. A reefer was definitely in order. As he sat smoking on his bed, he thought, *So Kate's been raped! Oh my God! Why did she ever allow that to happen? What a disaster for poor Kate! And for me too! I have to face it. I cannot marry her now. Son of a bitch Stud has ruined everything.* And he wept in sorrow but in anger too, and not just at Stud. *She is such a fool!*

I'll have to back away.

Chapter 18

The ten-year-old monumental legislative building rising in the treeless plain beside the manmade Lake Wascana was the pride of Regina and all Saskatchewan. It was designed in the Beaux Arts style by the prominent Montreal architects Edward and W.S. Maxwell, who were very close to the titans of the CPR who'd chosen Regina as the capital in the first place, and reflected magnificently the ambitions of glory of Canada's young and fastest-growing province. After all, it was already the third largest in the Dominion with a population of seven hundred fifty thousand, ten percent of Canada's total.

While the building's façade featured the soft mottled limestone from Tyndall in neighboring Manitoba, its interior featured hard exquisite marbles from Italy and elsewhere around the world. Its cavernous legislative chamber was sized to accommodate the one hundred twenty-five members which would be needed when the province reached its expected population. For now, however, there were only sixty-three members and all was far from glory in the chamber.

Cross was slumped uncomfortably in his mahogany chair behind his front row desk among the forty-seven Liberals on the right of the Speaker of the House who sat on a dais at one end of the chamber. The Premier was conspicuously absent and Cross was on his own. The press and public galleries looking down on the members below were full. Out of a cloud of cigar smoke from the small mixed-bag of an Opposition group across the red-carpeted aisle arose a successful farmer whom Cross knew to be deceptively clever behind his down-home exterior, a sort of a lay 'country lawyer'.

"Mister Speaker," he began, looking up at the Speaker rather than across the aisle, "I have a question for the attorney-general."

Then, looking across at Cross, he said, "When is he going to do something about the Yankee violence which is hammering the towns of southern Saskatchewan... the Ceylon bank robbery, the hijackings and now that flagrant murder in Bean Fate. Why isn't the attorney-general doing something to stop it?"

He sat down.

Cross rose and said, "Mr. Speaker, we're looking into those matters."

He sat down.

The Opposition member rose again and said, "Mr. Speaker, that's what he always says but he does nothing. Why? Let's follow the money. Is it because the government is too close to the boys who are making all this booze that's drawing the Yankees north? Is it because there's so much money being made? And so much money being spread around? Maybe to the Liberals? Did the Liberals receive donations from a man named Harry Bronfman?"

He sat down.

Cross stood and said, "There is absolutely no reason to connect that murder with the government's liquor policies. While the murder is obviously deplorable... and our hearts and prayers go out to the family... we have no reason to think it was anything other than a robbery that got out of hand. It might as easily have been the robbery of a grocery store. The provincial police are looking into it and I can assure the House that every effort will be made to find the killer, wherever that might lead, and bring him to justice."

There were jeers from the Opposition bench.

"As to donations," Cross continued after the jeers started to die down, "I'm not going to comment except to say that, like my honorable friend's party, the Liberal party has received donations from many different citizens for which we're grateful."

He sat down to more jeers from the Opposition benches.

Cross thought to himself, *this doesn't help the chances for Sir James.*

In his office later that day, Cross, Leech, and Harry discussed the firestorm.

"Jeez, Jimmy," said Leech, "they gave you a rough time this afternoon."

"Those sons of bitches were all over me."

Then Cross spoke to Harry, and not in the solicitous tones he'd used at the fundraiser.

"That murder of your brother-in-law seems to have set everyone off. And now it's getting ugly. Did you see this letter in the Saskatoon Star?"

"No, what does it say?"

Cross held up the paper and said, "It's from several Presbyterian ministers and they say:

'There are certain Jews in this province who could contribute a great deal to Saskatchewan by leaving it at once.'

That's you they're talking about."

"Anti-Semites!"

"Harry," said Cross, "I'm sure we have anti-Semites in this province but people know you're dealing with the Chicago Mob and suspect that you had a falling out and they killed your brother-in-law to get at you who, they think, brought all this violence on Saskatchewan. That's what they think. And they're not all anti-Semites."

Harry said nothing.

"So, do they have a valid point?"

"No."

"Are you sure?" asked Cross sharply. "Have you had any problems with the Mob? Any warning of trouble?"

"Well, a bit."

"A bit! What the hell does that mean?"

"They complained about a bad batch."

"What exactly happened?"

"They came to Bean Fate to complain."

"Goddammit, Harry! Who's they?"

"A guy named Al Capone and another named Dutch Schultz. They work for Johnny Torrio."

"Johnny Torrio! He's the head of the Chicago Mob."

"I know," piped in Leech. "Very threatening, but I set them straight Jimmy. Said we had the law on our side. This is Canada, not the States. That kinda thing."

"You were there too?" asked Cross, astonished.

"Yeah," said Leech, looking defensive.

"Shit. Better be sure that doesn't get out."

Turning back to Harry, Cross said, "And what about that story in the Winnipeg Tribune yesterday?"

"Which one?"

"Which one! Dammit, the one about a guy named Rabinovitch who's wanted for manslaughter in Minneapolis. They say he's your partner. Is he?"

"Yeah," said Harry ruefully, "but I didn't know anything like that about him."

"Harry, the public wants us to shut you down. And all this makes their case."

Harry looked nervous now and his hands were shaking.

"What do you want me to do, Jimmy?"

"The press is all over this, particularly the Winnipeg Tribune."

"You're right," added Leech. "I think they're trying to talk to my people. I'll try to stop that but you never know."

"Jeez," said Cross, "you better shut that down."

Turning to Harry, he said, "And you better talk to them and you know what to do: deny, deny!"

As Harry and Leech got up to leave, Cross said, "Can I have a word with you, Dick?"

After Harry left, Cross said, "I knew that bloody Jew would get us all into trouble. I wish you hadn't brought him around. Do you think he's telling us all he knows?"

"He's always been straight with me."

"I don't trust him. And what the hell ever possessed you to meet those hoods with him?"

"He told me they'd demanded a meeting and asked me to attend to show support and I thought I should. After all, we support his business."

"True," said Cross ruefully. *Dr. T. Albert Moore will not be impressed with Dick and me.*

"And it worked when it was starting to get ugly. I told them not to screw around with us up here. Fuckin' Yanks. And they backed off then."

Dick's a tough old bird, I'll give him that.

"What about Matoff?" he asked. "What was he like?"

"Not like Harry, or Sam either."

"Meaning?"

"To be honest, he was kind of a creepy guy. I don't think Harry liked him much. But he gave him a job because he was his brother-in-law."

"Maybe he was killed for personal reasons?"

"It's possible. Who knows?"

"Anyway, Harry sure looks like hell."

"He's taking it hard."

121

"What about Sam? Where's he?"

"Nowhere to be found."

"He's no dummy."

Chapter 19

Sure enough, the next day, Harry got a phone call from a reporter at The Winnipeg Tribune who said he was working on a story about the liquor business in Manitoba and Saskatchewan, particularly Saskatchewan, and wondered if he could come to see him for an interview. Harry agreed but said he'd come to their office in a couple of days.

Harry agreed to Winnipeg because he wanted to be cooperative with the reporter in hopes of more favorable treatment, plus he knew he had to give Sam a report on his meeting with Cross anyway and he had a sense that Sam wanted to avoid Regina.

If Harry had been superstitious, he might not have traveled on Friday, October 13. But he wasn't, and he did. He took a berth on the night train to Winnipeg, Canada's version of Chicago, only one-tenth the size but with the largest railway hub and stockyards in the British Empire. The next morning, he arrived at the CPR station, yet another magnificent Beaux-Arts building designed by the Maxwell brothers. It had been built by the CPR almost twenty years ago, well before the war, to facilitate Winnipeg's position as the 'Gateway to the West' for the hundreds of thousands of arriving immigrants.

He walked through the grand rotunda, down a grandiose corridor, and into the adjoining Royal Alexandra Hotel, also a magnificent Maxwell-designed building of seven stories and the CPR's largest hotel. The last time he'd been here was a few months ago for the huge reception and dance after Sam and Saidye's wedding where Allan, not Harry, had been the best man.

Harry checked in and went up to a grand suite on the top floor. He called Sam.

"I'm here at the Royal Alex."

"We'll be right over."

"We?"

"Allan and me."

"Okay." *Just as well*, thought Harry, *the kid's a lawyer*.

When they arrived, Harry told them about the meeting with Cross. Sam listened carefully.

Then Harry told them about his scheduled meeting with the reporter.

At that, Sam exploded, "Are you an idiot?! Why would you agree to meet with The Tribune? They're out to get us. Their goddamn editor is that asshole Knowles's brother Vernon. Vernon Knowles. He's their goddamn editor."

"Now you tell me."

"Do I have to tell you everything? Anyway, why speak to any reporter, Tribune or Free Press for that matter?"

"Because Cross had already asked me to. And we need his support."

"For what?"

"We still have a ton of product to get rid of. He can shut us down."

"Where's your big buddy Leech whose moose pasture you bought. Where's he?"

"He's there for us. But Cross is the main man."

"I don't like it. It's a setup."

"Well, I have to do it now."

"What're you going to say?"

"I'll just answer straight up as best I can."

Allan now spoke.

"The two things you have to be careful about are local bootlegging and compounding. Stick to the main thing, which is exports, and that they're legal and sanctioned by the government. Say they're our partners."

"No," said Sam. "They are but they won't like to hear that. Puts the pressure back on them, on your big supportive goy friends."

All the while Harry was thinking, *Godammit! Weren't we in this together? Now it's all my fault.*

"And," said Allan, "say you're talking on background only."

"What's that supposed to mean?"

"On the record but they don't quote you."

"Oh, that's a great idea. Sam, great to have lawyer in the family! They know these angles."

The next afternoon, Harry welcomed a young male reporter to the sitting room in his hotel suite. After brief introductions, the reporter said, "I started working on this story a few months ago. Then those bank robberies and hijackings, those kinds of things, started to happen all along the border with North Dakota. And then the murder of Mister Matoff made it a much bigger story. We anticipate a lot of interest. So, thanks for making yourself available, Mister Bronfman."

That's a good start, thought Harry. *The kid's showing some respect. This might be the opportunity I was hoping for before Sam made me nervous.*

"I'm happy to talk on background but I want my name to be kept out of it completely."

The reporter looked surprised and then almost amused.

"Mr. Bronfman, I've found it's impossible to investigate the liquor business without bumping into your name at every twist and turn. So it'd be impossible for us to avoid mentioning your name or disclosing your connection with it."

So much for my brilliant brother, thought Harry. *What am I going to do? Walk out? Tell that to Cross? I'm stuck.*

"Okay. Anyway, I don't mind being quoted that any slap at the liquor business in Saskatchewan at the present time I regard as a slap at me."

The reporter asked, "Why?" in a tone of surprise.

"Because, with the exception of two small concerns in Saskatoon, which have practically run out of stock, the liquor business in Saskatchewan is controlled by me."

The reporter could hardly believe his ears. What a scoop!

But for Harry's part, he'd decided to take the tack that everything was legal so he'd be absolutely open and confident about it all. He continued in the same vein.

"I've always done a fair business by everyone I've dealt with. I did it in the car business, still do, and then in the liquor business. And when that comes to an end, I'll be just a successful in the next business."

By now he was feeling ever more confident.

"You will find," he added, "that whenever I did business with rum runners…"

Again, the reporter looked surprised. Harry had used the charged words: 'rum runners.' But Harry was in full flight and didn't notice.

He continued, "… the people I dealt with always decided that so long as the stuff was from Bronfman, it was okay and that they'd take Bronfman's liquor when they'd reject the shipments from any other concern."

"But those people you dealt with, those rum runners, they weren't exactly Methodist ministers or Presbyterian elders, were they?"

"You know, I've met many white and square men among those who come from down south."

Harry wasn't about to get caught in the holier-than-thou trap of having to apologize for his business or the people with whom he had to deal. Sure, those punks from Chicago were rough and nasty people. Torrio presumably was too. But they were in the States. What he did on this side of the border was all legal and sanctioned by the government. He'd always felt just fine about that. He filed reports and they collected duties for God's sake. His evasive answer worked and the reporter changed his tack.

"Someone high in the management of the liquor commission said you're mixing liquor illegally at your Regina plant," said the reporter.

"That's wrong. We don't do that."

"Really? He said I could go any day to your plant and see liquor being made from alcohol and other ingredients."

"That man is a damned liar."

"So, if I went there?"

"However, what you might see is the mixing and blending of various ages and qualities of the same liquor, mainly whiskey. And that's perfectly legal. All our business is fair and within the law which, as you know, is quite specific on what's okay and what isn't. We stay completely within the law. Anyone says we don't is a damned liar and you can quote me on that."

"I've also heard that you have stacks of fake labels in your plant."

"Fake labels?"

"Yeah, like a label that says Johnny Walker, something like that, when it's only cheap booze you produced yourself."

Goddamn Chechik problem again. In a tone of almost hurt, Harry replied, "When I took over some other guys' stock for Dominion Distributors, and don't get me started, that included a vast quantity of labels, extracts, essences, and chemical coloring material. And some rotgut too. I can show you where I dumped all that stuff on the nuisance ground. On windy days when the wind was blowing from the north, you could smell all manner of extracts which, for my part, I would never consent to use. Never. And I opened those bottles of rotgut and poured the liquor away. And to my knowledge, I never sold any

126

liquor that did not carry the label it was supposed to represent. In other words, the right label."

Rotgut. Harry had it on his mind. He couldn't get over the thought, and Sam's criticism, that he'd screwed up by sending Chechik's rotgut to Torrio. But the reporter didn't pick it up. He seemed focused on a different aspect.

"So, for the record, you maintain that you're not compounding liquor?"

"Look, now I want to get out of this business. So why would I make liquor? I just want to get rid of the stock I have."

"You want to get out of the liquor business?"

"Yes."

"Why now?"

"I've paid sufficient price already. If anybody had told me that part of the price would be paid in the death of one of my family, nobody could have kept me in the business any longer than it would have taken me to get out of it."

"Then you attribute Matoff's death to the liquor business?"

Harry realized he'd got carried away. *This is not what Cross would want to see in The Winnipeg Tribune!*

"No."

"No?"

"If he'd been in any other line of business, people might have gone at him just the same for the sake of getting money."

Harry had slipped the hook. The reporter tried another tack.

"It was reported somewhere that you said you'd got your money's worth out of the politicians."

"That report's ridiculous. It's defamatory too. I never said that."

"Okay, but have you ever contributed to any political campaigns?"

"That's a private matter and I don't think I'll answer that."

And with that, Harry brought the interview to an end.

"By the way," he said, "when do you think this article will be out?"

"I'm shooting for Monday."

The same day, Mahoney arrived at Jack's office in Estevan in a big blue McLaughlin Buick motor car with a driver. He'd telephoned to tell Jack he was coming and to be there, which had made Jack curious yet anxious.

Mahoney sat in the chair across the desk from Jack.

"We have a problem, Jack."

"What is it, sir?"

"The public is in an uproar about what's going on down here. We have to do something."

Jack described what he knew so far, details of the murder scene and his various interviews. Where that left him at the moment was with no one to charge and no strong suspects. He had the involvement of two rum runners, Dillege and Lacoste, but they had ironclad alibis. He had his suspicions about a local cowboy who was linked to the Chicago Mob but no evidence yet.

"What's the deal about the cowboy? And the Mob?"

"There's a cowboy, Bill Studwell, badass guy, who lives around here. Fugitive from the States. I saw him at a big ballgame, actually that Dillege promoted—"

"Dillege promoted?"

"That's another story. Anyway, there was a big ballgame here on Labor Day, and Stud, we call him that, showed up with these two thugs who arrived on the Soo Line and left on the Soo Line. And they looked Chicago. In fact, I met them. Matoff introduced me to them. Apparently, they'd come up to deal with Matoff over in Bean Fate and were waiting for the train back."

"Nothing wrong with that. No one pretends these rum runners are nice people. The question is who killed Matoff. Do you have any link there?"

"Not yet. I'm just suspicious of this guy Stud."

"I haven't heard anything yet to make me suspicious. So, remind me again. What's so ironclad about the alibis of Dillege and Lacoste?"

"The telegraph agent, a guy named Rawcliffe, who was there when Matoff was shot, places Dillege right beside him when he was shot from outside. And the poker-players place Lacoste at Whites hotel when they heard the gunshot. So neither could have shot Matoff!"

"Well, how did the killer know Dillege was going to be there with cash? Maybe Dillege set it up? Maybe he was a draw to get Matoff there?"

"Everyone knows that Dillege has a standing order for Wednesday."

"Might not be known outside Bean Fate. It might suggest someone local. Like that fellow Lacoste, and his pal, Dillege, too."

"Or Stud."

Mahoney looked at Jack, recognizing checkmate.

"The other thing," said Jack, "is that I think it might have been personal."

"Personal?"

"Yeah, like a vendetta or something."

"What makes you think that?"

"A couple of things. Matoff's diamond tie pin was missing from his body but his diamond ring was still on it."

"So?"

"Why would a robber take one and leave the other?"

"I don't know, Jack," said Mahoney heavily. "What's the other thing?"

"There was blood oozing from Matoff's eye. Just one eye. Like he'd been pricked with a pin."

"I assume there was blood all over the place?"

"Yeah, there was, but—"

"Jack, you don't need to play Sherlock Holmes here. And we need to move fast. There's enormous pressure in Regina. You've already got guys at the scene you could charge."

"I get the pressure for sure," said Jack, dodging further pointless discussion about Dillege. "I'm feeling it here," and he told Mahoney about the threatened vigilante action and criticisms from his own pastor who said it's all happening because of higher-ups in Regina and also their relationship with the Bronfmans.

"Look, constable, it's bigger than you and me, and I'm just a cog in the wheel, and I have instructions from the attorney-general to get someone charged. Okay? So you need to get that done pretty quick. Tell me, do you need help?"

"Maybe but not just yet."

"Well, you let me know if you do. Time is short."

"Okay. By the way, sir, I heard something that maybe you ought to know."

"What's that?"

"Apparently, Mister Leech…"

Mahoney suddenly looked alert. "What about Mister Leech?"

"He's got a big bank account."

Mahoney looked at him.

"Apparently, he makes big cash deposits."

"Jack, what the hell are you saying? And where the hell did you hear this?"

"I'd rather not say, sir, but I thought maybe you should know."

"Listen, there's nothing wrong with having a big bank account or in making cash deposits. Most people make cash deposits."

"But big ones?"

"Oh, for Christ's sake, Jack, it's none of your damn business! Just concentrate on what is your business and get someone charged for that goddamn murder!"

And with that, the Commissioner of the Saskatchewan Provincial Police stormed out, got into his big blue motor car and ordered his driver to get going back to Regina.

Chapter 20

Harry had stayed in Winnipeg in anticipation that the newspaper article would be out on Monday. The 'Trib' usually hit the street at about four PM, so the brothers had agreed to meet at Allan's office at 3:30.

The office was that of A.J. 'Alf' Andrews, KC, with whom Allan had studied law and for whom he now worked as a junior lawyer. They were nice offices as befitted one of Winnipeg's leading lawyers and a member of the local WASP establishment, a Conservative in politics and Methodist in religion. It had been a bit of a coup for the young Jewish lawyer to obtain articles with Andrews but the growing Bronfman business had proved to be a bit of a coup for Andrews too.

When Harry arrived, he was shown into a small library with floor-to-ceiling shelves packed with leather-bound books of law reports. Around a big oak desk around sat Sam, Allan, and, he assumed, Andrews. Allan quickly arose and introduced Harry. Andrews was smooth and self-confident. But Harry could tell he was smart too, smart enough not to be condescending to his rich Jewish clients. They talked pleasantries for a couple of minutes and then Andrews left.

Harry was feeling a bit of an outsider. Allan looked sleek and elegant and at home in this WASP environment. *Allan is a different kettle of fish,* thought Harry. *Didn't grow up knowing the penury of our early days in Brandon. Went to university and got an education on the money I made for the family, got a law degree, and learned all those fancy terms. Hangs out with the big WASPS. Married into Jewish high society with a prominent Ottawa brother-in-law who's the president of the Zionist Society of Canada. All so sophisticated.*

"Where's that fucking paper?" asked Sam anxiously.

"My secretary's supposed to get it on the street as soon as it's there and bring it right up," said Allan. "I'll go and check."

Sam sat tapping his fingers on the table. Harry just sat.

131

"Where the hell did Allan go?" asked Sam after about five minutes.

He never changes, thought Harry.

Finally, Allan came rushing in and dropped a copy of the paper in front of each of them. By the look on Allan's face, Harry knew he'd have been better off going back to Regina.

"What does it say?" demanded Sam. He'd seen the look on Allan's face too.

"Long article. Why don't you guys read it for yourselves?"

Harry thought, *It looks like Allan doesn't want to be the bearer of bad tidings.*

Monday's afternoon edition of The Winnipeg Tribune featured a long expose article on the booze business with a focus on Saskatchewan, starting on the front page and continuing on for several more. It started off with a description of the history of the booze trade, the shifting regulatory environment, and the shocking increase in violence along the southern border. Then it moved to complaints about lax law enforcement. This included a curious section based on an interview with Col. Johnson, the U.S. consul. That drew Sam's attention.

Col. Johnson was reported as saying that in early 1922, an enormous seizure was made in Regina through the efforts of federal customs officers, in which fraudulent labels, U.S. counterfeit revenue stamps, chemical extracts, and aniline dyes used in coloring and flavoring of fraudulently manufactured liquors were taken into custody by federal authorities. Col. Johnson insisted that the subsequent prosecution was a farce, that the federal officer who made the seizure was in no sense supported by the customs officers in Ottawa, and that the whole situation was too ridiculous, fraudulent and impossible to warrant the U.S. government supporting the matter any further!

"That's Cyril Knowles," growled Sam.

"Keep reading," said Allan. "Harry's next."

Sure enough, the article went on with word-for-word quotations from Harry's interview. Harry and Sam read in growing agitation.

"So you control the business," said Sam. "Not the family…"

"I meant I run it here. In Saskatchewan, I mean."

They kept reading.

"You almost admitted Paul was murdered because of us."

"No, I made it clear…"

"After you'd almost admitted."

Then they got to the article's detailed and specific conclusions. They were in numbered paragraphs. This wasn't just the reporter speaking. This was the paper's editorial position as put forth by the editor, Cyril Knowles's kid brother. These were the paragraphs that Harry, Sam, and Allan read in growing consternation:

1. The liquor export business is substantially in the hands of Harry Bronfman and associates.

2. In the past, alcohol has been imported and illicit liquor made by exporters from alcohol, water, coloring, and flavoring essences, and the bottles were sealed with illicit labels.

3. High officials of the Saskatchewan government insist that the illicit making of liquor is still in progress, which Mr. Bronfman denies.

4. It is admitted that the rum running game is responsible for the epidemic of banditry, bank robbing, and murder now prevalent along the southern boundaries of Manitoba and Saskatchewan.

5. Col. J.A. Cross, attorney-general, indicates that the government is seriously considering requesting the federal government to prohibit absolutely the export of liquor.

The article concluded with comments from a Dr. John Nicol of Saskatoon, the director of Temperance and Social Services of the provincial government. He was convinced that the liquor business was, first, the center of corruption of many kinds and, second, the cause of the prevalent banditry along the southern border. "Liquor is a corrupter," he said, "of everybody that takes hold of it."

When he was finished, Sam threw the paper at Harry and screamed, "You totally fucked it up!"

Allan quickly closed the door.

Harry looked crushed.

"They didn't believe you and they're saying Paul's murder was because of us," said Sam.

"They didn't say that."

"More or less they did. And that Regina's gonna shut us down. Like I warned you against. Dealing with all those bums."

"One of their big issues was the compounding," said Harry, sort of suggesting that that was Sam's bright idea.

"You were supposed to say it was only blending!"

"I did. It's clear in the article."

"Well, you must have come across damn lame. And who's the official in high place? Your great friend Dick Fucking Leech?"

"I'm sure it's some goddamn bureaucrat."

"Wasn't Leech supposed to keep them in line?"

"I thought he would."

"You thought. Harry, you think with your head up your ass. My God, what a total fuckup! No quote from that useless bastard Leech. Instead, a quote from some nameless bureaucrat who's probably a communist. And your big man, Cross, he doesn't say we're great guys following the law and paying taxes. Instead, he's going to shut us down, run us out of Saskatchewan. Even worse, it fucks up our reputation in Winnipeg and it'll even be picked up down east. A total and complete fuckup!" he raged.

"At least," said Allan, the voice of reason not entirely unhappy about Sam's fury at Harry, "Cross only says he's thinking about shutting us down. He's given us notice. But not how much."

"You're right," said Sam. "What if it's one week?" Turning to Harry, he said, "You'd better blow out our stocks as fast as you can."

"It's all on me?"

"You said you controlled the business. Not us. You. So go fix it."

Harry was upset as he left the office, checked out of the Royal Alex, and headed back to Regina on the train. The newspaper interview had been, it seemed, a disaster, not only for the prospects of the business in Saskatchewan but also for his relationship with Sam. He had worked hard for twenty years to build the family's business and to bring his younger brothers along with it, all the while having to manage an older brother's screw-ups of one sort and the other. And they had achieved great success. Yet, now he had to turn to trying to wind up that Saskatchewan business in tough circumstances while Sam hovered over him in judgment. He wouldn't, he knew, be thanked for success in winding up the business but he'd sure as hell be criticized for any failings in doing so. And what of the future? It was just so much, and he wept quietly as he rocked from side to side in his berth.

Sam and Allan had stayed behind in the Andrews Library.

Sam said, "You know, this is really bad. Harry has really fucked up for us. He may wind up the business okay, probably will, with our help, and he's no

134

dummy on that sort of thing. But our reputation, the Bronfman reputation, will suffer. I've got big plans for us in Montreal. With our stake which I built up with Harry's help, and assuming we get it out, I want to set us up big, like the old established distillers. That's my dream, Allan. Like those guys in Scotland. Big guys and classy too."

"You've met them?"

"No, but I know about them. We've bought their products, Dewars, Johnny Walker, and I've heard about them from Mortimer Davis. I want to set up a whole new business based in Montreal to serve all of Canada but the states too when Prohibition comes off down the road, which it will. That's what I want. But if the name Bronfman is associated with bootleggers and rum runners and murder and the Mob, can I do that?"

"Sure, Sam, people will forget over time."

"I'm not so sure. I'm afraid there could be a stain we can never erase."

In some consternation, Cross read the article next morning when the paper came off the train from Winnipeg. The epidemic of banditry, bank robbing… and murder! The Trib was blaming the export trade for Matoff's murder. They hadn't zeroed in on the Mob but damn close. The kiss of death would be if they linked the government specifically to Torrio via Harry. It'd be fake news really but that wouldn't stop them and you could see how they'd do it if they knew about Harry's dealings with Torrio's thugs and their threats.

And Colonel Johnson… why the hell would he have waded in? Goddamn Americans are not good at minding their own business.

And who were the high officials who gave background? Government! So hard to keep control! The civil servants were there before you came and they'll be there long after you're gone. Some with their own agendas too. Who the hell was this Dr. Nicol? How did he get interviewed? Couldn't Leach have prevented that? Anyway, this article would only increase the public pressure on the government and, most importantly, on him. *Thank God,* he said to himself, *I mentioned the idea of closing the exports, which should indicate we're on it. Now we'll have to do it for sure.*

But that man Nicol's comments stung. *Liquor is a corrupter of everybody who takes hold of it. Was he talking about me? If that's the way people are thinking, I can kiss Sir James goodbye.*

The next day, he attended a black-tie club dinner at his exclusive men's club, the Assiniboia, not quite the Mount Royal but then, it was Regina, not Montreal. The club was housed in its own handsome three-story red brick pile just across the park. It was a chilly evening and as he entered the lounge room, he was glad to see a fire blazing and crackling in the great fireplace. Thirty or forty men were standing and talking with drinks in hand, and a couple of men were settled in deep leather club chairs in a corner. He assumed that most drinks were alcoholic drinks from the club's extensive stores built up during the mail-order era. He himself only drank soda water.

Across the room, he saw Colonel Johnson talking to Jasper Leask and he walked over. Johnson looked elegant in a crisp military-style tuxedo with a couple of medals. Jasper looked rumpled in a too-tight tuxedo that had seen better days, as indeed had he.

Cross said "good evening" to the Colonel, sticking out his hand for Johnson to shake.

"Good evening, Colonel. You know Jasper Leask?"

"Oh yes." Cross and Leask shook hands in a friendly manner.

"We were just talking about European politics," said Johnson.

"English politics? Lloyd's George's resignation?"

"No, Italian politics."

"You're going where angels fear to tread."

Johnson laughed but added, "We were talking about Mussolini and his likely march on Rome. With his black shirts."

"What's your thought on that?"

"It may be a positive development."

"You think that's a good thing?" asked Cross in some surprise. "I thought you career men didn't approve of militias, particularly private ones."

"Not normally, but it's not a normal situation. I hear a lot of officers in the Italian Army feel the same way. Italy's a disaster. Their parliamentary government... I forget what it's called. Seems weak. They've got general strikes trying to shut down the country. In fact, bolshie ideas are spreading all over the continent. What the Italians need is a firm hand to settle things down. Keep all those bolshies in line. And Mussolini seems like the man who could do it."

"I thought Mussolini was a socialist himself?" Cross was needling Johnson now.

"Was a socialist. Not anymore. Saw the error of his ways and has moved on."

"Yeah, to fascism."

"Right. They're anti-socialist and anti-trade union and think strong leaders are needed to take charge and establish law and order."

"I don't think that you need a strongman type to get firm leadership. Three years ago in Winnipeg, they put down a general strike by socialists and trade union leaders and, in fact, a couple of bolshies, without that kind of a leader. You just need the citizens to rally round."

"Oh? I wasn't here then."

"Yes. The citizens were led by a couple of lawyers I know. Leading citizen types. One was a former mayor. Alf Andrews. Not strongman types. Concerned citizens. They just got together and made it happen with the help of the government and the police."

"Yeah, but was it that big a deal?"

"It was a big deal, alright. Riots. They sent in the Mounties, shots fired, one fatality. Guys went to jail. All that kind of stuff. Alf in particular did a helluva job. But he was no strongman, just a concerned citizen."

"Well, good for them but that's in an Anglo-Saxon country. The Italians don't know how to do democracy. I mean liberal democracy, representative government. That kind of thing like you have and we have. They're unstable people. I mean they're fine individually, and I'm talking about the ones over there, not the ones we got up in New York, but they don't seem to know how to pull together, and so they need to be ruled by a strong man. Otherwise, they fall apart. And Mussolini's a strong man. But Jasper doesn't agree."

"You don't?" Cross turned to Jasper.

Jasper took the latest cigarette out of his mouth and stubbed it into a cigarette tray on a side table.

"There may well be," he said, "problems in Italy and all across Europe for that matter, mainly as a result of the war and the so-called peace treaties. But if the king lets Mussolini in, he'll live to regret it. He may think... as his industrialists and landowners seem to think... that Mussolini's the man to deal with the unrest in the country. But Mussolini's a thug and it won't end well. Pacts with the devil never do."

"Well, we won't settle that one this evening," said Cross.

Turning back to Johnson, he said, "But I see you were talking other politics in the Tribune yesterday."

"Not politics, Colonel, diplomacy."

Carter Johnson spoke in the soft drawl of tidewater Virginia. *Strangely similar to Jasper's drawl*, thought Cross. A West Point graduate, Johnson came from a long line of proud military men, both grandfathers having held commands under General Lee in what Johnson referred to as 'The War Between the States.' He himself had served in the last war about which he and Cross had swapped stories before. The consulship in a city of thirty-five thousand in the Canadian hinterlands was his reward from a grateful nation. Still, it was a job for someone retired while still relatively young. Meanwhile, he was an Episcopalian and his presence in the city and role as a pillar of the local Anglican Church was generally appreciated. After all, he added a little class to a plain world and Cross was well aware of the disparity in their social backgrounds, which the drawl seemed to emphasize.

"You think that was diplomatic?" asked Cross.

"It's part of my job."

"Really?"

"Yes, it's part of my job to speak to the press about contentious cross-border issues. When Canada allows a flood of banned product into our country, that's a diplomatic issue. And you must admit, Colonel, that that prosecution in the spring was an absolute farce."

"I wouldn't admit that, but in any event, it wasn't our prosecution."

"And I made clear that it was Ottawa I was criticizing. And you know, Colonel, with respect, as I hear you lawyers saying all the time, there really is so much hypocrisy in all this. A policy of prohibition at home while allowing exports." Johnson said it in a good-humored voice but with an edge betraying annoyance and even a hint of condescension towards the attorney-general of this two-bit province in which he was stuck.

"There's enough hypocrisy to go around, Colonel," said Cross, who picked up the nuance in Johnson's voice.

"Meaning?"

"Let's face it. Lax enforcement in the states and allowing exports of alcohol to Canada."

"What exports?" asked Johnson indignantly.

"Pure alcohol. You ship it up here and our guys compound it with other ingredients to make booze which gets exported back to the states."

"I never heard of any such thing!"

"I'm not surprised but it happens. One of our fine citizens, a man named Harry Rabinovitch, buys it in Minneapolis. Check it out, Colonel."

Leask watched with a bemused look.

"Well, gentleman," added Cross, "I see somebody over there I need to have a word with. Nice talking to you."

Cross took his leave. As he did so, he thought to himself, *Jasper's wise enough, nailing it about Mussolini. But he's boozing it up as usual for sure. Sad case really. When he first arrived in town, we all thought a London barrister would be a real asset. That's why I put him up for the club even though one member had wondered if Jasper were a homo. He was unmarried and had a very good male friend, also unmarried, with whom he stayed in Regina, the manager of women's clothing at Simpson's. But I had said, well, if he's a homo, he's discreet, which is good enough, and I talked the member out of blackballing Jasper. But the booze has got to Jasper. Maybe because he's conflicted about being a homo. Maybe he hates himself. Who knows? Too bad because he's a smart guy and an excellent lawyer.*

Jack also read the Tribune article, which he talked over with two people.

The first one was Jasper. He hadn't seen him since the murder but a couple of days after he'd read it, he saw Jasper at their favorite café.

"Haven't seen you for a couple of weeks," said Jack, sliding into the booth across from Jasper.

"I've been in Regina. Big case before the King's Bench. Just got back today."

"A lot's happened."

"Like that murder in Bean Fate," said Jasper.

"And then that interview with Bronfman in last night's paper. Did you see that?"

"Yes. It's a bit of a blockbuster. Big news in Regina."

"The whole thing's a bit of a blockbuster. I'm under a lot of pressure."

"That's why they pay you the big bucks, old boy," said Jasper, chortling. "Seriously, what's the story?"

Jasper's an officer of the court, thought Jack. *I can be open with him confidentially.* And he told him what he'd learned so far, basically that Dillege and Lacoste had alibis and he suspected Stud but without much to go one. Then he described his meeting with Mahoney and the pressure on him to charge someone, almost anyone but most likely Dillege and Lacoste.

"If you charge them, sounds like they'll be acquitted. Although, Dillege would have to be extradited."

"And you told me the other day that's a long and complicated process, right?"

"Yes, but that'd probably be just fine with the government."

"Why? Wouldn't they want to get to trial quickly?"

"Not necessarily. They might be happy to have it all tied up in court. Maybe all they really want is charges to show the public they're on it."

Huh. Jack hadn't thought of that. Jasper was a savvy guy behind that rumpled exterior.

"But if I were Dillege's counsel, I think I'd advise him to waive extradition," Jasper added.

"Why?" Jack was astounded.

"If his alibi holds up that is. Because he's better to get it over with rather than have it hanging over his head for the rest of his life."

"With that alibi, it just seems ridiculous that we'd even charge him."

"But," sighed Jasper, "when the pressure's on the politicians can't resist it."

"Surely, murder charges are not supposed to be political? I thought the attorney-general was supposed to stay out of them?"

"That's the theory, but in the end, everything's political. In life generally. You'll find that out as you grow older."

"But I have a lot of faith in Colonel Cross."

"You served under him overseas, didn't you?"

"Yes."

"I'm sure he was a good commander."

"He was."

"He's a good lawyer too."

"Have you dealt with him?"

"Oh yes, and he's a smart man."

"He'd do the right thing as attorney-general, wouldn't he?"

Jasper looked directly at Jack now. "You have to remember that now he's a politician. Not an army officer, not even a practicing lawyer. A politician. And the right thing in the eyes of a politician might not be the same as in your eyes or mine. They're always thinking of what the public wants. And the public isn't always right, impolitic as that may be to say."

Jack looked a little shocked at this assessment of his mentor.

"But enough of that, old boy. Now, what about your love life? How's that going?"

"Not so well at the moment."

"Sorry I asked. Are there any happy topics we can discuss?"

"Tell me about your case before the King's Bench."

"Ah, well, that is a happy topic." And Jasper went on to describe his latest victory in court.

The next day, Jack talked the Tribune article over with Sparling.

"It's what you've always said," commented Jack. "And that guy Nicol really nailed it."

"He's one of ours," said Sparling with a sly smile. "I've known him for a long time."

Bloody Sparling! thought Jack in surprise, and admiration too. *He's working it behind the scenes.*

Chapter 21

The pressure was on, no doubt about it after Mahoney's visit plus that newspaper article which had everyone talking. Jack let it be known he wanted to talk to Dillege and Lacoste in his Estevan office.

Lacoste showed up without Dillege.

"Where's Lee?"

"Dunno but I guess at home across the line."

"Tell him I'm looking for him," said Jack without much conviction, knowing he had no authority down there, adding, "but now I'd like to review what you told me about the other night."

Lacoste doesn't look as self-assured as he usually does, thought Jack.

"Start at Whites."

Lacoste took him again through his version of events from the time Matoff had left Whites to go over to the station until he, Lacoste, jumped in the getaway car with Dillege.

"Then what happened?"

"As I told you, we headed down the back road towards Portal. We soon caught up with the truck and stopped to make sure they had everything okay. Then we drove in front and they followed."

"Go on."

"But then, just before we got to the border, a big car pulled out of a side road and hailed us down."

"How?"

"Shone their lights right at us."

"On that back road, not the main road?"

"Yeah."

"So they knew you were going to be coming down that back road?"

"I guess so."

"How would they have known that?"

"I don't know."

"By the way, who was driving your truck?"

"I was in the car with Lee, not the truck—"

"I know," said Jack in some exasperation. "Who was driving that truck that had Lee's booze?"

"Oh. A couple of Lee's guys from down there."

So much for getting those interviews, thought Jack.

"Okay, go on."

"We stopped and these two guys jumped out with tommy guns and ran towards us. Even fired a couple of warning rounds. They shouted to get out. So we did and so did the two guys in our truck. One of them made us lie down in the ditch and covered us with his gun. The other two started unloading the truck into their car. It was a big car."

"That was quite a big job. How long did it take?"

"Not that long for the two of them. Maybe fifteen minutes."

"Two of them did the unloading?"

"Yeah."

"But another guy was covering you with the tommy gun?"

"Yeah."

"I thought you said two guys got out of their car."

"I did."

"But two guys were unloading and one was covering you?"

Lacoste looked confused for a moment.

"I guess three guys got out of their car," he said.

"Don't lie to me. I can send you up for that." Jack was bluffing but Lacoste wouldn't know.

"Send me up?" Jack could see he was sweating.

"You better not lie again."

"I'm sure it must have been three guys."

"So where exactly was this big hijacking?"

"Somewhere along the road near the border."

"Let's go down there and you can show me where."

"It was dark. I don't think I'd recognize it now."

"Jimmy, you've lived here all your life. You'll recognize ditches or fence posts. Something. Maybe the shells from the rounds those guys fired. Come on and we'll drive down there. You can try to show me."

"Look," said Lacoste, "I'll admit it didn't happen that way exactly."

"It didn't?"

"I mean the last part about heading to the border. We weren't stopped."

"What did happen?"

"Lee was worried."

"Did he have something to do with the murder?"

"No, no. But he figured it'd draw a lot of attention and the cops down there would figure he was bringing stuff back home and they'd nail him for that."

"So?"

"So he said we'll say we were hijacked while still in Canada."

Jack thought to himself, *So Lacoste was lying before. About anything else too? Is there a big lead somewhere in here?*

"Did Lee have the cash with him?"

"I don't think so! He used it to pay for that load."

"I know, but maybe he took it back after Matoff was shot?"

"I don't know anything about that. I didn't see it in the car. I don't think Lee would do that – steal the money."

"Did he mention anything about a diamond stickpin?"

"You mean like the one Paul wore?"

"Exactly."

"No."

"Okay. What did you guys do with all that booze?"

"We drove down to Lee's farm and buried it in a haystack."

"Let's go and see it. I'll call the sheriff and ask him to meet us. And bring Lee if he's there."

"Okay, I'll take my own car."

Jack followed Lacoste down south and across the invisible line into Burke County. It was now 'Indian Summer,' that period of autumn on the prairies when the weather has already turned cool but it's warm again and treasured because you know it won't last long. All seemed golden. The harvested fields lay golden in the sun's slanted rays. The poplars were now half bare but their remaining leaves were still golden too. It was a lovely day which belied Jack's mission.

Lacoste led to Dillege's farm where Tom awaited. But Dillege himself wasn't there. Tom said he hadn't been able to locate him but just as well as he would have demanded a search warrant.

"Do you know where he is?"

"No idea. But he often goes down to Minot."

Yeah, he'll be known down there, thought Jack.

Under Lacoste's direction, Jack drove across a field followed by Tom. Lacoste identified a particular haystack which did look irregular and attacked it with a pitchfork. He soon exposed cases of Black Horse.

Jack and Tom talked, standing apart from Lacoste.

"Interesting, but so what?" said Tom. "Would you charge Dillege?"

"I've got nothing to charge him for. I didn't catch him doing anything. Not bringing it across, not selling it. It's just sitting here."

"So, does this do anything at all for your investigation?"

"Not really," said Jack ruefully. "I'm kind of at a dead end. But, say, can you at least get Dillege to an interview with me?"

"I really can't force that. I can't deliver a suspect across the border."

Isn't that what he asked me to do with Stud? thought Jack.

"Maybe he'd agree to be interviewed by me down here."

"Not likely."

"I'm under a lot of pressure. I need any help I can get."

"Not really sure what I can do for you."

"If you can't get him for an interview, can you get me a rap sheet on him? Anything?"

"I've told you what I think of him."

"What about those Minot cops? Could you get me in touch with them and anyone else down here who might know something about Dillege? What about those prohis too? I need to be able to show I've done my homework."

Tom looked at him bemusedly. "Okay, let me see."

On his way back, Jack turned at a sign: *'WESTERN COAL MINE'* and took a well-traveled side road he hadn't been on before leading into coulees. *I should have done this before,* he thought, *but it's kind of out of the way.* The coulees were pock-marked with small tunnel openings surrounded by shanties. He'd heard mention of 'gopher holes,' unlicensed coal mines worked by miscellaneous local people. Then he came to a fence with a security guard on duty, who approached the lizzie as Jack stopped. Jack said he wanted to talk to Joe Bembury.

The heavily-freckled guard, who looked slightly familiar, said to follow the road and he'd come to his office. Jack drove on, marveling as another world was revealed. There was a railway spur line, repair shop, general store, and various buildings with cranes, hoists and other machinery, and, off to the side, rows of bunkhouses with white siding. He came to a small wooden building with a sign: '*MINE OFFICE.*'

He walked in. Bembury was seated at his desk and got up to greet him. They'd met before somewhere – before the murder. He was a hard-looking, no-nonsense kind of guy who'd started as a hard rock miner in Flin Flon in northern Manitoba.

"What brings you out here?" asked Bembury in obvious surprise. The mine had their own security and a visit from the police was rare in spite of the dozens of young itinerant men housed there.

They sat down in Bembury's office.

"I've never been here. Quite a place you've got."

"It works pretty well."

"How many people you got here?"

"Depends. About a hundred right now."

"Shift-work?"

"Yeah, two. Morning and afternoon. But I doubt you're here to discuss that."

"I just wanted to ask about Paul Matoff."

"Terrible thing that. But what about him?"

"I'm kind of at my wit's end. I don't have any leads and the pressure's on from Regina."

"I'll bet. Everyone says it was the Yanks from Chicago."

"Might have been. I don't know. But you have a lot of men working here. Sometimes they come to town. Sometimes they raise a bit of hell there, as you know."

"Sorry about that. We try to keep the lid on."

"You do a good job. But they do come in, they drink, and sometimes they fight."

Bembury raised an eyebrow as if to say, 'So?'

"And they gamble too. I hear that sometimes they gambled with Paul Matoff. I'm wondering if you've ever heard of anyone who might have been owed money by Paul. Someone who wasn't paid?"

"Yeah," and Bembury gave a dismissive laugh. "He owed lots of money over the years. Even to me."

"To you?"

"But he paid me off. This was before you came."

"Any problem collecting?"

"I told him I'd break his goddamn neck. He paid up right away after that. And then I stopped going there and warned my men against it too. To Whites to gamble. But I guess they still do sometimes. I can't control them off the premises."

"No, of course not."

"But look, Paul wasn't a guy to try to stiff you. He just lost a lot and took a while sometimes to pay up. You know, he'd try to win it back in the next game. But he wasn't too swift and he was a poor poker player. That might have been why he dabbled in bootlegging, which was surprising really, given the big operations the Bronfmans have got going to the states. At least I think he did."

"Think so?"

"Yeah."

"Know so?"

"I'll stick with 'think.' But maybe through Bill Studwell."

"What do you know about him?"

"Not much. Except the rumor is he's got booze for sale. We don't allow him on the premises. I'm sure he's a bad apple. That's about it."

"Okay. If you hear anything, please let me know."

As they went out and were shaking hands on the front porch, a group of miners trudged by, still wearing their helmets with attached lamps, covered in coal dust and looking exhausted and sullen.

"Morning shift coming off," commented Bembury.

As Jack drove away, he thought, *Jeez, poor bastards, what a helluva way to have to earn a living! Picking at rocks down in a hole. No wonder they come into town and piss it up.*

When he reached the gate, he slowed down. The guard waved him on but Jack stopped. The guard walked over.

"Didn't I see you at Whites a few weeks ago?" asked Jack.

"Not sure."

"I think I did. That big brawl. And when I asked who'd supplied the booze, you said it was Stud."

"Yeah, I guess I did."

"So, it was him?"

"Yeah."

"Would you testify to that?"

"Sorry."

"Is that a no?"

"Yeah, 'fraid so. I don't need that. I'm not even supposed to go to Whites."

"What do you know about him?"

"No more than anyone else around town."

"Well, do you know where he lives exactly?"

"I think I can help you with that," said the guard and explained in general terms how to get to Stud's remote cabin. There was a certain track to take off a side road. Then he added, "You won't tell the boss about me at Whites?"

"Not to worry. And thanks."

Early next morning, Jack's phone in his Estevan office rang. It was Tom.

"I got a meeting for you."

"A meeting?"

"This afternoon in Minot."

"Who with?"

"Town police chief plus the local prohi."

"Wow! Thanks."

"But don't mention anything about that incident a few weeks ago, you know, when we saw the Minot cops take down the bootleggers. The chief wouldn't want it discussed in front of the prohi."

"Got it."

"I'll meet you there. When you enter town, you cross over a bridge and take a hard right and the police station is right there."

Jack headed south, waving at the U.S. immigration agents as he crossed the border. The road to Minot was no better than the roads around Estevan, all gravel and lots of rough patches. *Must be hard on the springs of those cars and trucks hauling those big loads of booze,* he thought. He'd never been to Minot before but he'd heard about it, a town founded thirty years ago by, they said, some Canadian guy, as he'd built out the Great Northern to the coast. He knew it had always had a reputation as the most wide-open city between Chicago and Butte, which was surprising in a way because, apparently, North Dakota had always been a dry state even before the new national Prohibition a couple of years ago. But Minot was a railroad town with lots of itinerant young men passing through and known for everything from speakeasies and blind pigs to opium dens and prostitution.

The road dropped into the valley to reveal a city of ten thousand on the banks of the meandering river. It looked like a typical prairie city which could have been found on the other side of the line, except for the stars and stripes flying all over the place. As he crossed a bridge, he noticed a sign: *'MOUSE RIVER.' That's funny,* he thought. *It seemed like I was more or less following the Souris River all the way down here.* He turned hard right and found the city police station and saw parked out front the car of the Burke County Sheriff.

Tom introduced Jack to Minot's police chief and the local prohi who both had that typical American combination which he'd seen overseas – a breezy openness masking a certain anxiety. But they were accommodating a fellow law enforcement officer and he was grateful for that.

Tom opened the conversation by saying that Jack was investigating a murder over the border and wanted to ask about Lee Dillege who lived in Burke County and probably came down to Minot sometimes. Jack filled them in on the situation and why he wanted to talk about Dillege – he'd been at the scene of the murder and there was the question whether he'd somehow been involved; maybe been part of a setup with others. So he just wanted to know whether down here he had a rap sheet or was otherwise known to the police.

Tom said, "I've already told you what I know. Lee has a farm and is said to be a smalltime rustler and bootlegger, although I've never actually caught him."

Although you could have if you'd half tried, thought Jack.

"We know him," said the police chief, "but he generally keeps out of town. He may do a bit of local supply. Probably runs a few whores. Owns that ball team. It's minor league and so is he."

They all looked at the prohi. *He looks a bit different,* thought Jack. *Looks like a guy from a big city in a three-piece suit.* He had a lean and angular look and spoke like a college graduate. He also looked like he felt he was stuck in a boring meeting with a bunch of rubes.

"We have no book on him," he said.

"I wondered if he might be connected somehow to gangsters in Chicago," said Jack.

"Not that I've heard of. And I'm from Chicago. As I said, we have no book on him."

That hadn't taken long. The American cops just looked at Jack and then Tom said, "Well, I guess that's about it then."

"By the way," said Jack, "what about Bill Studwell? Anyone heard of him? Besides Tom, I mean."

"Oh, I've heard of him," said the police chief. "Son of a bitch skipped bail."

"He's up in Canada," said Tom. "Jack knows where."

"Anytime you want to unload him, just call," said the police chief.

Tom and Jack exchanged knowing glances.

"Been in trouble in Texas and everywhere in between," said the chief. "But I never heard he was a bootlegger. Total loner. Tough guy. You wouldn't want to mess with him but I never heard he killed anyone."

"Bill Studwell from Texas?" It was the prohi showing a bit of interest.

"Yeah," said Jack.

"I heard about him. Beat up Frank Hamer in El Paso pretty badly in a bar fight a few years back and been on the lam ever since."

"Frank Hamer?"

"Texas Rangers. He's pretty famous down there. Actually, works with us now."

"He's a prohi now?" It was the police chief.

"Down in Texas."

"Not many people mess with Frank Hamer from what I hear," said the chief.

"Not and live to talk about it."

"Looks like Stud did."

"Well, that tallies with my experience with him," said Jack bitterly. "But does he have any connections to Chicago?"

"Not that I've heard of," said the police chief.

"Me neither," said the prohi. "Why do you ask?"

"He drove a couple of hoods from Chicago around."

"Do you know who?" asked the prohi.

"A guy named Capone and another named Dutch Schultz."

"I know about them," said the prohi. "A couple of young punks who work for Johnny Torrio. He had a supplier murdered a few months ago for bad booze. Capone and Schultz did the dirty deed for him. We know that but

150

haven't been able to finger them yet. But they're mean bastards, both of them. If they were up in Canada, that means Torrio's looking for booze there. Why was this guy Matoff murdered do you think?"

"That's just the thing. The reason Stud was driving them was to meet with Matoff. In fact, I saw Schultz buying booze from Matoff once. He was a Bronfman guy and they're big suppliers."

"I've heard of them," said the prohi. "That could be it. Sounds like what happened to the guy in Chicago."

"That's what I'm thinking but I don't have much to go on."

"Neither do we. You hear of these things. Get some info. But not enough to build a case. These are tough cases."

As they were shaking hands goodbye, Jack said, "By the way, I saw a sign that said Mouse River when I was driving into town."

The men looked at him quizzically.

"Does it enter the Souris here?"

"There's only one river here and it's the Mouse," said the chief. "I heard Souris is the French word. You have a lot of French up there?"

"Oh. Yeah, some."

With that, the meeting broke up.

Driving back across the bridge, Jack thought, *I'm glad I came. It confirms my thinking that Dillege is not the prime suspect and, actually, Stud is... along with Capone and Dutch Schultz. But Stud's the connection. The problem is... I have nothing to go on and it's all suspicion on my part. I sure need a break. I can't keep Regina at bay forever.*

Chapter 22

The next morning, and in mounting frustration, Jack visited Adamchuk at his farm. He seemed surprised and nervous. He just looked at Jack, awaiting an explanation for his visit.

"I got a question for you, Borys."

Borys just looked at him, waiting for the shoe to drop.

"Where were you the night Paul Matoff was murdered?"

Adamchuk looked stunned by the question and then responded, "I was here with my wife and kids. Like always. You can ask her."

"Okay, let's talk about your friend Stud. Do you know where he was?"

"No! And he's not my friend!"

"He helped you with Walt when I charged you."

"I know nothing about Stud."

Jack exploded, grabbing Adamchuk by the collar. "Don't you fuck with me, you goddamn bohunk. Tell me about Stud. What's his deal?"

Obviously deeply rattled, Adamchuk said, "All I know about him is I have to pay him. I have to. Otherwise…" his voice trailed off for a moment, "… and he sells some whiskey too. Not to me. But please don't tell him I said. He's bad man. And why you ask me like this? I'm little man. Ask your friend Anderson. He's big man. Ask him where he gets his whiskey. Maybe he knows about Stud."

+ + +

As she arrived at school that same morning, Kate was reflecting on the fact that she hadn't seen Jack or heard anything from him since that day at church a couple of weeks ago when he'd had to rush off to his veterans' luncheon. *Maybe he's just waiting for my answer. Or*, she worried, *maybe he's heard about Stud and the dance.*

She opened up the school and the children started to file in. She went back outside and over to the outhouse. When she returned, the children were all sitting at their desks. They looked expectant and furtive somehow. She looked at them and then walked over to her desk. She froze. On her desk was a crude cartoon of a woman and a cowboy embracing.

She was mortified and turned away from the class for a moment. Then, she turned back and with a straight face ostentatiously crumpled up the piece of paper and threw it into the wastepaper basket. But it meant, she knew, that their parents were talking.

And that Jack would be hearing the same things.

+ + +

The next day, Jack drove over to the Anderson ranch and talked to Anderson in his yard. Somewhat hesitantly, Jack told his friend that Adamchuk implied that Stud supplied him with whiskey. Anderson looked at Jack for a few moments and then, with obvious reluctance, admitted that he made "the odd" purchase of booze from Stud "for medicinal purposes". Anderson was trying a little irony but Jack was in no mood for irony. Anderson also admitted that he submitted to Stud's extortion. "But please don't quote me on any of this," he said. "Stud's not a guy you want to cross."

Jack was disappointed. It seemed no one wanted to help him about Stud.

As they talked, Kate walked into the yard. She waved, seemed to hesitate, and then walked over.

Anderson seized the opportunity to take his leave.

Jack and Kate didn't embrace. They wouldn't have anyway in front of other people but they were awkward with each other. He was thinking, *How will I tell her?* She was thinking, *What does he know?*

"Shall we have a little drive?" he asked.

"Yes, I'd like that." *It'll be a chance to have the talk,* she thought.

Jack drove along a country road a little way and then pulled over and stopped.

It was a cool, cloudy, late-fall day.

"The leaves are almost gone," he said while looking straight ahead.

"Yes, they are."

There was a silence.

"I heard a bit more about the dance."

"What did you hear?"

"That you danced a lot."

"Yes, I did."

"With Stud," he said, turning to look at her accusingly.

She picked up his mood and it angered her.

"You weren't there. He was and he asked me to dance."

"It was more than that, Kate."

"I guess you know about me getting a ride with him."

"I heard."

"It was a mistake."

"I guess it was a mistake, alright."

"I'm not the only one with a problem around here!"

"What do you mean by that?" he asked sharply.

"Nothing. Please just take me home."

They drove back in silence, with Kate weeping.

As she got out of the car, he said, "Kate, I'm so sorry."

"So am I."

"That son of a bitch Stud," he muttered to himself as he drove off.

Chapter 23

The next day, Kate and Jack both made decisions.

Kate realized that it was over with Jack. *He's obviously been hearing things about the barn dance and me and Stud*, she thought. *Who knows what exactly? At the least, that I behaved badly at the dance and left with him. Maybe more. Maybe they even assume we screwed. Imagine! How awful! But what can I do about those kinds of rumors if they're around? Declare we didn't screw? Say he assaulted me but I fought him off? Press charges? That itself would be enough to ruin my reputation... even if they believed me. Anyway, it's clear that Jack has effectively withdrawn his proposal and I really can't blame him. The blame is entirely mine.*

If only I had someone to talk to but there's no one here. Not Mrs. Anderson. Not even Rev. Sparling beyond a point, like the details with Stud. That would be too embarrassing.

Thanksgiving at home doesn't seem so attractive either. I'd have to deal with the hints I threw out about Jack. Give some explanation. Mom and Dad would be too inquisitive. I just can't take that right now. I'll write them and say I'm not coming after all.

But I just feel so alone right now.

Jack had already made his decision about Kate. Today's decision was that the time had come to confront Stud. And he had the directions from the freckled kid at the mine.

He drove along a winding road across the prairie and turned off onto a track leading into a remote coulee near the Souris River. It was a spare yet lovely setting of Manitoba maples and poplars still sporting a few yellow leaves. There was a skiff of fresh snow.

He drove up to some small weather-beaten buildings, a cabin, a garage, a stable, and a small corral but no horse, although fairly fresh horse dung. No one came out of the cabin. Jack knocked. There was no answer. He looked around and noticed fresh tracks of horse hooves and sleigh runners leading to a path into the woods. He walked over to the garage and looked inside. The Packard was there. He looked closely but could see no gunshot marks. He looked in the stable; there were two empty horse stalls, a rack on which hung a saddle, and a large wooden cupboard which was padlocked.

Jack entered the cabin and looked around. Just when he saw a shotgun standing behind a wood box, he heard a noise and went to the door. Stud was approaching, walking beside and holding the reins of a horse pulling a sleigh with a big barrel on it. He had obviously been down to the river to get water.

He walked up to Jack.

"Why are you here?"

"Just looking around."

"You got a warrant?"

"No. Why? Is that a problem?"

"Yeah. As we say in Texas, time to vamoose, constable."

Ignoring that, Jack said, "I see you have a shotgun."

"I hunt birds, so what?"

"So Paul Matoff was killed with a shotgun."

Stud looked at him angrily.

Jack continued, "What's inside that locked cupboard in the stable?"

"Just some horse stuff."

"Not booze?"

"No."

"I'd like to have a look."

Stud suddenly reached down and pulled a little pistol from his boot while Jack's revolver was still stuck in his closed holster. Pointing the pistol at Jack, Stud snarled, "Now get the hell outta here."

Enraged, Jack drove off in his tin lizzie.

Arriving in Bean Fate, he stalked into Walt's store and asked him for a warrant to search Stud's cabin.

"Why?"

"I saw a shotgun there."

"So?"

"Matoff was killed with a shotgun."

"I know that but you have no reason to suspect Stud. He's probably a duck hunter."

"He pulled a gun on me, for God's sake."

"You were a trespasser in his home, for God's sake. Like you were at Borys's. Bad habit, Jack."

"He's not entitled to have a pistol."

"Do you know that? Maybe he has a permit. Maybe he has reason to fear assault. The law allows for that."

Furious, Jack ploughed on.

"I know Stud's bootlegging."

"How do you know that?"

"I talked to some miners." Jack didn't want to break Anderson's confidence, so he didn't mention him. "And he has a locked cupboard at his place where, dollars to doughnuts, he's got a stash of booze. Even worse, he's demanding protection money from citizens."

"Who from?" asked Walt sharply.

"From Borys Adamchuk for one," said Jack, again not mentioning Anderson.

"Oh, Borys, I wouldn't put much stock in what he says."

"That's funny you did before."

Walt gave him an angry look.

"Anyway, the big thing is," Jack continued, "everyone suspects the Chicago Mob is responsible for the murder. You know that."

"That's just wild rumor. Anyway, what's that got to do with Stud?"

"I think he works for them."

"What?"

"He was buddy-buddy with them at the ballgame. I even heard he drove them."

"Come on, Jack. You're just speculating, which is no basis for a warrant. What about Dillege and Lacoste? Here you're focusing on a guy with no known connection to a crime and they were right there. Why are you focusing on Stud?"

"Because he's a bad guy."

"Or because he stole your girl?"

Jack trembled in rage but took deep breaths to control himself. Then he said very quietly, "Walt, Dillege and Lacoste have ironclad alibis."

"Look, I'm not signing a warrant."

Frustrated and furious, Jack threw caution to the winds.

"Why are you protecting Stud? And by the way, where were you the night of the murder?"

Walt looked first astonished and then very angry.

"I was at home with Mrs. Davie that night, but you mind your goddamn mouth. I'm going to talk to Regina and I'm going to show you who's boss around here."

Chapter 24

Commissioner Mahoney summoned Jack to Regina.

In his office, Mahoney got right to the point.

"We want you to charge Lee Dillege and Jimmy Lacoste with Matoff's murder."

"Sir, I don't think that's right."

"It's not your decision."

"Sir, you're telling me to lay a murder charge against men who we know must be innocent?"

"Dillege is no sweetheart."

"He's got an ironclad alibi."

"He's all we've got. Throw in conspiracy and robbery with violence. As I said before, maybe he and Lacoste were decoys, you know, to suck in Matoff. All you know is that neither of them fired the gun. Maybe a third guy did and they were a part of it."

"Sir, there's no evidence of any connection between them and other guys. I even checked that out down south."

"Down south?"

"I met with the American cops in Minot. Even a prohi from Chicago. They had nothing. I mean, they know about Dillege around Burke County. But even in Minot, he's nothing. The prohi said they know nothing about him. So, it's safe to say there's no evidence he's connected to other Yanks who might be suspects."

"Good work, Jack," said Mahoney, sounding surprised. "But that doesn't mean he doesn't have connections. Did you check Butte? There's bad guys there too! He just seems a funny one. Furthermore, you don't even know he left the cash behind."

"There's absolutely no evidence of that," said Jack, although acknowledging to himself, *Mahoney has a point. Still, there's no evidence*

159

whatever. Neither the cash nor the stickpin has been found. Nothing on which to base a charge.

"And I have a better suspect."

"Who?" asked Mahoney is surprise.

"That cowboy, Bill Studwell."

"You mean because you saw him with a couple of guys from Chicago you didn't like the look of? Come on, Jack, you've got nothing but a suspicion with nothing to back it up."

"Maybe, but my suspicion has grown."

"Oh, and why is that?" asked Mahoney in an irritated voice.

"The guys he was with, Capone and Dutch Schultz, were involved in a murder in Chicago, sort of like the Matoff murder."

"Who told you that?"

"The prohi."

"Have they been charged?" Mahoney was suddenly on alert.

"I gather not."

"Ah… and why would that be? Maybe it's just suspicion, eh?"

"Yeah, maybe." Jack had to admit that.

"Look, Jack, we have to do something right now. Dillege and Lacoste are all we've got. So charge them like I said."

"Is that an order for me, sir?"

"Yes, it is."

"Does Colonel Cross know about this?"

"You don't need to know, but he'd like you to drop by his office."

Jack arrived at Cross's office in the legislative building. He was asked to wait. Then Leech walked out of the office, walked over to Jack, greeted him cordially and left, saying Cross was waiting for him.

Cross came out from around his desk and greeted Jack warmly, saying he'd heard Jack was meeting with the Commissioner and wanted to touch base with him.

Jack looked around. It was the biggest office he'd ever been in. Along one wall, the desk faced the room with a large window on the left of the person sitting behind the desk. Two armchairs faced it. Along another wall was a sofa with a coffee table in front of it and two armchairs facing across from it. The hardwood floor was largely covered by an oriental-looking carpet.

Cross suggested Jack sit down on the sofa and Cross sat down across from him.

"I heard you were going to meet with the Commissioner, so I thought we could catch up."

Jack was surprised and felt a little awkward but flattered too.

"I thought we'd have a sandwich," added Cross.

"That'd be very nice, sir."

The door opened and a woman entered carrying a rather large tray which she sat down on the table. There were some sandwiches and a pitcher containing a colored liquid.

"Help yourself," said Cross, motioning to the table. "To the lemonade too."

Jack was starving and happy to tuck in.

As he took a sandwich for himself, Cross said, "Just like old times, eh?"

As a private, Jack had not eaten overseas with Cross, who'd eaten in the officers' mess, so Cross was clearly referring to the time he'd dropped by to see Jack at the camp in England where Jack had recuperated before taking the return ship to Canada.

"Yes, sir."

"You look better than you did then!"

"I feel a lot better."

"Do you keep up with any of the other Tommies?"

"Occasionally, but so many didn't come back. And many of the ones who did, well, they don't get out that much, eh."

"Oh, I know," sighed Cross, thinking of the number of maimed and disfigured young men.

They sat, eating in silence for a moment.

"Garneau was a friend of yours, wasn't he?"

"Yes. He boarded with us, so we'd become close. Almost like another brother."

"You know, I think he could have had a career in the army too. Had a knack for it."

"That's really what got to me that day. What happened to him?" Jack had never told Cross about the other day, shooting the unarmed German in the face pointblank. He'd never told anyone about that, except Lenny.

"Terrible. But you've come out of it okay now?"

"Yes sir. And I really appreciate you getting me the job."

"Glad to do it. Cigarette?"

"Thank you, sir."

Cross lit Jack's cigarette as well as one for himself. They both drew deeply.

"By the way, I hear you have a nice girlfriend in Bean Fate," said Cross with a smile.

Jack was totally taken aback and it showed.

"Well, don't you? Kate Roberts?"

"Well..." stammered Jack.

"That's what I heard from her parents. Bob and Maggie Roberts. He and I are both stewards at the church. But she runs it. Wonderful people."

"I sure know Kate," said Jack, wondering what Cross would have heard about him.

"They were asking all about you, so I put in a good word." Cross winked.

"Oh thank you, sir."

"They're a wonderful family. Be a great connection for you."

Jack didn't know what to say to that.

"Anyway, how's it going down there, Jack?"

"Pretty well."

"You don't sound too enthusiastic."

"Oh sir, I really appreciate having the job. I really do. It's what I want to do. Make a career in the police force."

"But?"

"That murder in Bean Fate. It's on my watch. I'm trying to deal with it but I haven't found the killers and that's why I'm in town. The Commissioner called me here."

"I'd heard that," said Cross.

"He's ordered me to charge two men."

"Heard that too."

"Yes. But..." Jack hesitated.

"Is that a problem?"

"I believe they're innocent."

"Really!"

"Yes. So how can I charge them?"

"Jack, I don't know the details and I wouldn't want to get into them. That's for the Commissioner."

Funny, thought Jack, *Mahoney implied it was Cross's order.*

"But sir, I have to swear that I have reason to believe they've committed a crime. But I don't really."

"You're not trying the case, Jack. You're just laying out the facts you have which move it along to be looked at in greater depth. First a preliminary hearing before a magistrate. He'll do the deciding whether there are reasonable grounds. He might say there aren't and that'll be the end of it. Or, he might say there are and after that, there'll be a trial. That's where the real decision on guilty or not is made. Long way down the road. Lots of filters. What you're doing is just to get the ball rolling. You're advancing the cause of justice."

Jack was confused. *It doesn't sound quite right but the Colonel is so smart and so convincing.*

"Don't take yourself too seriously. You're not the judge."

Jack gave him a worried look.

"Now, if you really think you can't handle it, I guess the Commissioner would get someone else."

"You mean move me out?"

"Yes."

Cross looked at Jack very directly and knowingly as he said, "You understand, Jack?"

"Yes sir. I guess now that you've explained it."

"Good boy. It's called learning on the job. And Jack?"

"Yes sir."

"You be careful down there. Don't go running around insulting justices of the peace. Walt Davie is a good man, a friend of mine, and he should be a friend of yours too, and if he asks for help, give it to him."

Cross arose to indicate the interview was over and led Jack to the door, patting him on the back in a fatherly way as they said their goodbyes.

Jack sat on the train, listening to its clacketty clack sound and looking into the distance, thinking, *So I'm going to charge these guys who I really don't think are guilty or, at least, I don't really have convincing evidence that they are. But Colonel Cross says that's okay. Also, that my job's on the line. Somehow it doesn't feel right. I hope it is, but maybe Sparling has a point?*

The next morning, Jack attended at Walt's little office. Grim and unhappy, he signed the papers charging Dillege and Lacoste with murder or conspiracy to commit murder. Against his better judgment, he stated in those papers that he had reasonable grounds to believe they'd committed those crimes and signed an affidavit as to the supporting evidence, mainly what he had seen at the murder scene and Rawcliffe's testimony that Dillege was in the room beside Matoff when the murder happened.

"Not really much evidence of support," commented Jack.

"It'll do for now," said Walt as he signed the papers including for arrests.

Poor dumb Lacoste will be easy to arrest but Dillege is across the line, thought Jack. *Well, that's someone else's problem.*

"You finally saw the light," said Walt with a smug look on his face.

Chapter 25

The next morning, on Saturday, Jack had breakfast at the café. Thankfully, Jasper wasn't there because he wanted to be alone. He'd got to thinking overnight about Kate and what Cross had said about her. It sounded like she hadn't told her parents about her troubles with him, and maybe not her rape either. In fact, she probably wouldn't have told them about that. It was too humiliating. *And you know what?* he said to himself. *The fact is that she's far and away the best girl I've ever met. The best and the most beautiful. And I do love her. And she's having a tough time. It's not her fault she was raped, even though it was stupid to be with Stud in the first place. But she's young and naïve. And I think she knows about me too. She seems so understanding. Sparling was right. I should be supporting her, and we could be a great couple. Assuming she's not pregnant by Stud, that is.* That nasty possibility was still in the back of his mind. But surely, she'd deal with that if she had to. After all, her father's a doctor... but she wouldn't want to tell him. *Shit. Anyway, for now, I'm going to go to her and apologize and tell her how I feel.* There, he felt better already.

It was morning at the Andersons' house too. Kate was late for breakfast and Mrs. Anderson was waiting in some irritation. Finally, she heard an unusual sound from above like a chair scraping. After a few more minutes, she trudged upstairs and knocked on Kate's door. There was no answer. She opened the door, which felt heavy.

She saw first the knocked-over chair and then, behind the door, Kate's lifeless body hanging from the high clothes-hook.

Mrs. Anderson ran downstairs and called to Anderson who was out in the yard and called him over and told him the news. "We'll have to call Jack right away," she said.

"You won't have to call him," said Anderson grimly. "I see him coming down the road right now."

165

Anderson walked out on the porch to meet Jack, with Mrs. Anderson behind him. Jack immediately noticed the gravity etched on their faces.

"Is there a problem?"

"Yes," said Anderson. "It's Kate."

"Kate?"

"Jack, she's taken her own life."

Jack could not believe it. The timing was so cruel! He was just coming over to make it up with her. It was so cruel for both of them. He wept in front of the Andersons, which a man, let alone a cop, was not supposed to do.

But he had to deal with this professionally. It was the second time he'd had to contact the coroner and ask him to come over from Estevan. While waiting, he did a routine interview with Mrs. Anderson.

But when that was over, he just stood in shock himself, looking at the corpse.

Anderson came up and stood beside him.

"If only," Jack said quietly but couldn't continue.

"If only what?" asked Anderson gently, his hand resting on Jack's shoulder.

"If only I'd taken her to the wedding like she asked me to."

A week later, the dedicated phone line rang at the provincial police office in Estevan. This happened rarely and usually meant a call from Regina, so Jack picked up the receiver with some trepidation.

"Hello, Jack." It was Cross's voice.

"Sir! Hello."

"Jack, I've just come from the saddest funeral, for Kate Roberts."

"Oh," said Jack, choking up.

"I'm so sorry for you, Jack. She sounded like a wonderful girl. The church was packed. A lot of young people."

What could Jack say?

"Funerals of young people are so sad," continued Cross, "particularly because they assume they'll all live forever. Well, not you boys. You know all about that. But ordinary kids."

"She was a wonderful girl, sir."

"What happened anyway? I hear via the grapevine that she took her own life."

"Yes she did."

"That's terrible. Terrible for her parents. Terrible for you. Why would she do that?"

"I really don't know, sir. I guess the stress of a school and living in a small town was too much for her." Jack wasn't about to tell Cross about the rape which would only besmirch her memory.

"Anything else?" Cross had heard a rumor about a rape.

"Not really."

"Were you surprised?"

"I was. Totally."

"Well, you take care down there, Jack."

"Thank you, sir. I will."

Poor Jack, thought Cross. *He doesn't need more stress. Strange that she'd commit suicide from what he said. Maybe there was more to it. Who knows?*

+ + +

Monday, November 6 was Armistice Day and Thanksgiving Day too. Like all vets, Jack thought it was ridiculous that the happiness associated with Thanksgiving should be mixed with the sadness associated with remembering the Great War. But that's what those wizards in Ottawa had decreed – get together with the vets to remember their fallen and disabled comrades in the morning and celebrate with his family over turkey dinner in the afternoon. Ordinarily, this would have given him some conflict during the day. But this year was different, easier in a way, because there was nothing to celebrate.

He hadn't gone back to Regina to be with his family. He couldn't have if he'd wanted because it was not a leave day for him. He hadn't wanted to anyway. Nor had the Andersons invited him to join them. Maybe they weren't celebrating either this year. A death in the house can do that.

So, that night, he sat morosely in the usual café, rather hoping that Jasper would show up. When all was said and done, it'd be nice to have some company. Then Jasper did appear in the doorway and walked purposefully over to Jack's table but didn't sit down.

"Aren't you going to sit down?"

"I don't think I can, for a while actually."

"Why?" Jack asked in surprise.

"I've been retained by Lee Dillege. So it might not look right, for either of us."

"Really? How did that happen?"

"An attorney in Minot called me. Dillege heard about the arrest warrant."

"So he's going to appear in court?"

"Can't tell you, old boy," and Jasper winked. "We'll talk when this is all over. But I'll miss your sparkling company in the meantime." And Jasper took a seat at another booth.

Well, thought Jack, *Dillege has the world expert on extradition. And I think he'll be showing up in Weyburn after all.*

Chapter 26

Jasper had accepted the court's jurisdiction on behalf of his client and indicated that Dillege would appear to contest the charges.

One day, a typically weary-looking and overworked prosecuting Crown Attorney, who everyone simply referred to as 'the Crown,' had come down from Regina to Jack's office in Estevan. Besides Jack and the coroner, he'd interviewed several witnesses who'd come over from Bienfait, Colin Rawcliffe, the station agent and a couple of the guys who'd been at Whites who'd seen Lacoste there at the time they'd heard the gunshot. Afterwards, when the Crown had shaken his head at the evidence, Jack had said,

"There's no case against these guys, is there? You'll never get a conviction?"

"You signed the affidavit alleging reasonable grounds!"

"I know," had said Jack guiltily, "but I was ordered to."

"I'm not really surprised. I was ordered to take it too. This case is not about getting a conviction. It's about getting the legal process to start and then go on as long as possible. That'll keep the public at bay until the next crisis comes along and they forget about this one."

"Is Colonel Cross behind this?" Jack had asked.

"What do you think?"

On November 21, Jack took the Soo Line to Weyburn. He was met by a constable from the Weyburn detachment of the provincial police and driven over to the city hall, a handsome two-story red brick building with detailing in the ubiquitous Tyndall limestone. The courtroom was on the second floor.

The case had attracted enormous attention and the small courtroom was full. Jack looked around. The room had a spare elegance with a lot of wood, all oak, including wainscoting on the walls. At the front of the room was 'the bench,' a desk on a platform behind which was a high-backed chair. Down in front of the bench were two small tables at ninety-degree angles to it at which clerks were shuffling papers. Facing all this were two long counsel tables side-by-side with armchairs behind each facing the bench. Behind them was a wooden railing separating all this from several rows of bow-back side chairs facing the bench too, and these were all filled with spectators. The floor was carpeted in dark green.

Jack saw the Crown at one of the tables and went over to talk to him.

"You've got a full house," he said.

"Yeah, including the press."

"Oh yeah?"

"Those guys over there were on the train coming down from Regina. One's from the Leader, one's from the Star, and one's from the Tribune, all the way from Winnipeg."

"I thought the press was excluded from preliminary hearings?"

"Only if a party requests. The defense didn't and neither did we. Same with spectators. In fact, I think the government wants as much publicity as possible on this one."

"There's our JP," said Jack, nodding in the direction of Walt who'd caught his eye.

Jack saw Jasper walk in accompanied by Lee Dillege. They walked up to the other counsel table and sat down.

"Just so you know," said the Crown, turning to Jack, "we're dropping the case against Lacoste."

"Really!"

"Shh. You'll see," said the Crown, turning to look at Lacoste as he walked up to the other table accompanied by another man, presumably a lawyer.

Jasper looked over at Jack and winked.

Then the clerk called 'order all rise' and the police magistrate, a man in his mid-fifties, entered by a door behind the bench, stepped up, and took his chair. Unlike the lawyers, all male, who were dressed in business suits, he wore a black robe with a white dickie at his throat.

After the formalities associated with declaring the court in session and reading out the indictments against Dillege and Lacoste, the proceedings started in earnest.

The Crown opened by saying, "Your Honor, by the agreement of all parties, we are asking that the accused Dillege be allowed to sit at the counsel table, as he has voluntarily accepted the jurisdiction of the court which has saved the attorney-general the time and expense of extraditing him from the United States."

The magistrate nodded his approval. It wasn't an overly formal proceeding.

The Crown added that, "In all the circumstances, we agree that the same courtesy should be extended to the accused Lacoste."

Again, the magistrate nodded his approval.

"In fact, Your Honor, we are withdrawing all charges against the accused James Lacoste."

"I see," said the magistrate.

"Since we believe there is no realistic prospect of a conviction against Mister Lacoste."

There were murmurs in the courtroom and the magistrate called for silence.

"Very well," said the magistrate, "the accused James Lacoste may be released."

Lacoste got up and left the courtroom accompanied by his lawyer.

Jack looked over at Walt, who looked concerned.

The Crown then proceeded to the case against Dillege, calling only two witnesses. Rawcliffe testified as to the facts of the night of October 4 at the CPR station, the scene in the railway station office with cash changing hands, the shotgun blast, and Matoff falling apparently dead. The coroner testified as to the condition of the deceased victim of the crime consistent with a shotgun blast.

Jasper cross-examined Rawcliffe.

"You were in the station office the night of the murder when Matoff, the accused Dillege, and the agent came in?"

"Yes."

"To do the settling up of the transaction between Matoff and Dillege?"

"Yes."

"But before the gunshot, the agent had left and gone upstairs, right?"

"Yes."

"So there were three of you in the room, Matoff, the accused Dillege, and you, right?"

"Yes."

"And the victim was standing beside you, is that right?"

"Yes."

"Right beside you?"

"Well, I was standing at the desk and he was standing there too at my right."

"Facing the same way?"

"No, he was facing ahead, I mean at the window."

"So there was no one between him and the window?"

"No, the agent had been standing there before he left."

"So you were at the side?"

"Yes, I was at the side of the desk and he was at my right."

"But just a couple of feet away?"

"Yes."

"And the accused Dillege was across the desk from you, facing you?"

"Yes."

"So he was on Matoff's right?"

"Uh, yes."

"And he would also have been a couple of feet from Matoff?"

"Yes."

"And the desk was about ten feet from the window. That's what you said, right?"

"Yes."

"And the accused Dillege was just standing there, right?"

"Well, he'd just finished putting all that cash on the table and Matoff had just finished counting it."

"And then Matoff turned to you?"

"Yes, to pay the express charges."

"Right. And that's when he was shot?"

"Yes."

"And the shot came from outside the room, right?"

"Well, through the window from outside."

"Right. Did you hear anything else?"

"Just the sound of the glass being shattered. The whole thing was like an explosion."

"And the victim was hit while he was standing beside you, a couple of feet away. Is that right?"

"Yes."

"With the accused Dillege on the other side of him, right?"

"Yes."

"No further questions, Your Honor. And I will be calling no witnesses."

The Crown then argued that there had been a murder, facilitated by Dillege showing up with thousands of dollars in cash, that somehow the person who pulled the trigger had known Dillege was going to be doing that, which suggested Dillege was in on it somehow either as an accomplice or conspirator. There was a prima facie case against him and all the facts needed to be brought out at a full trial.

"Mister Leask," said the magistrate, looking in Leask's direction.

Leask arose.

"Your Honor, with great respect to my learned friend, the Crown has provided no evidence whatsoever to implicate my client in this sad case. A man is dead. Obviously, there was a murder. The victim was apparently killed by a shot from a gun thrust the through the window of that railway station. I don't dispute that. But by the Crown's own evidence, that gun was thrust through the window from outside the station while my client was standing inside right beside the victim himself. Indeed, my client appears to have been fortunate in not being shot himself! Accordingly, I urge Your Honor to find that there is no basis for sending this matter to trial."

That has to be right, thought Jack.

The Crown stood up and responded.

"You Honor, maybe it wasn't luck that prevented the accused from being hit. Maybe it was planned that way. We don't know yet. In any event, this is a sad case, as my learned friend says. There are unanswered questions that need answering. A man has been murdered. It represents an escalation in a pattern of violence down here. The accused is in the dastardly business which has led to all this violence."

"Objection, Your Honor", said Leask, jumping up with an agility which surprised Jack, "my friend has led no evidence on that broader topic."

"We all know what's going on down here," said the magistrate rather dismissively.

"You can take judicial notice of it," said the Crown helpfully.

"Exactly," said the magistrate. "Thank you."

"Maybe," said Leask, "Your Honor could also take judicial notice of the fact that shotgun blasts are notoriously imprecise."

"Please, Mister Leask," said the magistrate impatiently.

Jasper sat down. It was obvious where this was going.

The Crown continued, "As I said, the accused is in this business and just happens to be with the victim when the murder occurs. Just happens to be! I don't say he pulled the trigger himself, but the facts and the circumstantial evidence, which is not challenged, suggests he was involved somehow. He was there and he came out okay while Paul Matoff died. We don't know exactly how yet, but the public and, indeed, the administration of justice, needs a full trial where all the facts can come out."

As soon as the Crown sat down, the magistrate said, "I agree with the Crown's submission. The accused shall be committed to trial at a date to be determined."

Leask stood up.

"Your Honor, the accused elects trial by jury."

After court was adjourned, Jack went up to the counsel table to speak to the Crown.

"Congratulations, I guess, but aren't you a little surprised?"

"No. Like I told you from Day One, we'll get a trial. But we won't get a conviction. I just hope I'm not asked to waste my time on it."

"Regina will be very happy." Jack recognized Walt's voice and turned around to see Walt looking at him, smiling.

Chapter 27

The next day, Jack was morosely nursing a cup of coffee in his Estevan office. He'd pretty well failed at everything, his personal life and his job too. That's what he felt that morning. Maybe he should move on, he was thinking.

In walked the Soo Line Station agent.

"What's up?" asked Jack, politely if incuriously.

"Those hoods from Chicago we talked about? I asked our man in Portal. He says he thinks one of them was there a few weeks ago."

"Oh? When exactly?" Suddenly, Jack was curious.

"I didn't get any details. If you're interested, maybe you should go down and talk to him."

Jack left right away, driving down to the Soo Line Station just across the line in Portal.

The agent there confirmed that several weeks ago, he'd noticed a hood, who stood out, arrive one day on the train from Chicago and take the train back the next day. But he couldn't remember exactly when. But one other thing, he added, "Just before the train left for Chicago, a kid that works at the hotel came running over looking for the guy and gave him something."

"Like what?"

"I couldn't really see from inside and anyway I was busy."

"Okay, and thanks for the help."

As he walked out of the station office, Jack saw Tom parked in his car beside Jack's car and walked over.

"What are you doing down here?" asked Tom.

Jack explained that he'd been talking to the station agent about the Matoff murder.

"Can I be of help?" Tom said it with an edge and Jack was a little surprised at the hint of sensitivity over turf. *Weren't they buddies now? Of course, he was wearing his uniform complete with handgun in Tom's county!*

"Sorry. I meant to call you but I just thought I'd do a quick check-in on the agent and wouldn't waste your time. However, it's more interesting than I thought," and he explained what he'd found out. "I'm going over to the hotel. Why don't you come along... to my side of the line?"

They walked along Railway Street to the Grandview Hotel, a substantial three-story brick building barely on the Saskatchewan side. They entered the lobby and went over to the office of the manager. He looked up in some surprise to see two uniformed cops in his doorway.

"Hello, constable. And hello, sheriff."

They both answered amiably.

"Thanks for helping break up that fight the other night," said the manager, looking at Tom.

"No problem," answered Tom, avoiding eye contact with Jack.

So, he's taken action on my side! thought Jack. *But, so what? It's a fine line down here.* He ignored the comment and said, "The Soo Line agent told me about an incident a couple of weeks ago where you sent a kid over to the station to give something to a customer who'd just checked out. Remember that?"

"I do. A dangerous-looking guy too. He'd left a diamond tiepin in the room and was really glad to get it back. Gave the kid a fiver. He was just about to get on the train for Chicago."

"Do you remember anything more about him?"

"He was dressed like a guy from Chicago, you know? Except he kind of wore a satchel, you know, like with a strap... wore it like a school kid almost... as though he didn't want to lose it."

"Do you know his name?"

"Had a strange name... Let me check."

They went to the front desk and the manager looked through the registration book.

"Here it is. Flegenheimer, A. Flegenheimer."

"What's the date?"

"Checked in October fourth."

"The day of the murder," said Jack, exchanging looks with Tom.

"Checked out next day," added the manager.

"Do remember what he looked like? Big scar on his face?"

"I don't remember a scar. Little guy. Dark. Kind of cold and creepy actually."

"Maybe Flegenheimer is Dutch Schultz," said Tom.

"Sounds like him," said Jack.

Turning back to the manager, Jack asked "Was he here just that one night?"

"Just that one night," said the manager. "Thing was, now that I think back, the night clerk said he was out most of the night. The maid said he didn't even use the bed. But then he asked for a late checkout, saying he was waiting for the train to Chicago."

As they started to walk away, Jack turned back and asked the manager if he knew how Flegenheimer had travelled between the station and the hotel. Was he picked up in a car?

"When he left, he walked over to the station, I'm sure. But when he arrived, I think he was driven here in a Studie that had picked him up at the station."

"Driven by a cowboy?"

"Dressed like one."

"Maybe Stud, and maybe he drove Dutch up to Bean Fate too," said Tom, looking at Jack.

"Stud's not driving the Studie anymore."

"Since when?"

"Since the morning after the murder."

"Hmm. I wonder if he could have somehow switched cars," said Tom. Turning to the manager, he said, "Carl Schmidt's got the only Packard around here?"

"Who's he?" asked Jack.

"Elevator operator," said Tom.

"He's already gone to the coast for the winter," said the manager. "Took the Great Northern a few weeks ago."

"Let's check out his garage," said Tom, who got the directions from the manager.

They walked back to Tom's car and drove over to a little house at the edge of town behind some trees, a bit out of sight.

"It snowed not long ago… after he must have left," said Tom.

"But tire tracks!" said Jack.

They walked up the driveway. Looking closely, they could see that the lock on the garage door has been broken. Jack opened the garage door and peered in. There was no Packard. But there was a Studie with a couple of bullet holes in the rear end.

"Look at those bullet holes. I knew I'd hit the getaway car that night!"

"I think we're on to something here."

"I knew that son of a bitch was involved. But now I'll have to talk to my boss. He said to let him know if I needed help."

Jack drove back north to Whites.

Gordon White was in his office and said in a helpful tone, "Constable, what can I do for you today?"

"I'd like you to check something. Was either a Dutch Schultz or a guy named Flegenheimer registered here on Labor Day? Here with another guy named Capone."

White seemed to Jack to take a long time to check his book but he finally said, "There was no Dutch Schultz, but yes, an Arthur Flegenheimer. And Alphonse Capone."

Bingo! "Do you remember anything about them?"

"Tough-looking guys. Like big city hoods, which I think they were. I think they came from Chicago."

"Anything else?"

"They arrived with Stud. I think he drove them over from Estevan. Drove them back too next day. They met in their room with Paul now that I think of it. Never connected it before. And Harry Bronfman, he was here for that."

So this is where they met. Damn! I should have thought to ask before, thought Jack.

"And another guy," said White, musing aloud. "Come to think of it."

"Another guy?"

"Bronfman brought another guy with him."

"Do you know who?"

"No. An older guy. Looked like a bigwig of some sort."

Jack was getting even more out of this interview than he'd hoped for. *Might as well keep jogging White's memory.*

"Anything else?"

"I hadn't connected them to your investigation. I don't know if it's relevant but they all met here again a few weeks later."

"It's definitely connected. Tell me about it."

"Let me see. Here it is, September 29. Capone and Flegenheimer again. I remember they were here to meet with Paul and Harry and that older guy I mentioned."

"Do you remember anything at all about the meeting?"

"Not really, they met upstairs again. But I got the impression Bronfman and Paul weren't too happy when they left. Not like the first time."

Chapter 28

It was time to go to Regina. Jack arranged a meeting with Mahoney at police headquarters right away and decided not to wait for the next train but to take the lizzie.

But first, he drove to the Craftsman Building. On entering, he saw there was an office to one side and he could see Harry was in it. That was a piece of luck. He asked the young guy on the desk if he could meet with Harry and was soon ushered into his office.

"Well, hello, constable, what are you here for?" said Harry.

Jack hadn't seen Harry for several weeks and noted his changed state. He looked pale, thinner, and almost despondent. He looked like he hadn't slept for weeks, which, in fact, he hadn't much.

"I wanted to follow up on our discussion the morning after Paul's murder."

"I don't know what I can add. And I gave that interview to the paper which you probably read."

"Yes, I did."

"It was unfair the way it came out, suggesting that the murder was connected to our customers when it wasn't and I'd denied that."

"I just had one particular thing."

"What's that?"

"You told me about that meeting you and Paul had with Capone and Dutch Schultz."

"Yeah. But it had nothing to do with Paul's murder."

"That's what you said. And you said that was the one meeting with them."

"Yeah."

"At Whites."

"Yeah."

"But you didn't tell me you had a second meeting there."

"Second meeting?"

180

"On September 29."

Mr. Big Harry Bronfman looks like a deer in the headlights, thought Jack.

"Oh, maybe there was. I forget."

"Do you deny it?"

What the hell does this young cop know? thought Harry.

"No," said Harry slowly. "I don't deny it. In fact, come to think of it, there may have been a second meeting."

"Why would there be?"

"To discuss ongoing delivery issues, that sort of thing."

"Were there problems?"

"Nothing out of the ordinary."

"Why would two guys come?"

"You'd have to ask them."

"Who was the third man?"

"The third man?"

"The other man you brought with you to that meeting."

Who the hell has this damn cop been talking to? thought Harry. *Cross will be furious if that gets out.*

"I don't remember any third man that I would have brought."

"Mister Bronfman, this is serious, sir. Tell me the truth."

I'm not under oath, thought Harry as he said, "I don't remember any other man that I brought to the meeting."

So, Mr. Big is a liar, thought Jack as he said, "Let me know if your recollection changes."

As he left, Harry stood watching and thinking, *I better get over to Cross's office right away.*

But he wouldn't find Cross in his office.

Jack went straight to Mahoney's office.

On arrival, he was surprised but encouraged to see Cross there too and they greeted each other warmly, although formally, in the presence of Jack's superior.

Mahoney started off, "You said you had something important to discuss about the Matoff murder. Since it's now before the courts, I asked the attorney-general to be here too. So what is it, constable?"

Barely containing his excitement, Jack said, "I've got some new evidence."

"New evidence?"

"I've got leads indicating that the probable killers are two Yanks, that cowboy I told you about and a hood from Chicago called Dutch Schultz."

Cross and Mahoney exchanged surprised looks. "So?" asked Mahoney, turning back to Jack.

"So, now I need that extra help you offered me. To complete the evidence and track down Dutch Schultz. And we'll have to extradite him."

Cross sat stony-faced, thinking, *What the hell is Jack up to?*

Mahoney looked embarrassed in front of his boss and, looking at Jack, said, "A magistrate has just sent Dillege to trial for that murder!"

"He already dropped the charge against Lacoste. Dillege won't be convicted. No way. There's no evidence against him."

"Oh, constable, you know something the magistrate didn't know?" asked Mahoney sarcastically.

"I know this case better than anyone... ask the Crown attorney... and I know Dillege is not the killer. I'm onto the real killers."

"Okay," said Mahoney reluctantly. He had to be seen to give Jack a chance to make his point. "Be quick about it. What've you got?"

This was Jack's chance. He'd prepared for this, and he took his notes out of his chest pocket and started to read from them,

"One, the victim, Paul Matoff, had dealings with Dutch Schultz and Al Capone.

"Two, Schultz and Capone are hit men for Johnny Torrio, head of the Mob in Chicago, and they murdered a guy down there because he gave the Mob bad booze."

"How do you know that?" asked Cross.

"Oh, I told the Commissioner before. I heard that from a prohi... prohibition agent... in Minot."

"Okay," said Cross, surprised and slightly worried. He cast a glance at Mahoney who nodded.

"Go on," said Cross.

"Three, Dutch Schultz was in Portal the night of the murder, for one night, and returned to Chicago the next day.

"Four, Bill Studwell, a Texan cowboy called Stud, who lives near Bean Fate, drives a Studebaker and has driven Capone and Schultz in the past.

"Five, I shot at a car driving away from Bean Fate at a high rate of speed right after the murder and I know I hit it.

"Six, a dark green Packard was stolen from a garage in Portal. The owner is the local elevator owner who's been on the coast for weeks. Stud's Studebaker with bullet holes in the rear is now in that garage. And he's now driving a dark green Packard.

"So, I suspect that Stud was with Dutch that night, that he drove him up to Bean Fate and they murdered Matoff. On the way back, I shot at them. When they got back to Portal, Stud dropped him off and switched the Studebaker for the Packard. He drove back north and Schultz took the train back to Chicago."

Cross tried hard to hide his amazement at this, not only at what Jack had put together but the way he'd organized his thoughts. *Had he gone to law school in the last few weeks or what?*

"That's all very interesting," said Mahoney. "A good effort at trying to connect some dots. But what's the motive? You have to have a motive."

"I think I have one."

"Not that vendetta idea?" said Mahoney.

"What's that?" asked Cross.

"There was something odd about Matoff's corpse," said Jack. "His diamond tiepin was missing but his diamond ring wasn't. I thought at the time, that's funny. Why wouldn't a robber take both?"

Cross was listening intently.

"Maybe he couldn't get the ring off the finger," said Mahoney.

"Maybe. But that was one thing."

"Was there another?"

"Yeah. Like I said before when you came to see me, there was blood coming out of one of Matoff's eyes. Just a bit."

"Wasn't there a lot of blood around?"

"He hadn't been shot near his face. And what it looked like was like somebody had stuck something in that eye. Like maybe the tiepin. It was odd. It just didn't look like an ordinary robbery to me."

"Even so," said Mahoney, "it doesn't connect it to Dutch or this fellow Stud, does it?"

"In fact, it led me to the whole thing. I found out that Dutch made a big point of taking a diamond tiepin back to Chicago from Portal!"

"How the hell do you know that?" asked Cross.

"I talked to the guy at the Grandview Hotel. Dutch had left it at the hotel and they found it and a kid ran over to the train station and gave it to him and Dutch was so happy he gave him a fiver!"

"That's interesting," Cross admitted, "but why would Dutch want to harm Paul Matoff?"

"There's reason to believe that there'd been trouble between the Bronfmans and the Mob."

Oh oh, thought Cross as he said sharply, "Trouble between them? Why do you say that?"

"Because there were two meetings between the Bronfmans and Dutch and Capone. The first one was to set up the deal. The second one may have been to deal with problems between them."

"How do you know about these meetings?"

"I found out from the owner of Whites where both meetings were held."

"Whites?"

"The hotel in Bean Fate."

"You sure visit a lot of hotels," said Cross wryly.

"And the thing is that second meeting happened just five days before the murder. So I figure they might have been related. Like maybe the meeting went badly."

"Well, that's another stretch," said Cross. "We'd have to find out from Harry Bronfman what the meeting was about."

"Oh, he says it was just to discuss delivery problems."

"Sounds reasonable. When did you last talk to him?"

"Half an hour ago."

He's really on this, thought Cross.

"And the thing is," continued Jack, "I'm suspicious of what he says."

"You, Jack Ross, are suspicious of what Harry Bronfman says?"

Cross spoke slowly, an attempted putdown. But Jack was on a roll.

"He never told me about it... the second meeting... the first time I interviewed him right after the murder. In fact, he said there'd only been the one meeting. The first one."

"Maybe he forgot. People do, you know. Lying is a big allegation to make against a leading citizen. You'd have to give him the benefit of the doubt."

"I don't think we can, sir."

"And why would that be, Jack?"

"There's a pattern. He lied about something else."

"About what?"

"He denied there was a third man at those meetings. But I know there was."

Shit! Even Mahoney doesn't know about that, thought Cross. "Who was it?" he asked in some trepidation.

"I don't know. Gordon White, he's the hotel owner, didn't know but he said an older man was there, both times. Said he looked like a bigwig. Those were his words."

That stupid Dick Leech, thought Cross.

"Put it all together and here's what I think," said Jack. "There's reason to believe that there were problems between the Bronfmans and the Mob, maybe bad booze like the thing in Chicago, and Torrio sent Dutch to murder Matoff just like he did with the guy in Chicago. And Stud drove him."

Mahoney looked over at Cross, obviously not sure how to handle it.

Damn, thought Cross. *If this gets out, it's dynamite.*

Jack waited, looking expectantly at the two of them. He was proud of his work.

Then Cross said, "Jack, that's really neither here nor there, whether there was another man. And it's all high conjecture at the same time as a magistrate has decided there's enough evidence against Dillege to send him to trial. He's either guilty or he's not. We'll find out in due time. We shouldn't complicate matters by going off on some wild goose chase now."

Jack just looked at Cross. *What the fuck's happening?*

"And meanwhile," said Cross, "the whole issue of exports is old news now anyway because we're banning them."

"I heard that," said Jack, allowing himself to be momentarily diverted. "When exactly?"

"December 15."

"Sir, every day that goes by, we run the risk of more violence down there!"

Cross was annoyed. *Jack's getting above himself.* But he restrained his annoyance and simply said, "To be fair, we have to give the Bronfmans time. They have stock to get rid of."

"But we still need to pursue the leads I have now, don't we?"

"I don't think so at this point. See what happens. Leave it to me."

"But I think it's kind of urgent."

Cross looked at Mahoney and said, "Commissioner, please let me speak to the constable alone."

Mahoney left.

Cross said, "Look, Jack, I've got a lot of responsibility here. This whole thing is complicated. The public has calmed down, first with the prospect of a trial and then with the announcement we're shutting down the exports. No need to get them all excited again by going down another rabbit hole."

"But sir—"

"If Dillege is found guilty, that'll be the end of it. If not, we can have a look at these leads of yours about Dutch Schultz."

"That'll be in months if not years."

"Don't be difficult, Jack. I'm already hearing people say you're a secret Conservative."

That's Walt, thought Jack. *He's tight with Cross, alright.*

"I know you're not, but you're starting to look ornery and it's frankly embarrassing for me. I can't protect you forever. I'd appreciate it if you'd just back off for now and leave this Matoff thing alone."

"I don't see how I can do that, sir."

Cross, looking grim, said, "I thought I could count on you, Jack."

"You can but—" Jack was having difficulty.

"I've done a lot for you, Jack."

"Yes, sir, and I appreciate it. Very much. It's just that I know Dillege isn't guilty and I know who is. I don't see how we can just leave it." He looked at Cross questioningly. *Surely, Cross can see thi*s.

Cross looked at him coldly.

"Leave it with me," he said and showed Jack out the door.

Jack left, wondering what was going to happen, still hoping that Cross would see the light and that he was not as angry with him as he'd looked.

Cross wasn't as angry as he'd looked. He was angrier. He was bloody furious. Private Ross had just turned down his commanding officer! And there was no court martial available! *Goddamn Jack*, he thought. *After all I've done for him. Rescued him from that mess in France. Got him into Regina College and reinstated too after he'd screwed up. And then got him this job. And the one thing I ask him to do for me, the one thing, he turns me down. Here I am trying to keep the lid on an explosive situation… for the benefit of the public…*

and he won't help. What a foolish, ungrateful guy! thought the seething Cross as he paced back and forth in his office. He opened the door and, in an uncharacteristically abrupt manner she thought, asked his secretary to bring him a Coke. She brought it in and he sat down, took a drink, and leaned back in the chair behind his desk.

But slowly as he cooled down, he started to think, *You know, in a way, Jack's more to be pitied than scorned. He's basically a good guy. Just a bit of a blockhead. You can see he's got this bit between his teeth about the Matoff case, trying to do his job, and can't see the forest for the trees. A good guy and smarter and ornerier than I'd realized. But no judgment and too emotional. Maybe the shellshock after all. I shouldn't have sent him down there. Should have known it'd be too much for him. Not that I knew there'd be a goddamn murder, but it was the inherent dangers in the situation down there, with all that booze flowing through, that made me want to have my own man down there in the first place. But I sent the wrong man.*

It was a long drive back to Estevan and as the sun sank into the flat western horizon, the sky turned red, purple, and then black. The lizzie's headlamps shone weak beams of light on the gravel road. Then Jack noticed a distant glow in the dark which was soon revealed to be from bright flames in the distance. As he got closer, he saw that they were from Adamchuk's farm. He turned into the road leading down to the yard and, as he drove up, he saw Adamchuk standing there with his weeping wife and two small children. The barn's thatched roof was gone and the rest was going.

He jumped out of the lizzie and ran over to them.

"My God, Borys!"

Adamchuk turned to him forlornly. "I've lost everything. No barn, no animals."

"What happened? How did it start?"

"We were in the house and suddenly we saw flames. I ran out. It was dark but I'm sure I saw Stud." With a look of utter despair, Adamchuk said, looking at Jack, "That's why I didn't want to talk about him. You must have told."

The only person I told was Walt, thought Jack. *Jesus Murphy.*

What could he say? He looked at Adamchuk remorsefully. When pressed by Walt, he'd chosen to protect his buddy's confidence but not the bohunk's.

Chapter 29

Jack sat at his desk cleaning his gun and smoking. He was on edge, waiting to hear from Regina. The phone rang. It was Mahoney.

"We've considered your request, Jack. There'll be no further investigation."

"I see."

"One other thing."

"Yes?"

"You're being reassigned to Regina for further training."

"Further training!"

Jack let it hang there for a moment and then said, "When?"

"By the first train."

Jack slept fitfully that night. Images flitted across his mind – Lenny's bloodied head, the hole in the German's head, the hole in Matoff's chest, Kate's hanging body, and fire raging in the night. So did the image of Cross's speech on the parade square. He awoke sweating.

He got the reefer case out of the chest of drawers, lit up, and stood looking at himself in the mirror over the chest of drawers as the smoke swirled around his face. He was supposed to pack up and leave in the morning for Regina, his tail between his legs and knowing, he was pretty sure, that Stud was getting away with rape and murder. And knowing that his hero seemed involved in a cover-up. *I never would have thought that about Colonel Cross,* he thought. *He always seemed like such a fine man. And he has been good to me, God knows. But still, here I am, the one person, it seems, who knows who murdered Paul Matoff and that the killers are at large, one of them right here in Saskatchewan. But I'm just a lone cop. What can I do all alone? Yet, I've already put my life on the line for a country and values that I was always taught and I believe in. Was it all for naught? Is there really no justice? You know what?* he said to himself, *Maybe in my own small way, I could achieve some justice. Rough justice. Or maybe just revenge. Depends on how you look at it. What the hell?*

Chapter 30

It was first light and cold – very cold. Winter comes early on the prairies. Jack wore a police-issue short buffalo-skin coat and fur cap. He wound the crank to start the lizzie. There was no response. He tried again – still no response. After several more attempts, he went out back to the stable. Simmons had said there'd be a time and place that he'd need Dolly. This was it, and he saddled her up.

He rode for an hour or so in the pale light of a wintry dawn, steam coming in the cold from Dolly's nostrils and his too. She picked her way down the coulee bank and along the edge of trees, their branches encrusted with frost. He dismounted about fifty yards from the cabin and snuck up on foot. The garage door was open and he saw the Packard. Stud was chopping wood, which muffled Jack's approach. This time, Jack had his gun out of his holster.

He emerged from the bush and shouted.

"Stud! Drop the ax!"

Startled, Stud looked up, dropped it, and reached for his right boot.

Jack fired a shot and snow jumped at Stud's feet.

"Hands up!" shouted Jack.

Stud raised his arms. Jack walked over through the thin snow cover and cuffed Stud's hands in front of him. With his revolver in Stud's back, Jack reached down into Stud's boot, found the pistol, took it out, and flung it into the bush. He pushed Stud into the cabin.

"What the fuck is going on?" asked Stud.

"I just want to clear up a few things. First of all, I'd like to have a look in that cupboard you've got in the stable. Where's the key?"

"None of your business, unless you have a warrant."

"You don't seem to understand. I want the key."

"It's not handy."

"Don't you fuck with me." Jack slapped Stud across the face. "Where's the goddamn key?"

"Blue mug on the top shelf."

Jack got the key and, pushing Stud ahead of him, went to the stable and unlocked the cupboard. It was piled high with cases of Black Horse. A shotgun was standing in the corner.

"I thought so," said Jack and directed Stud back into the cabin. "Now let's have a little talk. For starters, what do you know about Adamchuk's barn?"

"I heard it burned down."

"That part I know. What happened?"

"Dumb bohunk probably blew up his own still."

"You burned it down because he talked to me."

"Don't you accuse me."

Jack slapped Stud across the face again.

"Big tough guy when I'm cuffed."

Jack slapped him again, this time drawing blood from Stud's nose.

"Okay," he said slowly, "I have a deal with Adamchuk."

"What kind of deal?"

"He pays me to protect him."

"From what?"

"Rustlers. Robbers."

"Arsonists?"

Stud just looked at Jack.

"Did he ask you or did you threaten him... to protect him?"

"My idea. I encouraged him. He agreed. It was mutual."

"I'll bet. Poor bastard. What he needs is someone to protect him from you."

Stud just looked at him sullenly.

"Do you protect anybody else around here?"

"Your buddy. Anderson."

"Uh huh. Now we're getting somewhere. That booze in your cupboard. Anderson told me you sold him Black Horse."

"He said that?" snarled Stud.

"The boys in that brawl at Whites told me the same thing. You were bootlegging for the Bronfmans."

"I helped Paul out a bit."

"Only Paul?"

"He didn't want Harry Bronfman to know. Paul wanted his own money."

"What about Walt? You fixed Borys's charge with him. Funny, since you burned down his barn the other day."

"You don't know that!"

Ignoring that, Jack said, "What's your deal with Walt?"

"You mean your boss?"

Jack slapped him again and said, "Don't get smart with me, you fucking Yankee bandit!"

"I collect from Paul for him."

"For Walt?"

"Yeah."

"You sure lead a complicated life."

"I do what I can."

Now Jack had Stud talking.

"What do you know about Paul's murder?"

"Nothing you don't know."

"You're lying. I know you killed him."

"What?" said Stud in alarm. "I did not. I had nothing to do with that."

"I know you did."

"You sure as hell do not!"

"I know you and Dutch Schultz met in Portal the night of the murder. I know you picked him up from the Grandview Hotel in that Studie and the two of you came to Bean Fate. You shot Paul. One of you picked up the cash and Paul's tiepin. You nearly ran me down on the road outside Bean Fate and you went on down to Portal. You dumped the Studie with the gunshot holes where I'd hit you at the back and you switched it for that Packard. In that garage by the elevator."

Stud looked at him, his face reflecting growing wonder.

"Oh and one more thing," said Jack. "I know that Dutch took Paul's diamond tiepin back to Chicago."

Jack saw that Stud looked thunderstruck. He didn't know about the tiepin and, so, he'd be wondering where Jack had gotten all his information from. Had he gotten a handle on Dutch somehow? Was Dutch setting him up? It was obvious that Stud now realized he was in a very bad spot, handcuffed by a cop who knew a lot and seemed to hate him.

"Okay," said Stud slowly, "I'll admit I was Dutch's driver. Just like I was on Labor Day."

Jack looked at him expectantly, letting Stud know that that wouldn't do it.

Then it came like a flood as Stud continued, "But that's all. Dutch killed Paul, not me. He and Capone were mad because of bad booze. They'd already warned Harry Bronfman but it wasn't clear he got the message. He had that asshole Leech with him and boasted it was his town and he owned you. They wanted to be sure the Bronfmans got the message by scaring them. So Dutch came back to do that, to show that Chicago could operate up here one way or the other. But Dutch is such a psycho and he just decided to kill him. Said he was pissed off when he saw that stickpin. It was meant to show a deal with Harry, not that chicken-shit Paul. He even stuck it in his damn eye."

"So you were there?"

"I saw it through the window."

"Maybe it was the other way around. Maybe Dutch drove and you shot Paul."

"That's crazy. Would Dutch come all the way from Chicago just to drive me?"

"Maybe he would to pick up six thousand cash."

"I was just the driver, okay?" said Stud almost imploringly.

"So you were an accomplice to murder."

"It wasn't supposed to be murder."

"You helped him escape."

"He's crazy. He would have killed me too. What could I do?"

"What happened to all the cash?"

"He took it."

"You got none?"

"Couple hundred, that's all. For driving him."

"Does Walt know about all this?"

Jack sensed that now Stud was willing to tell all, fearing a trap, setting him up for a murder rap.

"I went to see Walt right after you started questioning me at the garage in town. I warned him he needed to protect me. I had the goods on him."

"That was the morning after the murder. So Walt's known all along that you and Dutch were involved?"

"Yeah."

"Did Walt tell Regina?"

"I'm sure that's the last thing he'd do!"

"Why?"

"Then they'd know about his connection to me and they'd soon find out what he had going on down here!"

Makes sense, thought Jack. *At least Cross didn't know for sure that it was the Mob.*

Then Stud said, "But I'd never say any of this in court. I'd be dead like Paul."

"Who says you're going to court?"

Stud stared at Jack.

Probably thinks I'm looking for that couple hundred, thought Jack.

"Your story," continued Jack, "is that you're just a poor dumb bastard who got mixed up with the wrong people and was in the wrong place at the wrong time?"

"Pretty much."

"Bullshit! You're a killer. Plus, you ruined Kate and now she's dead because of you."

"So that's it!" said Stud. "Don't blame me for that. The little cockteaser asked for it."

Jack snapped. Trembling, he pulled out his revolver and pointed it at Stud's battered head and it looked like Jack meant to kill him.

"But I never fucked her if that's what you think."

"What?"

"I never fucked her. I tried. I thought she wanted it and when she resisted, I thought that was just part of the game. Like the senoritas down home. But she meant it! She fought like a wildcat! So I let her be. I don't need a woman who doesn't want me."

Jack looked at Stud in astonishment. *I never actually asked her,* he thought. *And she was too ashamed and everyone thought... Oh my God!* Shaking, he holstered his revolver and sat down at the kitchen table. He saw a half-full bottle of Black Horse on the table and took several guzzles.

"I never could figure out why she hanged herself," added Stud.

Jack sat there, stunned. Stud watched in wonder.

Then Stud said, "I need to take a piss. Outside."

Jack nodded 'okay' and stood up as Stud did. Stud walked out the door followed by Jack, who didn't really want to watch and stood behind him as Stud, hands cuffed in front of him, faked a fumble with his trousers' fly. Suddenly, in one motion Stud swiveled around and brought his arms up. Jack's slightly dulled reflexes were not quick enough. Stud's cuffed hands landed a solid blow to Jack's chest and he tumbled to the snowy ground. Stud kicked his stomach and Jack doubled over. Stud grabbed a shovel leaning on the wall beside the door. Jack had managed to stagger up and was just grabbing his revolver when Stud swiped at him awkwardly with the shovel, knocking the gun out of Jack's hand. But that swing with cuffed hands also put Stud slightly off balance. Jack, the old hockey player, nailed him with a solid right hand to the jaw and followed up with a good left. Stud crumpled.

Jack grabbed his revolver, pointed it at Stud, and re-cuffed Stud's hands, this time behind his back.

Chapter 31

When Tom drove into the parking lot beside behind a line of stores in Portal, Jack was leaning against the Packard, looking rough and disheveled with a black eye. Tom drove up, got out and looked at Jack quizzically.

"I came as fast as I could. How'd you get that Packard?"

"I've got something more interesting for you on the floor in the back."

Tom whistled in surprise when he saw the battered and bruised Stud.

"He murdered Matoff," said Jack.

"That's a lie!" shouted Stud.

"I've convicted him of maybe murder, at least accessory. Plus sexual assault. I'm handing him over to you for sentencing."

Tom looked at Jack, in a way his protégé.

"No more Boy Scout," he said wryly. "Well, your Honor," he added, "I'll see he's put away for a long time."

From the car's backseat, Stud said, "I know all about you, sheriff, so you better be careful."

Jack looked at Tom, who said, "Don't listen to that asshole."

They pulled the struggling Stud out and put him in the backseat of the sheriff's car.

"You better get out of here before I have to impound that Packard," said Tom.

"Okay, I'm off." Jack got into the Packard and turned the ignition.

A single gunshot rang out.

Jack stopped the car, got out and walked back to the sheriff's car, its backdoor still open. Tom was standing there with a gun in hand and Stud was lying in the backseat obviously dead from a gunshot wound in the back of the head.

"Son of a bitch was resisting arrest," said Tom as he holstered his gun.

Jack looked at Tom wordlessly, nodded and walked back to the Packard. *He could've waited till I'd left.*

Chapter 32

Jack drove into Anderson's ranch yard.

Anderson came out of the house and stopped in his tracks as Jack got out of the car. "Thought it was Stud!" he called out. "How come you've got that Packard?"

"He gave it to me."

"Gave it to you?"

"Yeah, asked me to drop him off in Portal and left me the keys."

They looked at each other.

"Uh huh," said Anderson dubiously.

"Just thought I'd come by to say goodbye."

Anderson looked astonished.

"Really? Come on in for coffee and tell me what's going on."

"How about whiskey?"

"I see you're not wearing your uniform but would that be wise?"

"I'm quitting."

"Okay, we both need a whiskey."

They entered the kitchen. "The wife's gone to town," Anderson commented as he walked over to a cupboard hanging in a corner, reached up and took a key from the top of the cupboard. Unlocking the cupboard, he took out a bottle of Black Horse.

They sat down at the kitchen table, each with a drink, the bottle of Black Horse standing in the middle of the table between them.

After their first guzzle, Anderson said, "So, Jack, what's going on?"

"I found out that the Mob murdered Paul Matoff and Stud was involved. But Regina doesn't want to believe me and were sending me back to Regina. For further training."

"Further training? That's bullshit. What's the deal about Stud?"

"Let's just say you won't be seeing him around here anymore."

Jack had quickly downed his drink and Anderson poured another which Jack started to drain.

"Funny about Paul. And Walt too," said Jack, looking at his glass.

"Walt? What about Walt?"

"Matoff was paying him off. Stud collected it for Walt."

"No!"

"And he protected Stud."

"You're kidding!"

"I'm not kidding."

"You think they knew in Regina?"

"Dunno. But actually, I doubt they know about Walt and maybe Harry Bronfman didn't know about Paul. Not his bootlegging around here."

Anderson was all ears as Jack continued.

"But the smart boys aren't as smart as they think."

"Yeah, but maybe not quite as bad as you seem to think?"

"They're bad enough. They set up the system, this booze-trafficking thing. That's what the big boys do. They set it up bad and then can't control it or at least know all the bad that comes out of it. Like Paul's murder."

Anderson nodded gravely.

"Like Kate," added Jack.

"Wait. How are they responsible for that?"

"Stud wouldn't have been hanging around here if they hadn't set up this whole booze-trafficking mess."

Jack's friends, the Andersons and Sparling, were worried about Jack. They'd talked about it after church. They knew he blamed himself for Kate's death and they all felt the need to suggest it wasn't his fault.

"Yes," said Anderson gently, "but Jack, she was a little unwise, getting mixed up with Stud. You tried to warn her about that."

"It wasn't like we all thought."

"What do you mean?"

"She wasn't raped."

"What?"

"He didn't rape her."

"You mean she went along with it?"

"No! I mean he didn't fuck her, goddammit!"

"But the wife saw her come in and—"

"She fought him off!"

"How do you know?"

"Stud told me."

"He told you?"

"Yeah."

"How come he told you that?"

"Long story. I don't want to get into it."

"But you believe him?"

"The way he told me, oh yeah, I do."

"My God, Jack. If that's true, we were all wrong."

"All of us. We let her down. But especially me."

They sat in silence. Anderson clearly didn't know what to say.

"Anyway, I got rid of him," said Jack. "Son of a bitch. That's for her."

"You said you dropped him off and he gave you the keys. Sounded voluntary?"

"Oh, well, I handed him to that sheriff, over the line."

Anderson looked at him questioningly.

"In a way," continued Jack, talking almost more to himself than Anderson, "that's some justice for the murder too. Not that I cared for Matoff personally. What pisses me off the most is that Colonel Cross covered it up. He sets up a system that leads to Matoff's murder. That's bad enough. What's worse is, he's even prepared to charge innocent men to cover it up. And when I won't go along, he pulls me off the case. He's the attorney-general and he's obstructing justice for fuck's sake."

Anderson looked in amazement at Jack's rant. Who knew he had this in him?

Anderson was watching Jack fiddling with a key and, noticing this, Jack put the key on the table.

"I don't know what to do with this," he said.

"What is it?"

"It's the key to a cupboard in the stable at Stud's cabin."

"You can give it to me."

"Why would you want it?"

"That cabin belongs to me."

"To you?"

"Yeah. I thought you knew."

"Right, you thought I knew." Now it was Jack's turn to be amazed.

"Well, I wasn't about to make a big deal about it. But that cabin came with the ranch and I just kept it in case I ever found a hired hand to cover that part of the ranch way down there. One day, I discovered Stud had just moved in. I didn't try to move him out. Wasn't worth it."

You never know anyone completely, thought Jack. He looked at Anderson and flipped the key to him.

"Dave, now you've got a lifetime supply of Black Horse."

Chapter 33

Jack parked the Packard in front of police headquarters in Regina and, carrying his duffle bag with his uniform and kit, walked into Mahoney's outer office. Approaching Mahoney's secretary, he asked to see Mahoney but was advised he wasn't there. He dropped the duffle bag on the floor in front of her desk and walked away.

"What should I tell him?" called the secretary.

"Tell him Constable Ross quit," he called back over his shoulder.

As he was leaving the building, he met Cross and Mahoney just arriving. They were not surprised to see him but were surprised at his civvies to say nothing of the black eye.

"Hello, constable," said Mahoney. "What happened to you?"

"Bit of a dust-up, sir."

"Where's your uniform?"

"I dropped it at your office."

Mahoney and Cross exchanged looks.

"You mean you've quit?" asked Cross.

"Yes sir."

"Why, Jack? Surely not because you were reassigned for further training?"

"Not exactly. I thought about the day you swore me in. Back in July."

Cross looked at him questioningly.

"You spoke about British values, the Rule of Law, and what we fought for at Vimy Ridge."

"Yes?"

"I realized you were full of shit."

Jack turned on his heel and strode away.

He got back in the Packard and drove over to a back alley near the Craftsman Building. He parked at a building which looked like a large garage. A rough-looking guy was standing beside its door. He nodded as though he recognized Jack and opened the door while saying, "It's been a while." Jack nodded and handed him a few bills of cash. It was dim and tacky inside with a makeshift bar. It was midday and there were no other patrons.

He walked over to the bar and the bartender spoke to him.

"Black Horse?"

"Sure. I'll just take the bottle."

"The whole bottle?"

"Yeah."

He sat down at a table, poured a straight shot into a glass, set the bottle back down on the table, and took the first drink of the day. *This won't be the last,* he thought.

Chapter 34

A couple of days and many reefers later, on a cold morning, Jack knocked on the front door of a substantial-looking house not far from Harry's, although Jack didn't know that. The door was opened by a woman of early middle-age, attractive if somewhat severe-looking. She was well-dressed, certainly better than his mother but not fancy. *She looks a bit like Kate,* he thought.

"Missus Roberts?" he asked somberly.

"Yes?"

"I'm Jack Ross."

"From Bean Fate?"

"Yes. I wondered if I could have a word with you."

She looked hesitant and then said, "Do come in. You can hang up your coat here." She opened a closet door.

He took off his overcoat and overshoes.

"Come into the parlor," she said. "Would you like a cup of tea?"

"That would be very nice, thank you."

She walked back to the kitchen.

Jack sat nervously on a settee looking around. The room was quite large, much larger than the parlor room at home and it was furnished with Edwardian furniture much nicer than the Victorian furniture at his parents' home. Of course, Jack didn't know anything about furniture. He just knew the Roberts' furniture looked a lot brighter and more cheerful. There was a brick-faced fireplace and over the mantle was a large painting of a mountain and what looked like camels and desert people on a plain in front.

She returned with a little tray on which sat a porcelain teapot, a porcelain jug, a small sugar bowl, and two china cups.

"How do you take your tea, Mister Ross?"

"Just clear, thank you. And please call me Jack."

"Very well, Jack."

He didn't know how to start, so he said, "That's a very nice painting over the fireplace."

"Mount Ararat."

"Where the ark landed?"

"Yes, so they say. It's an original. My brother brought it back from overseas."

"He was there? In the war?"

"Yes, in the Middle East. With a British regiment. He was seconded to it and they did some hush-hush work over there. I don't know what. I have no idea how he got it but he gave it to me that and the carpet on the floor in front of you."

"They're very nice. He lives here?"

"No, he never came back. I mean, not really. At the end of the war, he came back briefly, picked up his wife and two children, and took them to London."

"To London!"

"You see, I think he'd seen it and liked it. And he'd met someone, his commanding officer, who had a firm of some sort and offered him a good position, so he took it. I think it's wonderful for him to be there, at the center of the world really, but we miss him. You served overseas too, didn't you? Under Colonel Cross?"

"Yes."

"Must have been ghastly. He said so. And he's quite a man. It must have been good to be with him."

"Oh yes." He had to stop this line of conversation, so he blurted out, "I'm here about Kate."

"I assumed so."

"I don't know if you know about me."

"I heard a lot about you. I believe Kate was very fond of you, Jack."

"She said that?"

"Yes, she did. In her letters."

"Well, I was very fond of her too." *'Dammit!'* He'd worried whether he'd be able to keep it together and already he was choking up a bit.

Mrs. Roberts saw this and waited.

Jack was asking himself, *Why did I come here anyway?* He didn't know exactly. It was a loose end.

Finally, she said, "What happened down there to Kate? Why did she commit suicide?" She said it in a no-nonsense way but with a tremor in her voice.

What to tell her? thought Jack. *I have to find out what she knows. I don't want to add to her suffering or besmirch Kate's memory.*

"You know," he said, "I think she had a hard time fitting in down there. The job at the school wasn't easy, some of the mothers were very difficult, even nasty, and in a small town, everyone's looking at you and criticizing you. And she was sensitive to all that."

"What could they have criticized her for?"

"Oh, just stuff. I know one day, they were very critical because she lectured them on cleanliness and all that. They even complained to the chairman of the school board."

"Mister Anderson?"

"Yes."

"But they objected to that? I know the department even has a book on that. She showed it to me."

"Well, they did."

"Was it the foreign mothers?"

"I really don't know, but probably."

"Even so, I know Kate. She's strong. It just doesn't make sense."

There was silence in the room.

"What was your relationship with her, Jack?"

This was getting difficult. *How to answer that?*

"We liked each other a lot, at least I did. And I think she did."

"I know she did. But did it cool down? Was that part of her problem?"

"Yes maybe."

There was more silence in the room.

"Was she pregnant?"

Jack was a bit shocked. Mrs. Roberts asked that in her matter-of-fact way but her face was troubled.

"Missus Roberts, we did not have that kind of relationship... and I was hoping we might get engaged but we never quite got that far... unfortunately."

"Jack, I'm sorry I asked it that way. I know you're an honorable man. Kate always said so."

"She did?"

"She did. But I have to ask you whether you know anything about Kate and that dreadful cowboy."

"Did she tell you about that?"

"Yes, she did."

"If you don't mind my asking, what did she say?"

"Her letter just said she'd made a mistake about letting him take her home from a dance, since you weren't there. And that it had been a little unpleasant for her. But after she died, we heard rumors at church that maybe it was more than that and that maybe she was pregnant and that's why she'd taken her own life. In other words, that he'd raped her!"

There, she'd put it out on the table.

"Missus Roberts, I can tell you that he did not rape her. They did not..." he hesitated, searching for an acceptable word. "They did not have intercourse."

"Did she say that?"

"No, we didn't talk about it that directly."

"Then how do you know?"

"Because he told me."

"You talked to him about it?"

"Yes." That didn't sound quite right, like guys sitting around talking about screwing women, so he added, "It was not an easy conversation, believe you me."

"And you're sure?"

"I am."

"That's so good to know. But then I still don't understand why she'd be so upset, you know, to take her life."

"The problem was everyone thought she'd been raped."

"But why?"

"Her landlady... Missus Anderson... assumed it from seeing Kate upset when she came home after that cowboy... And I guess..." he hesitated, "I guess she looked pretty upset." Jack didn't want to mention the disheveled clothing and hair awry which Anderson had recounted to him. "But," he added, "I know now that although he didn't rape her, he did assault her."

"Oh my, he did?"

"Yes."

"My poor Kate."

"So Missus Anderson saw her after that but never actually asked and Kate never said, and Missus Anderson told some people… She wasn't being mean…. and her husband told me. I mean we all felt very badly. I tried to talk to Kate but she wouldn't talk about it. And it just kind of grew in people's minds. Even mine."

"She would have felt the shame."

"But it wasn't her fault!"

"Poor Kate! I should have realized when she changed her plans."

"She did?"

"Yes, she'd written that she was looking forward to coming home for Thanksgiving. She said she had something important to discuss. She mentioned your name. She sounded optimistic."

Oh no, thought Jack.

"But then she wrote again and said she wouldn't be coming after all."

At that, Jack broke down.

Mrs. Roberts sat looking at her hands.

"I'm so sorry, Missus Roberts. I loved her and somehow I let her down."

"We did too, Jack, somehow we did too."

At this, the formidable woman started to sob herself.

Then she came over to where he sat and put her arms around him and they comforted each other.

"Well, there's nothing we can do about it now," she said, dabbing her eyes. Her matter-of-fact nature reasserted itself.

"Missus Roberts, I'm afraid I made a mistake coming here."

"No, Jack. It's better that you did. Now I know what happened. And I know that you loved my girl."

Jack felt a bit better at that.

Finally, she said, "Jack, shall we have another cup of tea?"

"Thank you, but I should be going, Missus Roberts."

"I'm so glad you came by, Jack. I really am. I'm just sorry Kate's father wasn't here. He'd so like to meet you, I'm sure."

"I'd like to meet him too sometime."

"So please let us know next time you're back from Bean Fate."

"Actually, I'm back here now. For the moment."

"Reassigned somewhere else? I know it must have been difficult down there. That awful murder and all."

"No, I've quit the police force."

"What are you going to do?"

"I'm heading up to the Peace River country."

"Oh! When?"

"On the train tomorrow."

"So soon!"

"I want to be ready when spring comes."

"I hear it's a lovely country and it's finally opening up for homesteading."

"That's what I'm counting on. I'll give it a try."

"Doctor Roberts will be sorry to have missed you. Well, good luck then."

He walked out to the hall and put on his overshoes as she stood and watched.

"Jack," she said as he was putting on his overcoat.

"Yes, Missus Roberts?"

"What about that dreadful cowboy?"

"He's gone, Missus Roberts. He's gone."

Then he said goodbye, shook her hand, and walked out the door.

Chapter 35

Chicago was not called the Windy City for nothing. A Colorado Low was just arriving, an early-season blizzard with wind blowing off Lake Michigan at thirty miles per hour with gusts over fifty. Snow swirled around his car as Al Capone drove up to the building on South Wabash Street. He kicked the snow off his overshoes and trudged up the stairs. The thug on the door to Torrio's office searched him and took the pistol.

As he walked into the office, Torrio looked up from his desk.

"You wanted to see me, Mister Torrio?"

"Yeah. And Dutch too. Where's he?"

"I dunno. He left."

"When?"

"A while ago."

"We have a problem and he's a part of it."

Capone said nothing.

"We're not getting any more stuff from Harry Bronfman."

"That's what I heard."

"Fucking Canadians shut him down because Dutch did his brother!"

"Brother-in-law."

"Whatever. I told you guys not to kill him, just scare him. What the fuck happened?"

"Dutch said the guy pissed him off and he decided on the spot to kill him anyway."

"Dumb bastard. Where'd he go?"

"I heard back to New York. He knew you'd be unhappy."

"Damn right! Bronfman was a good source. But I may have a solution to our problem."

Capone was just listening.

"I hear there's another brother... Sam."

"Oh?"

"Yeah, in Montreal. They say he's the smart one anyway. And I hear that suddenly he's got stuff for sale. Brings it in from Scotland. Real stuff. Not like Harry's shit. Somehow, he brings it in through Cuba."

"Cuba?"

"Yeah, not sure how. I want you to go up to Montreal and check it out."

+++

Afterword

Paul Matoff was, in fact, murdered on October 4, 1922 at the CPR station in Bienfait by a shotgun blast from an unknown assailant through the window in the presence of Lee Dillege and Colin Rawcliffe. Dillege and Lacoste were charged with murder or conspiracy to commit murder.

A preliminary hearing was held in Weyburn on November 21, 1922. The charges against Lacoste were dropped but Dillege was sent to trial. He was acquitted in a four-hour jury trial in Estevan in March 1923. The murder was never solved.

Saskatchewan lore has it that both Al Capone and Dutch Schultz were seen at Whites and the Grandview Hotel, although not necessarily on the dates used in this story. Al Capone succeeded Johnny Torrio as head of the Chicago Mob and became 'Public Enemy Number One.'

Arthur Flegenheimer was the given name of Dutch Schultz, who later founded an infamous New York gang.

The quote from the Saskatoon Star is a real quote.

The article in The Winnipeg Tribune on October 16, 1922 is real.

Avery Erickson's murder of police officer F.S. Fahler in a 1921 shootout in Minot did happen. Mayor W.S. Smart of Minot was recalled in 1921.

Big Bill Thomson's parade opening the Michigan Avenue Bridge did happen. So did the parade with Amos Alonzo Stagg. And Charles Fitzmorris did make the statement attributed to him about fifty percent of the Chicago Police Force being involved in the booze business.

Dillege farmed at Lignite, North Dakota. He owned Dillege's Cubans who included the disgraced Swede Risberg. Dillege later served time in the federal penitentiary at Leavenworth, Kansas, for rustling and smuggling.

Leech was fired by Cross in 1925 after Leech lost a famous jury trial for libel against the Regina Leader arising from a series of sensational articles alleging Leech had been paid off by Harry Bronfman.

Cross was defeated in the 1925 provincial election due to the unpopularity of his political meddling in law enforcement. Another seat was soon found for him but he didn't run in the 1929 election in which a Conservative government was elected. They appointed a Royal Commission, whose counsel was John Diefenbaker, a future Conservative Prime Minister of Canada. It found that Cross had exercised improper political influence over the provincial police. Mahoney was described as Cross's 'rubber stamp.' But there were no sanctions. Cross left Regina in 1939 to take a Liberal appointment as Chairman of the Board of Transport Commissioners in Ottawa. He never returned to Regina.

Harry Bronfman wound up the Saskatchewan booze business by the end of 1922. He then suffered a nervous breakdown. In 1923, he moved to Montreal. In 1929, he was tried but acquitted on charges of attempted bribery and witness tampering related to his dealings with Cyril Knowles.

In 1924, with the large profits that they had made, primarily in Saskatchewan, Sam Bronfman founded Distillers Corporation in Montreal. While Harry was involved too and had a big interest, he was slowly pushed aside by Sam, who was haunted by their Saskatchewan problems. Allan Bronfman was brought forward until he, too, was pushed aside by Sam. Distillers eventually became Seagrams, the world's largest liquor distilling company and the basis for a family fortune worth billions. The Bronfmans became great philanthropists and, in 1967, Sam became a Companion of the Order of Canada. It wasn't quite 'Sir Samuel' but was as close as a Canadian could get by then.

+ + +

CPSIA information can be obtained
at www.ICGtesting.com
Printed in the USA
LVHW081748280122
709482LV00009B/187